OF PRINCES
AND
PROMISES

ALSO BY SANDHYA MENON

When Dimple Met Rishi
From Twinkle, with Love
There's Something about Sweetie
10 Things I Hate about Pinky
Of Curses and Kisses

OF PRINCES AND PROMISES

A Rosetta Academy Novel

SANDHYA MENON

SIMON & SCHUSTER BFYR

NEW YORK LONDON TORONTO SYDNEY NEW DELHI

SIMON & SCHUSTER BFYR

An imprint of Simon & Schuster Children's Publishing Division
1230 Avenue of the Americas, New York, New York 10020

SIMON & SCHUSTER BOOKS FOR YOUNG READERS
and related marks are trademarks of Simon & Schuster, Inc.
For information about special discounts for bulk purchases, please contact
Simon & Schuster Special Sales at 1-866-506-1949 or business@simonandschuster.com.
The Simon & Schuster Speakers Bureau can bring authors to your live event.
For more information or to book an event, contact the Simon & Schuster Speakers
Bureau at 1-866-248-3049 or visit our website at www.simonspeakers.com.
Interior design by Tom Daly
The text for this book was set in Janson Text LT Std.
Manufactured in the United States of America
First Edition
2 4 6 8 10 9 7 5 3 1
Library of Congress Cataloging-in-Publication Data
Names: Menon, Sandhya, author.
Title: Of princes and promises / Sandhya Menon.
Description: First edition. | New York : Simon & Schuster Books for Young Readers, [2021]
| Audience: Ages 12 up. | Audience: Grades 7-9. | Summary: Caterina is desperate to gain
back the popularity she once held at Rosetta Academy, while Rahul, desperate for a chance
with Caterina, discovers hair gel that turns him into suave RC, Caterina's dream boy.
Identifiers: LCCN 2020038932 (print) | LCCN 2020038933 (ebook) |
ISBN 9781534417571 (hardcover) | ISBN 9781534417595 (ebook)
Subjects: CYAC: Love—Fiction. | Popularity—Fiction. | Self-acceptance—Fiction.
Classification: LCC PZ7.1.M473 Ofh 2021 (print) | LCC PZ7.1.M473 (ebook) | DDC
[Fic]—dc23
LC record available at https://lccn.loc.gov/2020038932
LC ebook record available at https://lccn.loc.gov/2020038933

For the mislabeled frogs who were royalty all along

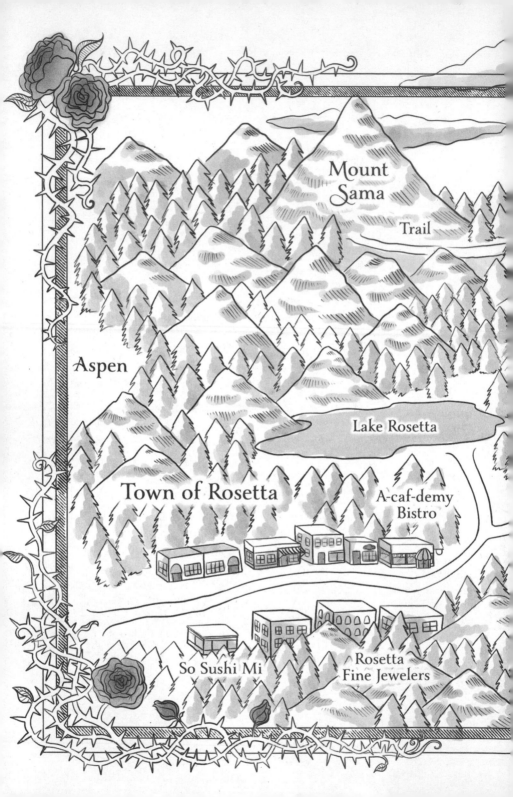

IT WASN'T A KISS THAT CHANGED THE FROG,
BUT THE FACT THAT A YOUNG GIRL LOOKED
BENEATH WARTS AND SLIME AND BELIEVED
SHE SAW A PRINCE. SO HE BECAME ONE.

—RICHELLE E. GOODRICH,
MAKING WISHES

OPEN THE DOOR, MY PRINCESS DEAR,
OPEN THE DOOR TO THY TRUE LOVE HERE!

—THE FROG PRINCE

CHAPTER 1

Rosetta Academy wasn't just her school, it was her *palace*. It was the place where Caterina LaValle ruled supreme, the queen of all she saw and surveyed. Nothing dimmed the shine on her crown, not fighting with her friends, not a bad picture in the *New York Times* lifestyle section (she'd gotten that photographer fired), not even a breakup with an inconsequential boy.

Not usually.

Winter break was the rest her soul had needed after the breakup with Alaric last year. She'd mistaken him for a prince, but he'd turned out to be decidedly amphibian. Still. It was nothing more than a setback, a minor inconvenience. She was back now, ready to rule with even more of a platinum fist—iron was such a plebeian metal—than before. She was going to walk into that brick-and-ivy structure with a sense of ownership, a sense of power, a sense of indestructability, as she never had. Her crown wasn't askew anymore.

Queen Cat was back. Rosetta Academy better watch out.

CHAPTER 2

CATERINA

The rumble of the private jet's engine soothed her. Her father liked to joke that all he had to do with baby Caterina when she fussed was stick her in the plane and fly to a different country. Easy-peasy.

Caterina took a deep breath and sipped at her freshly squeezed orange juice, proffered by the obsequious flight attendant in a crystal champagne flute. Normally, returning to school after break was something she looked forward to, something she'd have been planning for weeks with her friends. She glanced at her phone, at all the unread texts there from Heather and Ava. A small knot of something unpleasant sat in her stomach.

It was all *his* fault. She'd gone through the pictures on her phone, methodically deleting every single one that featured Alaric Konig, her ex-boyfriend, even if it was just an errant finger at the corner of the frame. It took an entire day—over the two years they'd dated, they'd taken thousands and thousands of pictures. Alaric was a ham; anytime he looked good, he wanted the world to know it. And he looked good almost all the time.

The strange part was, she hadn't even loved him anymore, not toward the end. Of course she did toward the beginning of their relationship, when everything still sparkled and he told her every day that she was the most beautiful, most intimidating girl he'd ever dated. (Caterina had liked that latter descriptor more than she'd expected to.) She'd felt like she had all the power then, like she could do no wrong. Alaric had needed her more than she'd needed him.

The plane began its descent, and Caterina's ears felt the brunt of the pressure. The thing was, she wasn't sure exactly when that scale, that imbalance of power between her and Alaric, tipped to favor him. When he began to look at other girls, thinking, *Hmm.* And of all the girls to cheat with—Daphne Elizabeth McKinley? The flamboyant daughter of the McKinley Hotel dynasty. A redhead who thought distressed vintage plaid sweaters were the height of fashion. Caterina's hand tightened around the stem of her champagne flute as the plane floor juddered with the release of the wheels. Alaric and Daphne Elizabeth had sneaked around behind her back, and no one had told her. She'd looked a complete fool. There were few things Caterina abhorred more than looking like a fool.

As the jet circled the runway, Caterina closed her eyes. Her soft false eyelashes pressed into the tops of her cheeks. She needed to get ahold of herself. Today was all about reasserting herself, about making sure her friends saw that she was still Queen Cat. That no one could ever take that away from her. Her father's words floated in her mind like skywriting: *It doesn't matter how you feel on the inside. What matters is what other people can see, and they must see the LaValle power. That's what defines us.*

As if he could hear her thoughts, her phone buzzed and her father's name popped up on the screen.

"Papa," she said, answering, her voice cool and controlled.

His deep baritone thundered down the line. "Are you in Aspen yet?"

"Nearly," Caterina said, looking out onto the snow-laden city, growing closer outside her window.

"Feeling invincible?" her father asked, a grin in his voice. It was their inside joke, ever since a journalist had once asked her, for a puff piece on "children of the wealthy," how she felt in her pretty new dress. Caterina, then only twelve, had replied seriously, "Invincible." Her answer had made the headline.

Now, although she felt anything but, she said carelessly, "Always. You know that."

"Good. Show them how the LaValles do it."

Caterina smiled faintly as her ears popped. "Just as you will when the elections roll around."

"Business, politics, finance . . . we'll be everywhere." He paused. "Senator LaValle does have a ring to it, does it not?"

"Absolutely," Caterina said as the plane touched down, jarring her in her seat. "Now I must go."

"All right. And remember, *topolina*, trust no one."

Caterina nodded, even though her father couldn't see her. He *had* seen the havoc Alaric had wreaked on her. For the first week of winter break, she'd been unable to so much as smile, even through all the wonders of Christmas on the Italian Riviera. Finally, her father had managed to coax out of her exactly what had happened. He was furious that she'd let herself get strung along in the first place, and secondly, that she was this upset over a boy. "Get angry, Caterina," he'd urged her, his deep brown eyes glittering. "Get angry. And then make a plan."

So that's exactly what she'd spent the rest of the winter break doing.

"*Ti amo, Papa,*" she said as the flight attendant moved toward her, beaming brightly. "Talk to you soon."

"Shall I get your coat, Miss LaValle?" the flight attendant asked. "Are you ready to deplane?"

Caterina smiled frostily up at him. "Oh yes," she replied. "I'm absolutely ready."

CHAPTER 3

RAHUL

His friends were speaking gibberish again.

"That's not what he said!" Jaya exclaimed, laughing. She was sitting at their polished oak table in the expansive Rosetta Academy senior dining hall, as they all were, but her chair was so close to Grey's that their seats practically qualified as a love seat. Her head was resting against his chest, and he was absently playing with her hair. Rahul didn't understand how that didn't drive her crazy. He hated people touching his hair.

"It was exactly what he said," Grey argued, rumbling a deep laugh. His Kopi Luwak coffee sat by his elbow, steaming gently. "'My universe would implode without you'? Come on. That's classic codependency."

"Or, totally romantic!" Samantha, Leo's girlfriend, countered, siding with Jaya.

Leo laughed and stuffed his mouth with another handmade almond biscotti while, beside him, DE was pulling up the exact quote on the newest iPhone that wasn't available to the public yet.

They were arguing about the dialogue in some romantic

comedy holiday movie they'd all watched over break. Naturally, Rahul hadn't seen it. But that wasn't necessary for him to know they were all speaking utter nonsense. Finally, not able to contain his thoughts any longer, he butted in, though he usually preferred to remain on the periphery in conversations where he lacked expertise. "Completely nonsensical. The universe cannot implode simply because one person has ceased to exist within it," Rahul said, watching his friends as they turned to him, their smiles slowly fading. "As it is, the multiverse theory states that everything that exists, to include matter, space, time—"

"Ix-nay ock-Spay," Leo said, putting his hand on Rahul's arm. When Rahul turned to look at him, he widened his eyes meaningfully.

That was their signal. Whenever Rahul got too literal or logical or went full-on "Robot Chopra," as DE called it, Leo would say the Pig Latin equivalent of "Nix Spock." It was a more polite way to ask Rahul to stop talking.

"Sorry," Rahul mumbled, feeling his cheeks heat. He'd gotten it wrong again.

"No worries, dude," Daphne Elizabeth said, clapping his shoulder heartily from the other side. She ran a finger along the Rosetta Academy insignia engraved along the edge of the dining table. "Some of us are complete morons when it comes to love. And I wholeheartedly include myself under that sad, lonely little umbrella."

Jaya and Grey smiled at Rahul kindly, but that just made it worse. The floor-to-ceiling windows on the far side of the dining hall let in waves of buttery golden winter sunlight, but Rahul's own mood was getting more dismal by the minute.

Just once, he'd like to be able to be one of the group. Not the one who was never in on the joke, not the one who made people laugh because of his idiosyncrasies, but the guy who deliberately made the jokes. The guy who directed conversation, not the one who stymied it. Like Grey. Or Leo. Or literally anyone else but himself.

"Shit," DE squeaked suddenly, slumping down in her chair. She attempted to pull her bangs down lower on her forehead, but they were short and barely did anything. "I knew I should've worn my ski mask in here."

Confused, Rahul turned in the direction she was looking, wondering whether this was yet another figure of speech he was unfamiliar with.

Caterina LaValle was walking in, flanked by those two girls she was always with. She looked like Princess Isabella of Portugal or a pale-skinned Jhansi ki Rani or some other fierce and beautiful queen. She wore an ultramarine-blue wool dress with bell-shaped sleeves that came to her elbows. Her slim legs were clad in shimmery tights and calf-length leather boots, her dark hair cascading in full, shiny waves down her shoulders—

"Yo." DE snapped her fingers in front of Rahul's face, probably emboldened as Caterina turned toward a corner table with her entourage, obviously not interested in a confrontation.

He blinked and looked at her, adjusting his glasses. "What?"

DE smirked at him, her pink lip-glossed mouth all shiny. "Dude. You have it so bad. Jaya asked you a question."

Rahul looked over at Jaya, who was grinning, her hand entwined with Grey's on the table. "I asked, did anything happen between you two over the break? After, you know, the winter formal . . ."

Rahul glanced at Caterina again, momentarily reliving what

had been one of the best moments of his life. She'd been so unlike herself that night, sad and hopeless and . . . almost kind of vulnerable. Rahul had wanted nothing more than to take her pain away, to wipe her tears, to tell her that jerk-off Alaric didn't deserve even an iota of her time. But instead, he'd just taken her in his arms and swayed with her, gently, half expecting her to snap at him that he was making her look like a fool, thanks to his uncoordinated, fawn-on-ice-like movements.

But she hadn't. She'd just let his hands rest on her waist while her arms rested on his shoulders. She'd looked into his eyes. There was a small smear of mascara at the corner of one of hers, which just showed how discombobulated she really was. And when he was thinking about that, she'd smiled softly and said, "Thank you, Rahul. You're really sweet, you know that?"

Caterina LaValle had called him, Rahul Chopra, *sweet*. No, actually, to be very precise, she'd called him *really sweet*. That was a superlative, was it not? That was evidence, was it not, of a burgeoning . . . something?

"Well," Rahul said, playing with the handle of his coffee mug. "I have a feeling things are about to become . . . more intense between us." He thought about his word choice, then nodded his head once. "Yes. Definitely more intense."

Jaya, Grey, DE, and Samantha all chorused with various versions of, "Wait, what?" while Leo leaned over the table to clap him on the shoulder and yell, at definite hearing-damage volumes, "*Quoi!* My man, tell me everything!"

Rahul looked around at all their eager, shining faces. He saw genuine joy there, and excitement. Had his friends known how he felt about Caterina all along? He thought he'd hid it pretty well, but maybe he'd been less suave than he'd thought. Big surprise. "I danced with her at the dance before winter break, as you know," he began. They all nodded, their eyes sparkling as they waited for more. "And she told me I was 'really sweet.' That's a direct quote. 'Really sweet.'" Smiling a little, he looked around at them all.

They glanced at each other, and he noticed they weren't really smiling anymore. DE was staring down into her waffles. Grey itched the back of his neck. Jaya bit her lip. Leo and Samantha both wore identical frowns.

"And . . . ?" Jaya prompted, leaning forward in her chair. "Did you speak to her over winter break? Did you text each other, perhaps?"

Frowning, Rahul took off his glasses and polished them on the hem of the orange turtleneck sweater that hung on his frame a little. Maybe he shouldn't have grabbed the first one off the rack at the store, but frankly, who had time for such banalities as shopping? "No," he said. "I didn't have her number. But that's immaterial, because I know she'll be ready to pick up where we left off."

He was pretty sure he heard DE mumble, "Left *what* off?" but he didn't respond because the answer was obvious from what he'd just recounted.

His gaze stole across the cafeteria again, to where Caterina sat with her entourage. As he watched, she grabbed a cup of to-go coffee that one of her many admirers was holding out (this was not uncommon; all Caterina had to do was sit down in the dining hall, and people would bring her food like she was an Egyptian queen and they her besotted servants) and then stood, her friends standing with her.

Rahul's fists clenched. Something inside him was churning.

This was exactly how he'd felt when he'd handed his gloves and hat to a homeless person he'd seen shivering on a bench one winter a couple of years ago. A feeling that he *had* to do something, that time was running out, that he couldn't just sit idly by and be some passive chump. And that feeling warred with the intense social anxiety that circled him at all times, like a dark vulture that refused to leave him alone. He cleared his throat and surreptitiously wiped his damp palms on his pants.

"Excuse me," he said, realizing only too late that he'd interrupted Sam's story about a vat of jam at her mom's factory that had almost eaten her scarf.

He could feel his friends' eyes on him as he stood from the table, the chair squawking a loud protest, loud enough that Caterina glanced his way. Dammit. This was not how he'd intended to get her attention. He raised his hand up to wave, but by the time his fingers had twitched, she was already turning away and gliding toward the main doors.

Rahul increased his pace, practically running toward her now, intending to intercept her path in a plausibly coincidental way. Puffing with the exertion, he made like a parabola and leaned into the turn that would place him directly in her way. Unfortunately, due to a slight miscalculation, he ended up running into her friend Ava instead.

"Ow!" she said, rubbing her shin. "Excuse you!"

The group came to a stop and Caterina was looking at him, no more than two feet away. She blinked those long, long lashes once, then twice. "Rahul?"

He opened his mouth to say something cool and collected. *How was your break?* Or *I like your dress—is it new?* Instead, he blurted out, "Dance."

This happened to him often. Even though he knew social etiquette required people to make at least one to two minutes of small talk before they launched into the topic du jour, Rahul's brain and mouth hardly ever cooperated.

"Excuse me?" Caterina frowned in that imperious way of hers, turning his blood to ice and molten lava at the same time. But then she was swallowed by a tsunami of seniors, all of whom chose that exact moment to walk through the dining hall doors, notice her, and immediately swarm her to demand her attention. And Rahul was spat aside like a hastily coughed-up hairball from the throat of a Persian cat.

For a moment, he felt the sting of rejection. But then he brushed it off. That was okay. They ran in different social circles. He'd observed hers enough to know that this was what was expected, nay, required, of her upon returning from a long absence. He could bide his time.

Rahul turned to make his way back to his seat and saw his friends staring at him with unabashed horror on their faces. It lasted only a brief second before they turned their expressions into smiles.

"What?" he asked, looking around at all their faces. He took a sip of his now-tepid coffee. "She's just a little busy right now. We'll talk later."

"Will you?" Jaya asked, glancing at Grey, who gave her a serious look Rahul couldn't read. Jaya glanced back at Rahul again. It was like she was waiting for a response to her question, which made no sense because he'd made it clear that they obviously would.

Rahul felt his frustration rise. Everyone was always speaking in code when things would be so much more efficient if they just said what they really meant.

DE ran a hand through her red hair. Over the break, she'd gotten it cut even shorter, with an undercut and a zigzag pattern shaved through it. "Dude, you . . . be careful with Caterina, okay? She's got really sharp edges, and I'm worried you don't see that."

Now, that, at least, he could understand. DE was wrong for a multitude of reasons, but at least she'd spoken plainly. "I can see why you might think that."

DE cocked her head, her fingers resting lightly on top of her coffee mug. "What, because of how she eviscerated Alaric at the yacht gala?"

"No." Rahul thoughtfully stirred more sugar into his coffee. "Because you were so oblivious to the fact that Alaric was using you and didn't care about you at all. You were completely humiliated at the yacht gala, and you're projecting that onto me now to warn me. But I have taken your warning into consideration and discarded it as not being relevant to this particular situation."

There was a sudden silence around the table. Rahul looked up to see all five of his friends staring at him, their eyes wide, their mouths open. It was a sure sign that he'd said something they considered wrong in some way. "What?" he asked when no one spoke.

DE bit her lip and looked away, and Jaya reached across the table to squeeze her friend's hand. Grey rubbed the back of his neck, and Leo and Sam just continued to stare at Rahul.

"Are you . . . mad?" he asked DE, frowning. Why would she be mad at him for speaking the truth? He wasn't mad at *her* for speaking what she thought was the truth.

DE snapped her gaze to him, her green eyes flashing. "What do you think, Rahul?" She pushed her chair back and got to her feet, picking up her books with quick, angry movements. "There's such a thing as being honest and then there's just being a shithead." Without waiting for a response, she turned and left.

Jaya stood. "I'll talk to her." Quietly gathering her books, she gave Grey a kiss on the cheek and strode after DE.

Rahul looked around at his remaining friends, his cheeks heating with confused shame and regret. Once again, he'd totally flubbed something and he had no idea why. "I . . ." He shrugged, but then the cafeteria lead was ringing her silver bell, signaling that it was time to make their way to their first class of the semester.

"Last semester of high school!" Leo said as he stood, and Rahul could tell he was trying to brighten the tone. Leo spent a lot of time doing that after Rahul's derailments. He turned to Rahul and smiled a little. "Let's make it a good one."

Rahul left his friends behind as he made his way across campus to the humanities building, the brisk wind catching at his clothes and hair. He needed the time to think, to dissect what he'd said to DE and why that might have made her mad. He could ask Grey later, or maybe even Jaya, but it was painfully embarrassing to have to do that all the time. He should be able to figure some of this stuff out for himself, dammit.

A group of freshmen passed him, laughing and talking as if it were the easiest thing in the world. As if social interaction wasn't infinitely more complex than AP Physics with Dr. Monroe, who used to be an actual NASA rocket scientist before Rosetta poached him away.

Rahul's phone dinged in his pocket. Shifting his psychology textbook to his other hand, he reached into his pocket and pulled it out. It was a Google alert, set up to inform him anytime his family was in the papers.

Chief Minister Arti Chopra attends celebrity wedding with husband, Malik, and sons, Vivek and Rahul, the photo caption read. Rahul clicked on the picture to enlarge it. He was looking at a picture of his family dressed in glittering wedding finery, all dark-haired and smiling broadly for the camera. There was his mom, his dad, his brother, Vivek—and his cousin Pritam.

It wasn't Rahul in the picture, it was Pritam, looking right at the camera, his smile just the correct amount of confident and humble, dashing and down-to-earth. Pritam was a year younger than Rahul, and his clothes—always designer—fit well.

His family had been using Pritam in their photo ops ever since Rahul had first been deposited at Rosetta in second grade. The first time he'd seen Pritam in his place in a photograph, he'd called home, wondering if the photographer or the newspaper had gotten it wrong. He'd been told promptly that it was no mistake, that this was what was best for the Chopra family. Two happy, smiling, socially acceptable sons.

It usually didn't bother him too much, seeing Pritam in his place. He'd had time and distance to accept this, that he was a shameful secret his family needed to hide. But after that debacle with DE . . . Rahul took a deep breath, his hand tightening around the phone, his chest aching with something he couldn't even name. Was there *any* place where he belonged?

Not bothering to answer his own silent question, Rahul put his phone away and continued his trek to class.

CHAPTER 4

CATERINA

"He's not in this class, at least," Ava said, side-eyeing Caterina. Her entire friend group spent 95 percent of their time side-eyeing her while talking about Alaric or even the topic of dating now, as if they were afraid direct eye contact might reduce them to ash. "That's good . . . ?"

Caterina maintained a carefully cultivated imperious cool as she studied Ava's profile—her pronounced brow and famous dark, curly hair (she ran a YouTube beauty channel with over a million subscribers). Ava was of Spanish descent, and her parents were big in oil. "It's neither good nor bad," Caterina explained. "I told you, I couldn't care less what he's up to. He has nothing to do with me anymore."

"Of course," Ava replied, but she and Heather exchanged a glance that Caterina wasn't meant to see.

"So I see they're still a couple." Heather aimed her cool blue gaze across the room at Leo Nguyen and Samantha Wickers. They were huddled up in the corner, laughing at something on his phone. "I honestly didn't think that'd last more than a week-end."

Heather and Ava both turned to Caterina, waiting.

This was the point in any conversation when she'd interject something sharp and witty, or derisive, depending on her mood, and her friends would laugh and agree. Caterina was like the motor to their conversational yacht; she kept things running; she gave them direction and momentum. But at that moment, she felt nothing but a deep, abiding sense of fatigue. As if just opening her mouth would cause her to lose precious oxygen and pass out. Her brain was blank; she found she didn't care about Leo and Samantha or Alaric or even the fact that she was, once again, dressed in the hideously constricting Rosetta Academy's maroon-and-gray uniform.

"Cat?" Heather said, her dirty-blond eyebrows knitting together. "You okay?"

"Fine," Caterina said faintly, wishing that for once in her life, she could actually say what she really felt. That, for once, her friends could really know what was going on with her. But her father's words echoed in her mind: *The face is more important than the flesh.* If she wanted to be the one pulling the strings, if she wanted to maintain control, it was imperative that her people saw her as unflappable.

Ms. Rivard, the AP Psychology teacher, chose to enter at that moment. She was dressed smartly, as usual, in a houndstooth pencil skirt and a gray chiffon blouse with a big loopy bow at the throat. She wore a discreet platinum-and-diamond Rosetta Academy teacher's pin attached to her shirt. Inscribed on the pin was the Latin motto *illuminare coronam*—"illuminate the crown." It glinted under the recessed lighting as she walked to the large oak desk. Ms. Rivard set her books down before turning to them.

"Good morning, everyone." She beamed around at them all, as if she were genuinely happy to be here. How peculiar. How could people *enjoy* jobs with rigid schedules and vacation time that you had to ask for and colleagues you had to pretend to like? "Welcome to your very first class of the semester, and for you seniors, the first class of your *last* semester in high school!"

There were a few whoops and hoots, the vast majority of which seemed to emanate from Leo's corner. Caterina gave him a withering look, noting briefly that Rahul Chopra was watching her, then turned back around. Decorum was a lost art.

Ms. Rivard paced the width of the room, from the door with an inset windowpane to the large bank of windows that overlooked the mountains in the distance, covered in snow and fog. "Psychology. The study of the human mind. Is there anything more fascinating or complex? Or impossible? The truth is, we won't ever learn everything there is to learn about the mind, not in this lifetime, anyway." She studied their faces, her back to the windows. "Who among you would say you know your mind completely? That *you* rule *it*, rather than the other way around?"

A few people raised their hands, including Caterina and Rahul.

"Mm-hmm," Ms. Rivard said, nodding as she walked toward her desk. "There are always a handful. Okay." She looked out at them again, her pale hands clasped under her chin, index fingers pointing upward. "Caterina. And Rahul. Why don't you both come up to the front of the class? Oh, and bring your chairs, please."

Caterina frowned. "Why?"

Ms. Rivard cocked her head, smiling. "I'm proving a point."

Knowing she wouldn't get any more out of her, Caterina stifled a sigh and carried her chair to the front of the room. Rahul was a few steps ahead, carrying his chair in one hand, his feet clomping in shoes that were scuffed at the toe and heel.

"Set the chairs up here, facing each other." Ms. Rivard stepped aside and pointed to the vast empty space between her desk and the door to the right. "And then have a seat."

Caterina and Rahul did as they were asked. Rahul kept glancing at her, his big Adam's apple bobbing as he swallowed nervously. Caterina looked up at Ms. Rivard, waiting.

"Now I want you both to stare into each other's eyes." Ms. Rivard walked over to the light switch and dimmed the lights in the airy room. There were titters around the classroom.

Caterina narrowed her eyes. "For how long?"

"Ten whole minutes," Ms. Rivard replied.

"B-but why?" Rahul asked, his voice cracking. He licked his lips. "I mean, what's the purpose behind all this?"

Caterina almost felt sorry for him. But mostly, she just felt annoyed at being paraded in front of the class like a show pony.

"I'll tell you when we're done, I promise," Ms. Rivard said, patting his shoulder. She pulled her phone off the desk. "I'm setting a timer now. Look into each other's eyes when I say 'start,' and don't stop until you hear the timer go off. Got it?"

They both nodded.

"Start," she said, and Caterina looked into Rahul's brown eyes.

RAHUL

Why was he being forced to do this? It didn't make any sense. If humiliation was what Ms. Rivard was after, there were so many other ways to carry it out. Asking for his opinion on the current winter fashion trends, for instance. Or making him perform the floss. Besides, Ms. Rivard didn't really strike Rahul as the sadistic type.

But Caterina was gazing into his eyes with her big, brown ones, like big bowls of melting, warm chocolate, and he had no choice but to stare back at her. It was weird. The longer he let himself look into her eyes, the looser he felt. Like some internal barrier that he hadn't even known he had was crumbling, bit by bit, molecule by molecule. As minutes ticked by and he continued staring at her, the more intensely he felt that Caterina and he were the same person. Maybe not literally, but somewhere deep inside, where nerve fibers and bits of tissue lay. They were made of the same stuff. They weren't so different after all. When they'd danced, she'd seen it, she'd felt it, just as he had. Of this he was sure.

Another minute folded and melted and dribbled down, followed by another and another.

And then things got *really* weird. Rahul began to . . . see things. Like a hairy mole, at the corner of Caterina's mouth, that he was sure hadn't been there before. And . . . wait. When had she grown that handlebar mustache? He blinked, but it was still there. Caterina looked extremely familiar now, except she wasn't Caterina at all anymore. But who *was* she? The answer was on the tip of Rahul's tongue, but it evaded him, jellylike and fluid.

CATERINA

As the minutes slipped by, Caterina lost track of them, scattered like grains of sand on a windy beach. The rustling and quiet coughing in the room vanished too, as if down a dark, silent tunnel. All that was left was Rahul's deep brown eyes.

She'd never noticed the strength there before. They emanated a light, almost, a quiet and steady brightness that she'd never seen in anyone else's eyes. Suddenly she was flooded with memories of them at the dance, only her memories had the texture and quality of a moment that was taking place directly in front of her. As if she were watching a holographic projection of herself and Rahul. She saw him hesitantly wrap his arms around her waist, as if she were a very expensive, fragile glass doll, or the most precious thing he'd ever held. She saw herself put her arms around his neck and gaze into his eyes then as she was now. He'd said something that had made her laugh, though she couldn't remember what it was now. She remembered the way it had made her feel in that dark moment, though—normal, almost happy.

Rahul had been one of the only people who hadn't judged her—either silently or out loud—for the things that had happened with Alaric and Daphne Elizabeth. He was one of the few who hadn't watched in gleeful shock as she'd fallen from her throne, her Valentino dress billowing out, her crown flying off her head. He'd been tender. And comforting. And still authentically himself. He'd been exactly what she needed.

Caterina blinked. Of course, Rahul was . . . so very Rahul. What made him all those things—tender, comforting, authentic—were things that placed him firmly outside her social circle. She was in the process of rebuilding her throne, and Rahul was an extra piece. There was no place for him.

The timer rang out.

RAHUL

"Okay. Now, I want you to share with the class what you saw." Ms. Rivard turned the lights back to their original brightness, which now felt searing to Rahul's retinas. Ms. Rivard smiled at Caterina and then Rahul. "I'm willing to bet there was some weird stuff. Rahul?"

"Uncle Bipin!" he heard himself blurt out, because the answer had just arrived in his consciousness, now that his mind and time were melting taffy. "That's who you looked like!" He grinned, relieved at finally having the answer. But Caterina didn't smile back. In fact, she looked kind of mad.

"I look like . . . your uncle?" she asked, her pointy nose in the air.

There were a few laughs around the classroom, which Caterina silenced with a single glance.

Oh shit. Maybe that was too much honesty. "No, no!" Rahul leaned forward in his chair, eager to have her understand. "It was the hairy mole at the corner of your mouth. That, and your mustache."

Caterina folded her thin arms, her glare intensifying. "You are clearly not in control of your faculties, so I'll wait for the episode to pass before I address what you just said to me."

Ms. Rivard laughed and clapped her hands together, as if she was delighted. "Rahul, what you experienced is actually pretty common! In an experiment run by researcher Giovanni Caputo, fifteen percent of healthy young individuals who had prolonged 'interpersonal gazing'—aka eye contact—hallucinated a relative's face in place of their partner's face! Isn't that fascinating?"

Actually, it was. But Rahul couldn't help but notice the coldness in Caterina's gaze as she regarded him, as if he were a complete stranger. Dammit. He'd blown it. Why couldn't he have kept his mouth shut?

"Caterina," Ms. Rivard continued, oblivious, the big bow on her shirt bobbing, "what did you notice? Any strange hallucinations? Or thoughts and realizations you'd never had before, perhaps?"

Caterina continued the glacial treatment, bathing Rahul's skin in ice. "No," she said slowly, as if to make sure Rahul would hear. "Not a single one."

They returned their seats to their desks then, Caterina not even glancing at him as they walked back. Dammit. *Dammit.* He'd have to make this right.

His chance came right after class. Caterina's friends Heather and Ava rushed off to their next class, which was across campus, leaving her alone. Rahul hurried out into the hallway and waited by the door for her, rehearsing what he'd say in his head as students from other classes rushed by. *Keep it simple, Chopra,* he told himself as he shifted from foot to foot. *Keep it casual and cool and laugh it off. You can still salvage this. Talk about the dance. She has positive associations of the dance, which you need right now.*

Caterina came gliding out a moment later, engrossed in her phone, her hair cascading forward and hiding part of her beautiful face as she stared down at the screen.

"C-Caterina," Rahul said, annoyed that he seemed to always develop a stammer when he spoke to her. "Hi."

She looked up at him, her brown eyes blank at first. Then, slipping her phone into the pocket of her uniform skirt, she came up to him. "Hi. Are you going to tell me more about your Uncle Bipin?"

She didn't smile when she said it, which made Rahul nervous. Was she serious? He forced a laugh. "Ha. No. Um. Sorry about that. I was just—"

"Hallucinating." Still no smile. God, she was making him sweat.

"Right." Rahul pushed his glasses up on his nose. "Listen, I just wanted to say, about the dance, I had a good time." Whoa. That came out relatively well. No stammering, no anxious gulping, just a bit of sweat. A solid B performance. Rahul smiled to himself, pleased.

Caterina continued to stare at him.

His smile faded. "Um. And I was wondering—"

"Rahul. Let me stop you right there. The dance was *just* a dance, okay? It was just the one night and it doesn't mean anything else." Her eyes softened for a moment just as his heart went crumbling to dust in his chest. "It can't mean anything else. I'm sor—"

"Caterina. I need to speak with you at once."

They both swiveled toward the male voice to see Alaric standing behind Caterina, looking slightly annoyed. A range of expressions crossed Caterina's face that Rahul caught only because he'd spent so much time staring at her. Curiosity, annoyance of her own, anger, distaste. She turned back to Rahul. "Just a minute, Rahul."

He nodded and stepped off to the side, pulling his phone out to play a round of speed chess against *kingedyourass*, a Russian chess player he hadn't managed to beat yet.

CATERINA

It was the first time she'd really *looked* at Alaric in weeks. She'd been made aware of his presence in the dining hall and hallway by Ava, Heather, and her other friends, of course, but she'd pointedly looked away in those moments. Now she had no choice but to take him in fully.

He was beautiful; there was no denying that. His tall, lean physique, his shiny blond hair, and those plump pink lips were all picture-perfect. He had better lips than hers, even when she overlined. It wasn't fair.

Alaric batted his long blond eyelashes at her and sighed petulantly. "You're looking well." His eyes ran over her hair, her nails, her skin.

So that's what was bothering him. Caterina pulled herself to her full height and looked him square in the eye. "Yes. I am. Better than I've been in years, in fact."

He scowled, a mannerism that had always greatly annoyed her. "Are you going to the Hindman Foundation Gala in two weeks?"

Her head spun at the sudden change in topic, but she kept herself poised as always. "Yes, of course I am. I never miss it." The gala was an annual event, and all the usual socialites would be there. The major lifestyle and fashion papers and magazines would be filled with pictures from the event for a few issues afterward. It was a good place to go after a breakup, too: Caterina's friends called it the "Find Man" Gala because of the number of hookups that happened there.

Alaric smirked as a group of juniors walked by, talking about skiing in Aspen over the weekend. "Well, then you should know I will be there as well. And for my date, I'm bringing Lizel Falk."

The name sounded familiar. Caterina frowned, trying to place it before it came to her. She jerked her gaze back to Alaric. "Lizel Falk? As in, the Australian model?"

Alaric's eyes sparked with delight, knowing he had her. "*Super*model, actually." He gave her a complacent smile; he'd had his teeth whitened over the break. "That won't be a problem for you, will it?" He put on a faux air of concern and leaned in to graze her chin with one smooth finger. "Being all alone while I'm with her?"

Fury, loud and hot and powerful, washed over Caterina. Before she could think twice, she heard herself saying, "Who says I'm going to be alone?"

It was worth it just to see Alaric's smile fade. "What? Who will you be going with?"

Caterina's pulse raced. The only thing worse than her trite little lie would be for Alaric to figure out she was lying. She'd looked completely pathetic and weak, eager for his approval, actually caring what he thought of her. Tucking a lock of hair behind one ear, she shrugged in what she hoped was a gracefully insouciant manner. "Oh, just someone from a very well-connected family. I don't think he's ever been near disgusting assorted animal byproducts in his entire life. Not all of us can say the same now, can we, Alaric?" She was purposely hitting him where it hurt. The Konigs were very sensitive about the fact that they made their fortune from commercializing rarely used cow parts. "So you can go Falk yourself. And I'll bring my own prince."

He drew himself up, ugly splotches of red appearing on his cheeks. "Fine. I suppose I'll see you then." He turned and stalked off. Caterina could practically see the steam emanating from his ears.

She smiled to herself for a long moment until reality came seeping back in. Now what? She had to somehow come up with a well-placed boy to take to this thing. There were plenty of options at the school, of course, but . . .

But what, Caterina? she asked herself, annoyed. *There shouldn't be any "but." Just ask one of them to go.* She knew no one would deny her.

Caterina stood there as dozens of eligible boys walked past her, guffawing at jokes their friends were telling, showing off pictures of the new Ferraris they'd gotten for Christmas or Hanukkah, so shiny and perfectly Alaric-like in the uniforms their maids had pressed for them back home. The idea of approaching a single one, let alone allowing him to be her date for an entire evening in the spotlight, exhausted her to the bone. She was tired of the Alaricbots, fresh off the line, each one just like the other, and each one just like his father before him. What she wanted, she realized, her gaze bouncing off each one and going on to the next, was someone . . . completely . . . real.

Her eyes came to rest on Rahul as she thought the last word. He was still standing where she'd left him, simply because she'd asked him to wait and he was someone who was good for his word. His thumbs were moving quickly along his phone screen, and his glasses had slipped to the tip of his nose. He was biting his lower lip so hard, it was a wonder it wasn't bleeding. His uniform was terribly ill-fitting; it must be at least three years old. One of the buttons on his shirt was hanging on by a thread, but he didn't seem to have noticed.

He was, to put it quite bluntly, a mess. Rahul Chopra was *not* the kind of boy you took to the Hindman Foundation Gala, not if you wanted to reestablish yourself as Queen Cat, not if you wanted to pick up that crown, polish it, and set it back atop your head. Rahul Chopra was all wrong, as ill-fitting as his uniform.

Caterina found herself walking up to him. "Rahul."

His attention snapped to her immediately.

She took a breath. "I have a proposition for you."

CHAPTER 5

RAHUL

"Come with me," Caterina said, heading in the opposite direction of where Rahul needed to go. The wooden double doors leading outside lay a couple of yards ahead of them, beyond a cluster of juniors.

"What . . . what about class?" he asked, his feet already picking themselves up and following her across the maroon-and-white checker-tiled floor, even if his brain wasn't sure yet.

Caterina smirked at him over her shoulder. "I think you can afford to miss one class. You already have over a 4.0 GPA, don't you? You'll get caught back up soon enough."

"That's true," Rahul mused, pushing his glasses up as he and Caterina neared the end of the hallway. "But what about you?"

Caterina laughed a little as she circumvented the juniors, pushed the doors open, and headed outside, toward a little picnic bench and table in the distance. It was cold but not snowy, the grass stiff with crystal flakes. "I'll be okay. Italian is sort of my first language."

"Oh." Rahul glanced at her in the sudden quiet, away from the bustle of the other students. He heard the bell ping softly inside the building as they walked quickly toward the table, signaling the start of the next class, but he already felt far away, removed from it all.

They sat on the wooden bench, the cold seeping through his uniform pants and into his skin as he watched Caterina curiously. She perched beside him, her skirt swept under her. Setting her textbooks on the table, she took a deep breath, not looking at him.

All around them the Rosetta campus sat peacefully, still not fully adjusted to being overrun with students again. It felt more like home to Rahul than his own family's house: the Rocky Mountains in the distance, always signaling west. The stately buildings around campus, including the ballroom with its domed roof where he'd danced with Caterina. The sprawling dorms, closer, that had been his home for most of his life. And here, in front of him on this chilly picnic bench, the only girl he'd ever loved, looking right at him now, as if she were evaluating something.

Rahul sat up straighter, adjusting his glasses surreptitiously, smoothing his hair back just a touch, wishing it looked more like Alaric's or Grey's or really anyone else's than his own.

"Do you know what the Hindman Foundation Gala is?" Caterina's voice was as crisp and cool as the air. She wrapped her arms around herself as if she were cold, and Rahul wanted to immediately give her his blazer too. But he stopped himself. Intuitively he knew Caterina didn't like to be seen as weak, and him offering her his blazer would definitely be misconstrued as a judgment on her strength.

"Um, is that like a dance?"

Caterina winced a bit, and Rahul was sure he'd said the wrong thing. "Yes, but it's much more than a dance. It's a society affair, where all the most influential people come together to celebrate the Hindmans and give their foundation a lot of money and basically parade around their wealth."

Rahul knew he shouldn't ask the next question on his lips, but he couldn't help it. He was a collector of data, if nothing else, and he had to know. Adjusting his position a bit on the cold wooden bench, he said, "Right. Um . . . who are the Hindmans, exactly?"

Caterina stared at him silently, unmovingly, for a long minute. The chill wind picked up a strand of her hair, but she didn't smooth it back down. Finally, she closed her eyes for just a moment. "This is going to be a lot more challenging than I had thought," she mumbled, as if she were talking to herself.

"What is?" Rahul asked, frowning.

Caterina opened those luminescent brown eyes he'd spent ten minutes and a lifetime staring into that morning. Propping one elbow on the table, she said, "Rahul . . . the Hindmans are the most connected, most powerful family in the US, and probably among the top five most powerful in the world. People like us always want to know the Hindmans. Surely you've heard of them. Paul and Amelia? They have two daughters and a son who go to boarding school in Switzerland? One of their daughters recently launched a fashion line partnering with Chanel, and it's become iconic. There are memes on the internet about the Hindmans."

Rahul wanted to say yes, of course he knew exactly who they were. If he could say the names of the children, that would be extra impressive. This was why he'd told Grey and Leo he thought tiny computers embedded in people's brains would be a good thing, the technological advance we all didn't know we needed. Instead, he shrugged. "Sorry."

Caterina exhaled slowly. "Okay. Well, never mind that. You're a quick learner, right? You have a photographic memory?"

"Eidetic," Rahul said automatically. "'Eidetic' is the correct term for exceptional visual recall. But I can also remember other things that aren't visual for much longer than most people can, yes."

Caterina narrowed her eyes. "Right." Then she straightened her shoulders. "I mentioned a proposition, before." She nodded her head toward the building they'd left.

"Yeah." He'd almost forgotten that, swept up in the trance of being led away by Caterina LaValle, like he'd been in his dreams a million times before. (In his dreams they always ended up playing chess on the green, Caterina laughing as she castled him while he was in check. Which wasn't even a valid chess move.) "Okay, yes."

She frowned. In the distance, a lone winter bird cawed. "'Yes' what?"

"Yes to your proposition."

A brief look of amusement flickered on her perfect face. "You don't even know what I'm asking yet."

He could see, from her perspective, why she'd find it amusing that he wanted in without more information. But Caterina couldn't see into his heart. He'd seen her without her mask on. He'd seen the *real* her no one else knew. And he'd follow *that* Caterina anywhere, no questions asked.

Now Rahul leaned forward to rest his elbows on the wooden slats of the picnic table. "Unless you're going to ask me to murder someone—which I am 99.87 percent sure you're not, as I don't think it aligns with your previous actions, which are the most consistent predictors of future behavior—I'm going to say yes."

The amusement morphed into a faint smile. If Rahul were a painter, he would spend eons in his room, painting it to get it right. "But don't you want to hold back a little? Maybe think about something you might want from me in return?"

She was talking about social bartering, something Rahul would never, ever understand. "But why would I do that?" he found himself saying, instead of keeping it to himself like he'd learned to do with most people. "I want to spend time with you. I want to give you whatever you want. To pretend anything else is the truth would be disingenuous."

Caterina studied him, a look between alarm and intrigue on her face. There was a sudden break in the clouds, and a thin, weak beam of winter sunlight hit her brown hair, dappling it with gold. "You're quite possibly the oddest person I've ever met."

Rahul nodded. The way she said it, as a matter of fact rather than judgment, didn't embarrass him. "I've heard that sentiment expressed in much meaner ways."

Caterina leaned forward. "But wait, what you said just before. You don't hold back the truth . . . ever? You just say what you mean. You never lie."

"Well . . . I would *like* to lie to preserve people's feelings. To protect people I care about. But things don't always work out like that." Rahul shrugged and polished his glasses with his tie before popping them back on his nose.

He'd barely finished speaking when Caterina said, "Go to the Hindman Foundation Gala with me."

And his eyebrows shot up into his hairline.

CATERINA

He sat there with his eyebrows invisible for a long time. Finally, Caterina reached forward and touched his hand. He reacted as if she'd pressed a live wire into his skin.

"Are you all right?" she asked, frowning. "What's the matter?" He looked ill.

"It's—I'm—so, you're saying you want me to be your date. To the biggest event in socialite land."

Caterina shook her head and tapped her fingernails on the hard cover of her Italian textbook. "No. Not my date. My . . . escort, or companion, I suppose. I'm trying to prove a point to someone."

"Alaric," Rahul said. "I saw him talking to you. He got that look on his face he always gets when he's trying to make someone feel inferior."

Caterina went still. "What look?"

Rahul waved a hand. "I don't know how to describe it. There's a little smirk at one corner of his mouth, and he uses his height in a certain way, looming over the person." He shrugged and shifted his feet on the stiff grass. "I'm not the best at reading people, in case you haven't noticed, though, so I'm probably wrong."

Caterina shook her head slowly. "Au contraire," she said, "you might be the only one who's ever noticed that." Why hadn't *she* ever noticed that? She'd gone out with him for two years. That was plenty of time for her to realize he was manipulating her or others, trying to make them feel less than. Had she been so focused on the superficial—his looks, his well-placed family, the presents he bought her—that she'd forgotten to pay attention to Alaric the person? The idea didn't make her feel very good about herself, so Caterina quickly changed the subject. "In any case, do you think you could keep Saturday the fourth free? That's in two weeks."

"Well, sure," Rahul agreed immediately. "But, um, I don't know how to dance. And you might have noticed that I'm not exactly gala material."

"I have noticed," Caterina replied as her phone buzzed in her pocket. She pulled it out without looking at it, swiped to silence it, and slipped it back into her pocket. Whoever it was could wait. "And that's why I need to tell you the condition of my proposition. I'm going to give you a makeover so you'll fit in better. So Alaric can see I've moved onward and upward." *So you won't embarrass me and completely negate what I'm trying to accomplish*, she didn't add. There was no reason to be cruel.

Rahul sat up straighter, tugging at his tie. "A makeover? What, like, *My Fair Lady* or something?"

"Exactly like that. Hair, fashion, social training, all of it. Now, we only have two weeks, so it won't be quite as thorough as I'd like, but it's a start. As long as you leave the talking mostly to me, we'll be fine. What do you say?"

He didn't hesitate even a moment. "Yes. I still say yes." Then, pausing to look down at himself—his horribly ill-fitting uniform, his messily done tie, his untied shoelaces—he said, "When do we start?"

RAHUL

As he watched her walk away, back into the building in time for the next class, Rahul couldn't help but smile. *Caterina LaValle* had asked him to the Hindman Foundation Gala. Not as a date, but still. He'd get to spend time with her, not just at the event in two weeks, but in the intervening time as well.

Not to mention, her training him could only mean good things. He'd be able to fit into her social circle better—he'd be able to fit into his *own* social circle better. No more wondering what his friends were talking about, or if he still wondered, maybe he'd know when to speak and when to hold his tongue. He wouldn't hurt people like he'd hurt DE that morning. She'd forgive him soon enough, he knew—his friends always did—but he didn't want to be in a position to require their forgiveness anymore. He wanted to be more attuned to their needs, more careful of their feelings.

With Caterina's help, he could be more polished. A neater, classier version of himself. Maybe if he fit in really well with all of Caterina's friends at the gala, she'd want to date him for real. He could be Alaric's equal. Hell, with his personality, he could be Alaric's superior. He'd never lie to Caterina or cheat on her like Alaric had done.

Rahul got up from the bench and walked toward the towering mathematics building in the distance. For the first time since he'd been enrolled at Rosetta Academy, he whistled as he walked.

CATERINA

13 Days until the Hindman Gala

She didn't like to think of it as *spying*. Spying was what palace maids did in the old days at the bidding of their mistresses. Spying was what undercover agents did in exchange for a paltry paycheck.

Spying was beneath her. Caterina was merely . . . observing Rahul in his natural habitat. Nothing more, nothing less.

She sat in the darkened observatory and planetarium at the top of the natural sciences building, not paying the slightest attention to Dr. Patton, the astronomy teacher, prattle on in her monotone about some celestial oddity or other that was playing out on the large domed screen above Caterina and the rest of the students. Normally, she wouldn't be able to keep her eyes open, staring at the stars and the meteors and other space debris from a million miles away, but that was okay. Tonight she was here under cover of the open invitation issued by the astronomy club—of which Rahul was a part, naturally—for all the Rosetta students to come marvel at "a presentation chronicling the wonders of the heavens above" with them, according to the flyer. There were about two dozen students present, which was perfect. Caterina arrived late, once the lights had been turned out, and took a seat in the back so as not to catch Rahul's eye.

She knew he put on a little bit of effort when she was around. She was used to it; most people did that around her. What she was really interested in was seeing exactly what she was dealing with. How was he when he thought no one was watching? What might she have to work on with him in the ensuing two weeks? Surely being the son of a high-ranking politician would have imparted *some* social training in him, if only by osmosis.

Currently he was sitting in a theater-style seat off to the left, a few rows down from her. As she watched, Rahul pulled his feet up onto the seat and hugged his knees, as if he were a child watching a movie about Santa Claus. Sighing, Caterina scribbled a note to herself on the back of the flyer. *Lessons in how to sit appropriately when in company.*

"Caterina?" a voice from over her right shoulder whispered.

She turned to see Ava staring at her, the whites of her eyes glowing in the near-dark room. Lights from the movie shone purple in her brown hair. "Hello."

"What are you doing here?" Ava asked, still looking completely thrown. "Are you . . . watching the movie?"

"Of course I am," Caterina answered, sliding the flyer down to where Ava couldn't see the note she'd made. "Just like you, I imagine."

"Yeah, but I only came because Zahira wanted to come, remember?" Ava said, gesturing slightly to a Pakistani girl with a thin face who was staring avidly at the screen above them.

That's right; this was her new girlfriend, Zahira, a junior. Caterina had only somewhat listened as Ava had filled them in at lunch that day. And naturally, she hadn't told Heather or Ava about the deal she'd made with Rahul earlier in the day. She couldn't trust them to keep the information to themselves. It was a motto she held dear: if you want to tell someone a secret, tell yourself. Rahul was the clear exception; she couldn't execute the plan without him being in on it.

"Oh, well, yes," Caterina said, smiling coolly. "I'm here for a similar thing, actually. A boy who's taking me to the Hindman Gala is very interested in astronomy. I'm just picking up a few facts so we can talk about it together."

Ava gasped and grasped the back of Caterina's seat. "Who is it? You didn't tell us you were bringing a date to the gala!"

Caterina brushed her aside as a boy in big glasses, probably a sophomore, turned to glare at them. Normally, she'd freeze him with an icy stare, but she was glad for the interruption this time. "Later," she promised, turning back around.

Just in time to see Rahul stick a pencil down the back of his shirt in an effort to scratch a place that wasn't easily accessible to his fingers. As he scratched, he closed his eyes, as if to fully appreciate the sensation of doing something so private in public. He looked like a mangy mutt getting its ears rubbed. Appalling. Caterina barely restrained herself from running over and snatching the pencil out of his hand. Instead, sighing, she made another note on her flyer: *Scratching of any kind is* not *permitted when there are human beings within sight.*

12 Days until the Hindman Gala

Day two was worse. So much worse.

Caterina walked a few people behind Rahul in the mathematics building after his advanced Boolean logic class. Another senior, a well-coiffed Black British boy named Will, whose family were real estate moguls, was attempting to engage him in conversation.

"Did you have a good break, then, Rahul?" Will asked, smiling at Rahul as they walked, books in hand.

Rahul looked straight ahead. "Yep."

"Did you go home? Your family's from India, aren't they?"

"Yeah."

A long pause, with Will presumably waiting for Rahul to supply something of his own to the conversation, as all well-bred children of well-placed parents would. But there was nothing but deflating silence. Caterina sighed.

"Ah . . . what do your parents do again? Isn't your mum in politics?" Will asked, rallying valiantly to revive the conversation.

"She's a government worker," Rahul replied flippantly, and

Caterina almost choked on the air she was breathing in.

A government worker?? His mother was the chief minister of Delhi! Why wouldn't he say that instead? Why was he determined to be viewed as some wallflower when he could present himself as so much more?

"Caterina! What are you doing here? I thought you were finished with all your mathematics requirements. You made such a fuss about it junior year." She stopped to find Vanya Petrovic, a blond-haired senior and one of Alaric's friends, looking at her in astonishment. The stained-glass windows high up on the walls cast pink-and-yellow squares in his pale hair.

"Taking pictures of the architecture," Caterina replied with her practiced answer, holding up her phone. "It's for photography class. How have you been, Vanya?"

"Very well, thanks," he said, smiling. "Looking forward to seeing your fabulous sartorial choices at the Hindman Gala soon." Then, his smile slipping, he added in a conspiratorial whisper, "But I feel I must warn you about Alaric. He's got—"

"A date with Lizel Falk. Yes, I know."

Vanya looked pained, the expression sweet on his square face. "I'm sorry, Caterina. I tried to tell him it was much too early to be—"

"Don't worry." She smiled a somewhat genuine smile. Vanya had always been the most tolerable of Alaric's friends. "I'm bringing someone too, and I couldn't care less what Alaric does. Really."

Vanya searched her eyes with his blue ones for a moment and then smiled back. "Well, good. I'm happy for you, then." Squeezing her arm gently, he added, "But I must go now."

Caterina turned back around to see that Rahul had disappeared. Annoyed, she slipped her phone into her blazer pocket and made her way down the hall, Vanya's words playing in her mind. So Alaric had told everyone about Lizel Falk. He'd made it seem like he'd moved onward and upward while Caterina was still pining after him, wringing her hands, waiting for a text with haunted eyes.

Screw him. Screw them all. She slammed the door open with the heel of her hand and strode out into the cold sunshine. At the Hindman Gala, they'd see just how spectacularly she'd moved on.

11 Days until the Hindman Gala

The last phase of observing Rahul in his natural habitat had commenced. He was sitting at his usual table in the dining hall, about to eat his lunch. His friends Grey, Leo, and Samantha were already there, all of them with plates of food of their own. Caterina had taken a seat toward the kitchen, a table that was usually unoccupied because of its undesirable location. Hopefully, Rahul wouldn't see her there.

She waited with bated breath as he picked up his sandwich. Perhaps this was one area where she wouldn't need to coach him. Perhaps he'd have the genteel table manners of an English duke. Perhaps—

Rahul's method of eating could only be described as "violent snarfing." He stuffed the bread into his mouth, chewing and swallowing in record speed before shoving even more of the bread in. It didn't look to Caterina like he could breathe. Bits of olives and pickles fell off his sandwich onto his plate, and like some kind of circus juggler, he managed to pick those up and reintroduce them into the rotation while he continued to feed bread to his gnashing teeth. Completely unacceptable. He was eating like he was a starving prisoner with a cruel guard about to snatch away his daily allotment of dry bread and watery broth. Caterina couldn't even *imagine* taking him in his current form to the Hindman Gala. They'd be the laughingstock of the entire—

"Caterina? Why are you sitting here?"

Oh, for God's sake. Why couldn't people just leave her alone?

She turned to see Jaya and Daphne Elizabeth gaping at her, plates of food in their hands. Jaya was the one who'd spoken, but Daphne Elizabeth looked equally startled to see Caterina sitting in such an unfavorable spot.

Caterina smiled at Jaya. "Hello, Jaya." Then, letting her smile vanish, she turned to Daphne Elizabeth and stared at her in cold silence. Daphne Elizabeth continued to gawp at her, looking much like a bird hypnotized helplessly against its will by a predatory snake. To facilitate the breaking of Daphne Elizabeth's paralysis, Caterina raised a recently threaded and powdered brow.

"Um, I better get, um, just going to . . ." Daphne Elizabeth gestured vaguely around her, turned on her heel, and sped off.

Jaya cocked her head at Caterina, her long black French braid brushing her arm. "That wasn't very nice."

Caterina smiled again and crossed her hands neatly in front of her. "Haven't you heard? *I'm* not very nice."

Jaya's expression softened at that. "Well, neither of them treated you very well. But for what it's worth, I really do think DE regrets that quite a lot."

Caterina waved her comment away; she wasn't interested in what Daphne Elizabeth felt, not even a tiny bit. The girl was immaterial.

Setting down her plate of what looked like avocado salad, Jaya took a seat. "Seriously, what are you doing here? You looked very intent on whomever you were watching." She looked in the direction Caterina had been looking. "That's my table." She turned to Caterina. "Who were you watching at my table?"

Caterina blinked and looked away out the window, as if a bird pecking at the frozen ground had caught her attention. "Nobody. I was sitting here for some peace and quiet, which it's clear I'm not about to get."

But Jaya didn't take the hint. She propped her elbow on the table and her chin in her hand. "Rahul? Are you watching Rahul?"

Caterina glared at her. "No, I'm not."

"Yes, you are." Jaya smiled a half smile. "What's going on? Why don't you just go over there and say hello?"

"I don't *want* to go over and say hello." Why was Jaya so exasperating with her social graces and her wish for everyone to be as sickeningly happy as her and Grey? "And I wasn't watching him."

Jaya's face got more serious as she took a beat to absorb whatever she thought was happening. Sitting up straight, she said, "He's my friend, Caterina."

Caterina kept her expression cold as she adjusted the jade bracelet on her wrist. "I'm well aware."

"Don't hurt him, whatever it is you're doing. Rahul is . . . He likes you. A lot. He'll follow wherever you lead."

Caterina didn't respond.

The two looked at each other for a long moment, and then Jaya nodded and stood, grabbing her untouched avocado salad. "All right. I'll leave you to it, then."

"Goodbye." Caterina watched Jaya walk away to join her friends for a moment before she stood and began making her way to the doors, wondering why she spent so much time feeling so alone when she was always surrounded by people.

But never mind that. She had all the information she needed. Now it was time to build herself a new boyfriend.

CHAPTER 6

RAHUL

Rahul looked in the mirror and smoothed his hair back. It sat there limply, never quite able to muster enough oomph to do anything interesting, like Alaric's hair seemed to do so effortlessly. He sighed and, abandoning his hair, tugged on the sleeves of his tan sweater. It was the only garment he had in his closet that fit him well, because it had been a birthday present from Leo, who had an impeccable fashion sense (though he didn't like it if you assumed it was because he was French; he said he'd had to work at it like anyone else and that Rahul should too).

His pants were a different matter. He wasn't sure when he'd purchased them, but it had been at least two summers ago because pants shopping was one of his least favorite activities in the world. For basically just being temporary leg coverings, people fussed over them way too much. Grabbing his phone off his dresser, Rahul walked out of his dorm room and shut the door behind him, feeling the first flurry of nerves.

It was Thursday, and to be precise, T-2 days until the Hindman Gala on Saturday. Caterina had been meeting with him nearly every day until now, and today marked one of the last of his social training classes. He was meeting her in the senior common area, which, like the rest of the dorm, would be empty. They had the next day off, so the seniors were all on an optional skiing trip that the school administration had organized; as far as Rahul knew, he, Caterina, and a couple of seniors who'd been unlucky enough to get sick were the only ones who'd opted to stay behind. He'd just told Grey and the others that he felt a little under the weather. The benefit of having a reputation of being honest to a fault was that no one thought to question you when you actually lied.

Him and Caterina, alone. Caterina and him, by themselves. Talking. Laughing. Growing closer? His brain couldn't wrap itself around the concept. Anytime he thought about it, he went into a mild state of shock.

Doing one last check in the mirror to confirm he looked decent, he turned and walked into the common room.

Caterina stood by the floor-to-ceiling windows on the far side, staring out at the mountains in the distance. Her dark brown hair cascaded down her back like thick ribbons of silk. She was wearing a shimmery gold sweater with voluminous sleeves and dark jeans that hugged her skinny legs and butt. Her shoes were so high and pointy, Rahul wondered at her ability to walk in them.

He cleared his throat and she turned, looking a little foggy, as if she'd been light-years away. "Hey."

She looked at him inscrutably for a moment and then walked a few steps forward, holding up one long index finger. "Lesson one: You do not greet people by saying 'hey.' Instead, try, 'It's a pleasure to meet you,' or if you know them, 'It's so nice to see you again.'"

"Right. Sorry." Rahul took a step forward. "It's so nice to see you again."

Caterina nodded. "That's better. Also, don't say 'sorry.' You should say, 'Excuse me.'"

"Right," Rahul repeated. "Excuse me." After a pause, he added, not able to help his curiosity, "Do people really care about that?"

"About what?" Caterina asked, cocking her head.

"The minutiae. 'Excuse me' rather than 'sorry' seems a little . . . I don't know. Who really keeps track of all of that?"

Caterina raised one thin eyebrow, and Rahul knew he'd stepped in it. "I do. As do many others. Etiquette separates us from animals, Rahul."

"Really?" he said. "I thought that was opposable thumbs."

For a moment, he was aghast. He shouldn't have said anything. He was being rude; she'd change her mind about helping him with these lessons. But then Caterina smiled a half smile, and Rahul's heart sang.

"All right," she said, turning toward a small table that had been set with two chairs, napkins, silverware, and plates. "Let's say we've been led to the dinner portion of the evening and they've shown us to our tables. Demonstrate how you'd proceed."

"Okay . . ." Rahul glanced at Caterina, as if there might be some trick she was playing on him. "I mean, it's pretty straight-forward, right? I'd . . . go sit down?"

Caterina held one hand out as if to say he should do what he felt was right, so Rahul nodded, walked quickly and decisively to the chair, and sat. Looking up at her hopefully, he said, "How'd I do?"

But Caterina was already shaking her head. "No. Firstly, you have to wait for me to take my seat first."

"Oh, right. Sorry." Rahul shot up from his chair and joined her at her side. "I mean, excuse me."

Caterina walked, gracefully and surely, to the table and looked at him, waiting.

"Um . . . go ahead?"

Giving him a withering look, she said, "Hold my chair back, please."

"Oh, okay." Rahul rushed forward and held the back of one of the chairs, but Caterina didn't move.

"The lady always gets the better view," Caterina said, nodding her head toward the bank of windows meaningfully.

Rahul walked to the other chair and held its back.

Smiling, Caterina walked over and took a seat. "Perfect."

Feeling a lot more pleased than he should, Rahul took a seat opposite her.

Caterina reached into a small purse thing she had with her and pulled out a Lara Bar. Reaching over the table, she set it on Rahul's plate. "Eat it, please."

Rahul glanced at it uncertainly. "Um . . . should I unwrap it first?"

"Yes!" Caterina said after an incredulous pause. "How will you eat it if you don't unwrap it?"

"I don't know," Rahul replied. "I wasn't sure if unwrapping was a faux pas or something."

Caterina took a deep breath and let it out slowly. "Please unwrap and consume the Lara Bar."

"Okay." Rahul unwrapped it and took a bite, and then another, and another, until the bar was gone. He looked at Caterina while chewing (with his mouth closed; he wasn't a total troglodyte), his eyebrows raised.

"Say your name," she said, gazing at him steadily.

"Mmm?" Rahul asked, frowning.

"Say your name. Right now. Don't bother swallowing first."

So he did, in spite of his misgivings. As he'd known it would, a disgusting spray of Lara Bar landed in front of him on his empty plate.

"Sor—excuse me," he said, rushing to wipe it up with his napkin.

"That's a lesson in eating etiquette," Caterina said calmly. "If you can't comfortably say your name with food in your mouth, you have far too much food in your mouth. Slow down and take smaller bites. It's not a contest."

Rahul nodded. Caterina reached into her purse and pulled out yet another Lara Bar, then set it on the napkin on top of his plate. "Let's do that again."

Rahul unwrapped the bar and, this time, took a tiny bite of the corner. Looking at Caterina, he said, uncertainly, "Rahul Chopra."

She smiled, a real smile, and he nearly fell off his chair. "Excellent, Rahul Chopra," she said, and he'd never heard anything as beautiful as his full name in her mouth. "That's another lesson down."

CATERINA

"Handshakes are how men are judged at this kind of thing," Caterina explained. They'd moved on from the dining table. Now they were standing, facing each other, in front of the windows. Outside, a blanket of snow had started to fall, coating the rolling hills of the campus in pure white. It was Caterina's favorite kind of weather.

Straightening her shoulders, Caterina held out a hand. "It's a pleasure to meet you," she said, smiling the gracious, elegant smile she used in high society.

"Oh, you too," Rahul said, grabbing her hand as if it were a malfunctioning water pump handle and jerking it enthusiastically up and down. His maniacal grin slowly faded at her stony expression. He paused the jerking and then let go of her hand. "Um, too much?"

"*Far* too much," Caterina said as calmly as she could manage. How could a Rosetta student be *so* undereducated in proper etiquette? "Your mother *is* the chief minister of Delhi, is she not?" she asked, suddenly afraid that Rahul was actually a street urchin who'd just wandered in for warm meals and a bed and this was all a case of mistaken identity.

"Yep. We don't talk a lot, but I did get a Google alert saying she was headed to Canada for a speaking engagement, and the article did reference her formal title, which is 'Mukhyamantri' or 'Chief Minister.'"

Caterina frowned. "You don't talk a lot? Why not?"

Rahul flushed a faint pink and looked away. Curious. "She's, ah, busy. It's always been that way with her and the rest of my family; my father and older brother, too. They're all jet-setters, very engaged in my mother's career." He managed a weak smile, then took off his glasses and focused intently on cleaning them.

Caterina felt a tug of pity in her heart. What Rahul wasn't saying, but what she was hearing anyway, was that his family was ashamed of him. Perhaps his . . . odd . . . way of being in the world was something they'd tried and failed to fix. Perhaps Rosetta Academy was a way for them to sequester him from the public eye without feeling guilty about it. She thought of her own father, always eager to have her on his arm at various events, and realized how lucky she was to have the relationship she did with him.

She cleared her throat delicately. "Right, of course. Politics is very demanding." After a pause, Caterina broached a topic she'd been meaning to broach since she'd asked him to do this. "So . . . I was wondering, ah, about your social relationships. Do you have, that is, is there a diagnosis?" It was clumsy, but she'd never been trained on anything like this. In her usual circles, she'd never dream of bringing it up, but this was important.

Rahul looked confused for a moment, but then his brow cleared. He wiped his palms on his pants. "Are you asking if I'm on the autism spectrum?"

Caterina nodded.

"I'm not." Rahul looked her steadily in the eye, but he licked his lips as if he were nervous. "People often wonder that about me, but Ari—um, the school psychologist—says I have social anxiety and am supremely logical, which is different from being on the spectrum."

"Ah." Caterina studied his expression; his cheeks were stained pink. This was hard for him to talk about. He was probably afraid she'd judge him, like almost everyone probably did. "Thank you for sharing that with me. I wanted to be sure I was being sensitive to your needs."

He rubbed the back of his neck. "I appreciate that."

Sensing that they both needed to move past this, Caterina said, "So. Back to that handshake."

Rahul appeared relieved at the change in subject. "Back to the handshake."

Caterina held her hand out again. "Take it gently, but with a firm pressure," she advised.

Rahul paused, regarding her hand as if it were a complex advanced calculus equation he was trying to solve in his head, before taking it between two fingers, like he was afraid it would break.

Caterina sighed. "No." She withdrew her hand. "Hold out your hand. I'll demonstrate."

He did, and she took it, wrapping her fingers around his hand, feeling the warmth in his skin. Her hands were always too cold. "Like that," she said. "Do you feel the pressure?"

Rahul was turning a flamingo-pink color. "I—I do feel it. Pressure," he said, his voice cracking.

"And how is it?" Caterina asked, not understanding why he was having such a reaction to hand shaking. Was he a secret germophobe? But he'd had no issues taking her hand the first time around.

He cleared his throat. "Ah, it's—it's gentle." He licked his lips again, as if they were dry. "But, um, f-firm."

"Right. Good." Caterina pumped his hand once. "One or two pumps, *max*. Anything else is too much. Do you understand?"

He was still staring at their hands. "Yep. I got it."

"And study my hand. Where is it in relation to yours?"

"Um . . ." He kept staring at their hands until Caterina was concerned he was going into some sort of weird trance. "Your hand is in mine," he said finally, faintly, as if he were having trouble believing it.

"Yes," Caterina replied impatiently, "but what else?"

"Um . . ."

Ugh. This strange Rahul trance had gone on long enough. "The webs of our fingers are aligned, do you see? My hand isn't on top of yours, which would imply that I'm in control of you."

Rahul looked up at her at last, still looking like he was in a daze. "You're in control of me?"

What was going *on* with him? "Yes. And you don't want to offend anyone at the gala, so keep your hand in line with theirs."

"Okay." He smiled a little moonily at her.

"Okay." Caterina withdrew her hand. "Now. On to the next thing."

"Which is . . . ?"

"Air-kissing," Caterina said matter-of-factly, and Rahul collapsed back against the window.

RAHUL

"Are you okay?" Caterina said, frowning, reaching for his elbow. "Do you feel faint? There's some kind of flu going around. . . ."

"No, no, I'm fine," Rahul insisted, righting himself and forcing his body not to sway.

First she'd held his hand for what felt like an hour, her skin all soft and silky and cool against his. And now she wanted to air-kiss him? Okay, so that wasn't a *kiss* kiss, but still. She would be up close to his body. He'd be able to smell her *perfume*. Oh God. The thought made him want to simultaneously run away and sing a hymn about the wonder that was Caterina LaValle in a quavery, religious voice. She wanted to *air-kiss* him. Voluntarily. What else could a guy want in life, really? Rahul had the distinct sense that if a lightning bolt came through the window right now and struck him in the heart, he'd die with a smile on his face.

"If you're sure . . ." Caterina eyed him up and down

suspiciously. He had to get over his starstruckness if he wanted her to continue her lessons.

Forcing a more solemn expression and broadening his shoulders, he said as confidently as he could manage, "I'm sure. So. We're on to air-kissing."

"Right." Caterina took a step closer to him, and Rahul forced his heart to stop its useless spluttering. "Now, if you were at an event in New York City, you'd do just one air-kiss on the right cheek. But since our event is in Denver this year, we'll be doing two air-kisses on the right cheek, just like everywhere else in the world."

Rahul frowned, his curiosity piqued in spite of himself. "Why is it different in New York City?"

"Because they think they're special," Caterina said wearily, as if she were tired of New York's shit. "Anyway. Two things to keep in mind: Absolutely no lip or skin contact. They call it an *air*-kiss for a reason. And two, it's always right cheek to right cheek."

"Okay, got it." Rahul's mouth had gone completely dry. Why were his spit glands malfunctioning right now? Traitors.

Caterina stepped forward once more, until she was just a few inches away from him. Then, placing one hand on his upper arm, she leaned forward, so close that her luscious wavy hair tickled the side of Rahul's right cheek. Her perfume wafted over him, gentle as a spring breeze—just a touch of rose and something else, something fresh and pure. He heard her make a kissing sound, and in spite of the fact that his entire body had seized up, Rahul forced himself to follow suit. He had to prove a good student, or she might just give up and take one of Alaric's perfect human mannequin friends to the gala.

Caterina pulled back and studied Rahul's expression. He

hoped she didn't see his deranged muskrat expression (that Leo had informed him he got when he was nervous), but rather, a human who appeared to be quickly learning all the lessons she was imparting. "How was that?"

"Good," he said immediately, his voice about three and a half octaves too high. Clearing his throat, Rahul tried again. "That, um, I think I got it. Yeah."

Caterina took a step back, and Rahul immediately regretted not saying that he needed to practice it two or three more times to get it down pat. That's what Leo would've done. Unfortunately, Rahul Chopra had absolutely zero game. The day the universe was handing out a heaping ladleful of guile and charm, Rahul's genes had gone in for a second helping of every flavor of social inadequacy instead.

"Excellent." Caterina clasped her hands together, a faint smile at her lips. "I think we should stop there today. I don't want to overwhelm you with information. Are you sure you don't need to write it down?"

"I'm sure," Rahul replied. "I have an—"

"Eidetic memory," Caterina finished. "I remember."

"Maybe you have one too," Rahul quipped, and then was inordinately pleased with himself. Usually that joke would've come to him hours later, when he was in the shower or about to fall asleep.

Caterina's faint smile turned into the real thing, and Rahul couldn't help but stare, transfixed. "I sincerely doubt that." She turned and pulled out her cell phone, typing a message to someone. "So, tomorrow, then? Same time?"

"Tomorrow," Rahul agreed, his heart pounding. She wanted to see him again. He hadn't messed it up. Yes! "At Nyx, for lunch."

"Right," Caterina said. "We'll work on table manners some more. See you then." And she swept out, still texting.

Rahul stood for a long minute, staring after her. Then he pulled out his phone, meaning to text Leo. And realized he could do no such thing. He was sworn to secrecy. Dammit. He slipped his phone back into his pocket and turned to the window. The entire campus was quiet, huddled under a fresh coat of snow, devoid of all signs of life. It seemed he was the only one in the world. And yet, right then, Rahul didn't feel alone.

CHAPTER 7

RAHUL

"Come shoot some hoops with us."

The next morning, Rahul looked up from his book (the latest etiquette book by Myka Meier—with a dust jacket from his chess manual to disguise it) to see Grey and Leo in his dorm room, Grey spinning a basketball on his index finger. Jeez, every time Rahul looked at him, he couldn't help but notice that the dude had gotten even *bigger* during winter break. What had Jaya's family fed him? Rahul closed his book. "I think I'll sit this one out, but thanks." He was meeting Caterina at Nyx for lunch in just a couple of hours; he couldn't afford to get all red and sweaty before then. Besides, he'd rather spend his time reading the etiquette book anyway.

"Oh, come on." Leo bounded over and sat at the foot of Rahul's bed. "We need one more to make an even team against the juniors. They—how do you say? Oh, *oui*—they whooped our asses last time before break, but I have been practicing all break long."

"I need to read." Rahul gestured to his book. "Sorry."

Grey walked in and leaned against Owen's, Rahul's roommate's, dresser, making it creak in protest. Thankfully for Rahul, Owen was an overenthusiastic, overly social dude who liked to spend as little time as possible in his dorm. "What's going on, man?" Grey frowned. "We've barely seen you since school started."

Rahul laughed a little. He'd been practicing for this question. "School only started two weeks ago."

Grey quirked one corner of his mouth, his blue eyes piercing in that eerie way, as if he could read your mind. "That's not really an answer to my question."

Rahul shrugged, starting to feel a prickle of uneasiness. He wasn't the *best* liar, given more to logic and facts than smoke and mirrors. "Nothing's going on. I'm just . . . you know . . . reading and stuff. Busy."

Leo was frowning now too. "Busy reading? But you have always been a reader." He looked up at Rahul's collection of chess posters on his wall. It was something of a joke with him and Leo; he'd been adding them so steadily over the years, destroying every inch of blank wall in every one of his dorm rooms over the years, that they practically qualified as wallpaper. "Have you added any new posters yet?"

Rahul followed his gaze. "Um, I don't think I have room for any more posters. Besides, like I said, guys: We've only been in school for two weeks."

Leo looked at Grey like, *You see?? He hasn't added any posters yet; clearly he is in the process of dying from a very rare and protracted illness that has affected his brain.* Thankfully, Grey wasn't nearly as hysterical.

"Okay," Grey said in his unflappable and cryptic way. Rahul could tell he wasn't buying it.

Rahul began to sweat under the weight of Grey's gaze.

Rolling his eyes, Leo said, "Thanks for that contribution, Grey. Very helpful." Looking at Rahul, he added, "Maybe later this weekend we can all get together and do something?"

"Sure," Rahul said. "What about Sunday evening?"

By then the gala would be over and he would be returning to real life. Rahul felt a shot of despondency at the thought of Caterina going back to not really seeing him in the hallways anymore, but it was what it was. There had been a part of him that had hoped, by being the best student ever, that Caterina might slowly begin to see that Rahul could fit in her world. But so far that hadn't happened, and Rahul had to admit that it wasn't likely to happen in the short time they had remaining before the gala. Oh well. At least he'd gotten to spend all this time with her.

"Sunday it is." Grey pushed himself off the dresser and strode with his ridiculously long legs out the door.

After a brief moment, Leo nodded, stood up, and followed him.

CATERINA

Caterina prided herself on being someone who was rarely, if ever, impressed. And yet, in this moment, she had no choice but to admit she was, in fact, *extremely* impressed.

On Friday afternoon, the day before the Hindman Gala, she sat back in the booth at Nyx, the restaurant at which she and Rahul had just eaten lunch. Caterina studied him, shaking her head slowly.

"What?" he asked nervously, leaning forward. "Did I do okay? How many this time?"

Caterina consulted her phone quickly, breaking an etiquette rule, but this was important. Looking back at him, she said, "Not a single etiquette mistake or grievous social faux pas that time."

Rahul gaped at her. "Seriously. Not one? Not even a tiny half mistake?"

"Not even that." Caterina took a deep breath and released it slowly. "I think you're ready for the gala."

"I'm ready," Rahul said in wonder, the lights of the restaurant glowing purple in his black hair. It was always nighttime at Nyx; the ceilings were made to look like the night sky, using fiber-optic lights and special panels. Normally, Caterina didn't go in for gimmicks, but this was the only remotely "fancy" restaurant in the area. It crossed her mind that she could buy the place; it had potential. She'd talk to her people about it later. "I'm really ready."

"Good thing, since it's tomorrow." Caterina signed the receipt the waitress had deposited at their table a few minutes ago. She'd insisted on paying. One, this wasn't a date, and two, she knew for a fact that the LaValles were much, much wealthier than the Chopras. "We need to get you cleaned up."

After a lengthy pause, Rahul asked, "Will there be a lot of cameras there?"

Caterina put the pen down and looked at him. "Yes, there will. As I said, all the society pages and a few lifestyle magazines were invited. Why?" She crossed her arms and studied him. "You're not changing your mind at the eleventh hour, are you?"

"No, of course not!" Rahul said immediately, and Caterina relaxed a bit. It would be nearly impossible to find a suitable date this late, even for her. "It's just that . . ." He played with his napkin, which was definitely an etiquette breach, but Caterina held her tongue. She wanted to hear this. "I'm not really great with cameras. I kind of . . . seize up."

Caterina cocked her head. "But surely you've done a few professional photography sessions for your mother's campaign, gotten some media training. I know you said she's busy, but politicians like to trot out their families for photo ops."

"I've forgotten everything they taught me as a kid," Rahul explained. "And after a few really bad pictures . . ." He cleared his throat, a faint pink hue coloring his cheeks. "Um, my parents began using one of my distant cousins as a stand-in for me. Apparently, we have the same bone structure." He pointed to his nose and jaw, but kept his eyes averted. The funny thing was that Rahul had a strong jaw and an aquiline nose. They could be handsome if he were to own them with just a little more confidence.

Caterina's heart contracted in her chest as the waitress swung back around to pick up the check. "They . . . use someone else in pictures. You mean like a body double?"

"Yeah, I guess." Rahul nodded solemnly, his gaze on hers defeated and heavy.

Caterina kept her voice neutral. She suspected the last thing he wanted right now was her pity. "I'm surprised the media hasn't caught on."

Rahul waved a hand, attempting to appear insouciant. But Caterina saw the vestiges of hurt there, lingering on his face. "Ah, they're much more interested in my brother, anyway. He's on track to continue the family political legacy." He paused. "But, um, I guess you wouldn't know anything about that. People using body doubles for you in pictures, I mean."

Caterina frowned, not understanding, as she grabbed the

handles of her Chloé bag. "What do you mean?"

Rahul looked at her again, his cheeks staining an even brighter pink than before. "Um, because you're—it's like—" He gestured at her, at a loss for words.

Realization dawned, and Caterina smiled a little as she sat back in her booth, letting go of her bag. "Do you mean because you think I'm pretty?"

"Uh. Yeah."

She continued watching him, though he was having trouble making eye contact. In spite of herself and the very businesslike nature of this transaction, Caterina couldn't help but be charmed. When Alaric had fed her lines, they very much had the feel of lines: meant to impress and maybe even get under her dress. But with Rahul, it was obvious he was just speaking his mind, as much discomfort as it caused him. He truly, genuinely thought she was beautiful. "Well, thank you, Rahul. I appreciate that sentiment."

He studied her face frankly and then took a sip of water. A nearby table of four adults laughed loudly and utterly obnoxiously before subsiding again when they caught Caterina's withering glare. "Do you ever get nervous? About the people, the cameras, all of that?"

Caterina looked at Rahul in surprise. He wasn't one for emotions, she knew. It was one thing they had in common. "No, I don't. It's important to my father and our businesses that I attend these things, so it's important to me as well. It's work, in a way. Emotions don't really come into it."

"Emotions complicate things," Rahul said thoughtfully.

"They make things messy. And the last thing I need in my life is mess." Caterina was glad she didn't have to explain. Most of the people in her life—Papa excluded, naturally—thought it was odd that a girl, especially, was so emotion-averse, as if emotionality was a gendered trait. Ridiculous. "So, are you ready to go shopping?"

Rahul took a breath. "I'm ready."

RAHUL

February was living up to its title as the cruelest month of the year (according to the *Farmers' Almanac* that Rahul had perused for fun earlier that day). It was bitterly, achingly cold even though it wasn't snowing, and the five-minute walk from Nyx to this western hemlock-lined street full of stores felt like risking his neck on an ice slide. Rahul was huddled into his coat, trying not to shake, but Caterina stood beside him, tall and imperious and graceful as ever in her sweeping pale blue cashmere coat with big wooden buttons.

"This is it?" Rahul looked at the artfully arranged storefront of the small boutique—a bronze-and-gold sign declared that it was called CASSA DEL TESORO—Caterina had led him to. It was filled with impractically small vintage trunks and lacy dresses that would probably disintegrate to wisps in a washing machine.

"Yes. I've known Oliver Lemaire for a couple of years now. He's a dear friend." Glancing over her shoulder, she added, "Oliver's good for many things, not just what he has on display in his shop. He's helped me in many different ways over the last couple of years—*and* he's discreet."

"Okay . . ." Rahul was not convinced of Oliver's ability to procure things that would be practical to wear, but he held the door open for Caterina nonetheless.

At least it was warm inside the store. Rahul took off his coat and looked around the small, but not cramped, space. He guessed this was what a Realtor would call "cozy."

The walls were exposed brick—fly ash colored to look like sand lime, from the looks of it. Fun fact: fly ash bricks were also self-cementing due to high concentrations of calcium oxide. There was also, confoundingly, an unused fireplace filled with decorative lit lanterns. "If he wants light," Rahul murmured, "why doesn't he just light the fire?"

"Shh." Caterina stepped to the right to examine a silk scarf draped over an undressed cloth dress form. "Oliver has very good hearing."

Curtains in jewel tones, both heavy and sheer, hung from rings in the middle of the room, but as far as Rahul could tell, there was no purpose to the curtains either. Oliver must be an artist. That was the only explanation. Creative people did weird, impractical shit all the time that Rahul couldn't fathom doing himself.

"Did someone say my name?"

Rahul turned to see a tall, thin, tan young guy approaching them. He was probably around twenty-four or twenty-five years old, with dark brown hair swept back into a low ponytail. His expression was serious, his brown eyes on Rahul. But the moment he saw Caterina, his face broke into a smile and he walked quickly to cover the distance between them.

"Caterina, my sweet bird!"

Sweet bird? An interesting choice of phrase for an endearment. Birds were not particularly known for their intelligence, unless Oliver was speaking about very specific species.

Caterina smiled back at him and even accepted a hug, which Rahul had never seen her do before, so she must not be well versed in ornithology.

"Oliver," she said warmly—or as warmly as she'd ever said anything within Rahul's earshot, anyway. "How are you?"

"Magnificent now that you've visited me," he said smoothly, speaking in an accent that seemed to be a blend of different European accents; Rahul detected English and German and Italian and French. Oliver wore a sheer black shirt with giant sequined flowers appliquéd on it and pants with legs wide enough to fit ten of his legs in them. Was this the kind of thing Caterina expected Rahul to wear? He would, without question, if that was what she wanted. But there would be *cameras* there. He hoped she was considering that. "What has kept you away?"

Caterina made a face as she pulled off her gloves and took off her coat. She was wearing a velvet dress underneath, with cutouts along her collarbone that were deeply sexy, somehow. Her skin was perfectly smooth and a little glittery, as if she'd patted on sparkly powder. Rahul made an effort not to stare. "Winter break, unfortunately. I've missed my shopping trips these past three weeks."

"Ah, of course! But you are back now, so all is well." Oliver snapped his fingers, and a tremulous female assistant with mint-colored hair suddenly appeared out of nowhere, rushed up to take Caterina's coat and gloves, and disappeared into the recesses of the store again, never once making eye contact with any of them.

Caterina gave Oliver a half smile that would've brought Rahul to his knees if directed at him. Yet oddly enough, Oliver seemed unfazed. "I'm not so sure you even noticed I was gone. I hear you have someone new in your life already." She cocked her head. "How long did the last girl stick around? Two weeks?"

Oliver chortled as if Caterina had told the best joke. "You

know better than to listen to idle gossip," he said, his eyes shining. "I'm nothing if not loyal. Have I not been a faithful servant to you, bringing you whatever your heart desires?"

Caterina laughed a little, allowing this. "All right. You have me there." She paused and glanced at Rahul, standing by her side. "Speaking of which . . ." Turning back to Oliver, she continued. "I'm here with a mission that you must promise to keep secret."

Oliver immediately nodded, all business again. "But of course. You know what happens within CdT stays within CdT."

Rahul frowned, wondering what the hell CdT was, and then it came to him: Cassa del Tesoro. The name of the store. The abbreviation was so trendy it almost didn't make sense, which, Rahul knew, meant it was probably very fashionable to most people.

Satisfied, Caterina walked over to Rahul. "Oliver, I would like you to meet my friend Rahul Chopra. He is to be my date to the Hindman Gala tomorrow, but we're in a bit of a pinch. He's got absolutely *nothing* suitable to wear."

"Ah." Oliver turned to Rahul, a twinkling smile on his face. "I wondered about your companion. So this is to be a makeover—rags to riches, that kind of thing." He clasped his hands together and grinned.

Rags? Rahul looked down at himself. He wasn't really raggedy, he didn't think. But then looking at Oliver in his impeccable (at least, he knew they were impeccable to Caterina, even if he couldn't see it himself) clothes, he realized that was beside the point. He wanted to be more like Oliver, more like Caterina, more like anyone other than himself. And this man could help him get there.

"Exactly," Caterina said.

Rahul stood up straighter as Oliver approached and walked around him in a circle, observing him from every angle. He pushed his glasses and the waist of his pants up and stood staring straight ahead, feeling a little bit like a soldier in formation being inspected by a military sergeant.

"Where do you buy your clothing?" Oliver asked, coming to stand in front of Rahul again.

Rahul adjusted the neck of the yellow sweater he'd put on that morning. (He wasn't wearing his uniform; they'd had the day off for teacher planning.) "Um . . . I don't know. I think this one was from Target? A few years ago? It was on sale—I do remember that." His eidetic memory did not, unfortunately, extend to fashion; the only reason he remembered the sale was because he bought everything on sale. It didn't matter if it was three sizes too big; spending a lot of money on clothes was something Rahul had never understood.

There was a collective gasp from Oliver, Caterina, and the mousy assistant who peeked at Rahul and then ducked back behind a rack of military-style, presumably fashionable, coats.

"Mm." Oliver regarded Caterina solemnly. "It will be a monumental task."

Caterina took a breath. "Do you think you can do it, though, Oliver?"

Oliver bowed a little and closed his eyes. "I will try my valiant best for you, Caterina."

The next couple of hours were a breathless series of trying on shirts, tuxes, pants, and bow ties in the confines of a dressing room in which Rahul couldn't even stretch out his arms all the way.

After surveying himself in the latest silken tux by an Italian designer he'd never heard of, he sat on the bench (made from a chopped-up tree trunk) in the fitting room, his head between his knees, trying to breathe. It was a technique he'd learned from the school psychologist, Ari, when he was in sixth grade. He'd been terrified to go speak to her, imagining her as some scary old lady in a severe bun. Instead, she'd turned out to be a young, bookish nerd with a cool Cheshire cat tattoo on her forearm who knew all the obscure comics he read. *And* she'd helped him with his anxiety, something no one had ever done before.

It is quite possible, Rahul Chopra, that you are in over your head. Way, way over your head. Rahul held his head between his hands and took slow, deep, controlled breaths. Wearing a tux? *That* was supposed to make him someone else? Wasn't that a bit like putting a wig over a computer screen and asking people to believe it was human? Who in their right mind at the very high-profile gala would buy this?

But you need the training, he told himself. And the cold, hard truth was that he did. Desperately. If he had any chance of salvaging his friendships or of ever recapturing what he'd shared at the winter formal with Caterina at all, this was it.

Taking another deep breath, he said, "Caterina?"

"Yes?" Her cool, imperious voice floated in.

"How much longer? I may not have mentioned this before, but I'm kind of claustrophobic." The curtain rattled back and Caterina stood in the doorway, looking at him, as he peered at her from under his knees. He was lucky he'd put his pants on before he sat down.

"Are you all right?" she asked, and although there was still that touch of icy authority in her voice, the place between her brows held a crease, as if she were really concerned.

"Yes, fine." Rahul sat up and took a shuddering breath.

Caterina turned and spoke, presumably to Oliver. "We've had enough. Let's go with the first tux he tried on; I think that'll do nicely."

Rahul stood shakily, grateful that he could leave the tiny coffin of a dressing room. He followed Caterina out as the assistant ran in and began to take the clothes he'd already tried on. (Oliver had insisted Rahul leave them for her; apparently, customers only "ruined the vibe" of CdT by jamming things on racks where they clearly didn't belong.)

"Oliver, I do like the tux," Caterina said, once they were at a little seating area made of velvet, fuchsia-colored armchairs. "But . . ."

Oliver held up a hand. A pinkie ring glinted in the light. "Say no more. There's something missing."

Caterina sighed and crossed her legs. "Yes. I'll be doing his makeup tomorrow, of course, but I have a feeling that's not going to be enough. Do you have *any*thing else that might help complete his transformation?"

Makeup?? She'd never mentioned makeup before. He had an image of Caterina dusting his face with her glittery powder. No, if she tried that, he'd have to put his foot down. He drew the line at sparkles.

Oliver took his time, tapping his finger against his chin, pacing around the armchairs. And then, finally, he looked up, a small smile on his face. "I have it. Come with me."

They followed him to the far end of the store, around tiny side tables stacked with old books, tree branches hanging from the ceiling with fishing wire, and even, inexplicably, a giant stuffed tiger (artificial, hopefully) with reindeer antlers on its head. A taxonomist's nightmare.

Oliver, unbothered by his atrocities against science, went around a large ornate cherrywood desk where he checked out customers. He pulled what looked like a small, squat glass jar from one of the drawers.

"I haven't had a chance to put this on the floor yet," he explained, holding the jar in the palm of his hand and extending it toward Rahul. The label was black-and-white, and the wording was in a language Rahul didn't recognize. For just a moment, the letters appeared to glow as if made from flame. But then Rahul blinked and the effect was gone. Huh. Must be low blood sugar or something.

Oliver continued. "This is a very special hair gel, from a small fishing village in Estonia. I got it from my cousin, who traveled there and met a woman at a night market." Leaning closer to Rahul, his dark eyes gleaming like wet stone, he added, "They say it's made from wolfsbane and has magical properties. That it will bring the wearer the ability to disguise himself as whatever his heart desires."

Setting his palms flat on the desk, Rahul narrowed his eyes. "Wolfsbane is toxic. Why would I want to touch that?"

Oliver laughed, though his face flashed annoyance for a tiny beat. "The toxins have been taken out through a very lengthy process."

Rahul raised an eyebrow. "What process? Boiling? Or distillation? Or—"

"Does it work?" Caterina interrupted quickly from beside Rahul. "Have you seen it yourself?"

"I have," Oliver said immediately. "My cousin, he was not a musical man. And yet, once he began to use this . . ." He shook his head. "I have not seen such ability, not even in the masters. Now he travels the world playing his harmonica for enormous crowds. He won't go a day without using the gel."

That was anecdotal evidence, based on nothing more than one man's experience (if it was even true) as opposed to a controlled, scientific study designed to look at statistically significant trends within populations. Clearly, the story was designed to part Caterina from her money. But before Rahul could open his mouth to say that, Oliver extended the jar toward him again. "Take it as a trial. No charge this time. If it doesn't work for you, no harm, no foul." A smile licked across Oliver's face.

Tucking her hair behind one ear, Caterina spoke. "Well, that's very generous of you, Oliver. Thank you. We'll certainly give it a try." Seeing Rahul's skeptical face, she narrowed her eyes. "Won't we?"

"Um, sure. We'll definitely try it." He took the jar from Oliver and pocketed it, hoping it wouldn't cause all his hair to fall out.

"Excellent." Oliver bowed. "I know you'll find it . . . transformational."

Going bald *would* be transformational, but Rahul didn't think he'd say that just now. He had a feeling neither Caterina nor Oliver would be amused. As the assistant packed up the things Caterina had purchased for him, Rahul studied the packages. Caterina was spending a lot of money and time trying to gold-plate his dull exterior. Rahul glanced at her, feeling his heart thrum with nerves. What would happen if he remained stubbornly brass-hued in spite of all her ministrations?

At least you had this time with her, he thought, *even if she never speaks to you again. Be grateful for that.*

And in spite of the sinking feeling in his heart at the thought of never hearing her say his name again, Rahul promised himself he would be.

CHAPTER 8

CATERINA

Caterina did not like being nervous. It was an odd, uncomfortable, unfamiliar feeling, as if an olive pit had gotten lodged in her diaphragm and was waiting to be coughed up. She felt like she couldn't get a deep-enough breath, even though her custom Balenciaga evening gown was perfectly fitted to her form.

She turned to Rahul in his hotel room in Denver. The Hindman Gala was a mere hour away now, which meant Caterina had exactly sixty minutes to make him presentable. And so far . . . it wasn't working.

He stood there before her in the tuxedo that Oliver had so carefully picked out. It was impeccable, as were all of Oliver's curations. Caterina had purchased all-new designer makeup for his exact skin tone, and that, too, was top-of-the-line. Rahul promised he had freshly washed his hair. She'd gotten him into contacts, even though he insisted stabbing his eye with his finger was completely unnatural. And yet . . . yet he was still so very *Rahul*.

Somehow, he managed to make the tux look ill-fitting, even though Oliver had tailored it (at record speed; he was such a lovely person) to suit him. The makeup did accentuate his strong jawline, but his hair refused to cooperate, no matter how much she'd fiddled with it. And it was clear he had no confidence. He kept rubbing his palms on his trousers, though she'd warned him not to about a thousand times so far.

"I'm sorry," he said, rubbing his palms on his trousers again. Caterina stifled a sigh. "I know it isn't working, but I'm not sure why. Should I stand up straighter?" He adjusted his shoulders, and she could see the reflection of his back in the floor-length mirror behind him. He had a playful whorl in the middle of his head that she hadn't noticed before; it showed a pale scalp. Not to mention, "playful" was all wrong for the gala.

"No, that won't help," she said, rounding the sharp edge out of her voice. It wasn't his fault this wasn't working. She should've known it was too much to ask of him. And now it was too late to call in a backup. All the suitable ones would already be at the gala with other dates.

A sort of numbness took over Caterina then, forcing the nervousness away. Alaric would see her fall tonight, spectacularly, with all the cameras flashing. He'd get plastered all over the magazine pages with Lizel Falk, his supermodel, and Caterina would get photographed with Rahul, with a snide caption something along the lines of "Millionaire Heiress Caterina LaValle Seems to Lag in the Rebound." Alaric would *really* enjoy that. He'd probably frame the page.

Rahul was staring at her desperately, as if he were upset. And maybe he was, Caterina realized. He wasn't like any of the guys she'd dated. He probably really did care how this night went for her, without much thought about how it would affect him.

Caterina forced a small smile. "Let me just fix your hair a bit." There was no need to suck him into her vortex of unhappiness and dissatisfaction. He'd done nothing wrong. In fact, he'd made a valiant effort to help her achieve her goals. She walked around behind him and tried to get a strand of hair to lay over his whorl, but it kept snapping back into place.

"Oh," Rahul said suddenly, turning around to look at her. "We forgot. The hair gel, remember?"

She hadn't forgotten. Yesterday, at Oliver's shop, she'd been overcome by the possibilities of what Rahul could become. She'd been swept up in Oliver's vision and optimism, sure that they could make something of Rahul together. But tonight, seeing him in all of the Oliver-sanctioned finery, Caterina had to admit she'd been a tad overzealous. And so she hadn't bothered putting the gel into Rahul's hair. What good would it do now, honestly?

But he was looking at her with a mix of hope and desperation, and she couldn't dash that. "Oh yes." She walked over to the bed and grabbed the pouch that contained Rahul's makeup. Pulling the pot of gel out of the bag, she held it in her palm for a moment, noticing that the glass had an iridescent shimmer she hadn't noticed before. It caught the light and winked at her. "Let's try it."

Caterina walked back over to Rahul and opened the jar, holding it out to him in the flat of her hand. He peeked in at the milky white substance. "Do I just . . . take some in my fingers and put it in my hair?"

"Yes," she said. "And kind of style your hair as you go."

"Style it . . ." Rahul looked as though she'd asked him to open a wormhole in the hotel room.

"Just run it through your hair," she said, not able to edge out the touch of impatience this time. "It really doesn't matter." His face fell. God. It was like kicking a puppy. She added, "It'll look good no matter how you do it."

Looking happier, Rahul reached his fingertips into the jar and came away with far more than she would've advised. "Whoa," he said, bringing it to his nose. "It smells weird. Like lilies and metal and almonds. And dirt."

Dirt? Caterina tried not to let her irritation show. "Just put it into your hair. I'm sure it'll fade once it's in there." She sighed and began to fiddle with her jewelry. This was hopeless. They were going to fool exactly no one at the gala, and worse, she was about to become a laughingstock. Dammit. Why had she *ever* thought this was a good idea?

"Um . . . Caterina?"

"Yes, what?" She blinked and refocused on him. He was turned away from her now, looking into the mirror in front of him. From this angle, she couldn't see his face anymore. "What is it?"

Rahul turned around slowly, to face her once more.

And Caterina found herself staring.

Something was happening. Something very strange was happening.

RAHUL

Something was happening. Something highly unusual and that Rahul was fairly sure defied every law of physics he'd ever read up on in his free time.

The flabbergasted, suspicious, alarmed look on Caterina's face mirrored his. Well, except that he wasn't sure his face was . . . *his* anymore.

Rahul turned slowly back around to face the mirror. Caterina took a step to her left so she was beside him, also looking at him in the mirror. "Is that . . . ," Rahul began, not sure how to finish that sentence. Is that real? Is that a hallucination? Is that magic? Ridiculous. That last one was absolutely ridiculous. "Is that . . . *me*?"

"I think it is," Caterina said faintly, her fingers reaching forward to the mirror, then settling back down again. "It's you."

Except it wasn't. Not as he'd previously existed anyway. None of his atoms or molecules had ever arranged themselves to look like *this*. This was not his genetic code. This was someone else's phenotypical expression of superior DNA. He didn't look like himself at all, but maybe a distant cousin who modeled in his spare time. Not Pritam—he looked way better than Pritam had ever looked in his best pictures.

Somehow, Rahul's face had taken on a chiseled quality it had never had before. His skin looked clearer, his hair thicker and lusher and shinier. Even his shoulders were broader, though he couldn't tell if that was simply because he was naturally standing straighter because he felt more confident looking like *this*. Casually he stuck one hand in his pocket, the way he'd seen Grey and Leo do before. He looked like a freaking *GQ* model. How was this possible?

"How is this possible?" Caterina frowned. "Am I dreaming?" She tugged on a lock of her hair, her expression unchanging, and then slowly put it back with the others where it belonged. "No. That hurt. I'm awake."

"It—it has to be a shared delusion. A folie à deux. It's a well-documented phenomenon in the psychological literature. People begin to believe the same things, and—"

"But why? Why would we suddenly begin believing you look like Tom Holland?"

Unable to stop a grin—a confident, easy, graceful grin!—from spreading across his face at the comparison, Rahul turned to Caterina. "The smell. The smell that wafted off the gel. What did Oliver say was in here?"

"I don't remember; some plant."

"Wolfsbane. Maybe it causes hallucinations in its essential form. I'm not aware of that ever happening before, but . . . Or maybe there's something else in here, that when inhaled or ingested in some fashion—say, through the roots of your hair— causes hallucinations."

Caterina shook her head and stepped away from him, looking effortlessly like an A-list celebrity headed to an awards ceremony in her midnight-blue gown. "It sounds really far-fetched. I don't know. And does that mean when they take your picture tonight for the pages, you'll look like you? Since the people can't smell the gel through the pages of a magazine? What about people who are too far away to smell the fumes?"

Rahul pinched the bridge of his nose. These were all excellent questions, ones he had no answers to yet. "I don't know. I guess we'll just have to go out and see how this goes."

Caterina's eyes ran over every part of his face and body in a way that wasn't at all unpleasant. "Yes," she said thoughtfully, folding her hands on the silky skirt of her dress. "I suppose we should."

CATERINA

What the hell was going on with Rahul? Was it the gel? Was it wishful thinking? Or the folie-whatever Rahul had called it, a psychological phenomenon? But something inside Caterina told her that this was real. This new Rahul was a flesh-and-blood person standing in front of her. Neither she nor Rahul was prone to hysteria. So why would tonight be different? Caterina had been in many far more stressful situations before, and she'd never lost her cool. She was sure that what she was seeing was really happening.

Rahul was . . . handsome. Actually, literally quite gorgeous. He was the kind of man Caterina would flirt with at any event, and she'd let him dance with her and hold her close all night.

As she studied Rahul looking at himself from every angle in the hotel mirror, her gaze traced his broad shoulders, his narrow waist, the large hands that suddenly looked graceful and strong. Had he always looked like this? Was it just covered up under bad clothes and no grooming whatsoever? Had he been a diamond in the rough, just waiting to be mined?

She couldn't wait to take him to the gala. Because if her instincts were right and he really *did* look like this to everyone, then . . . then it would change everything for her. This could be her comeback, not just with Alaric but with her entire social circle. Showing up with *this* Rahul on her arm would tell everyone that she had truly landed on her feet, as Cats do.

Caterina picked up her clutch. "Are you ready to be the belle of the ball, Rahul?"

He turned to her, smiling a dashing smile that, if she were being completely honest, made her heart skip a beat. "Let's go."

RAHUL

If having a near anxiety attack in that claustrophobic dressing room of Oliver's shop had been bad, this right here in Caterina's private limo was a veritable tsunami of pain.

Trying to calm himself, Rahul attempted to talk to Caterina like she was a normal girl with a normal boy on a normal date. "I . . . uh, I really like your ring."

Caterina smiled and leaned back against the cushioned leather limo seat as she gazed down at her gold, sapphire-encrusted ring. "Thank you. It's an antique—Victorian era. My father gave it to me on my eighteenth birthday. It used to belong to my great-great-grandmother."

Rahul nodded in what he hoped was a casual way, though his mouth felt parched. "It goes well with your dress, too. You're just really good with all the fashion." *All the fashion?* God. He couldn't even string together a sentence right. How was he supposed to survive the night surrounded by well-bred socialites?

Caterina shrugged as the limo rocked them gently back and forth. "Thank you; it's a passion of mine. I think I might minor in Victorian-era fashion in college, actually. With a major in business, of course."

"Of course." As Rahul sipped his Acqua di Cristallo Tributo a Modigliani water from a crystal flute (the water was stored in an actual 24-karat gold bottle in a mini-fridge; as if he needed any more reminders how little he really belonged here), the limo began to slow. He stared out the tinted windows at the rows and rows of journalists and other media personalities who were standing around with mics and cameras, thrusting said mics and cameras into people's faces. Some of whom he recognized. He was pretty sure the tall dude with the dazzling smile was Vanya Petrovic, a friend of Alaric's. And that short-haired blond girl over there, showing off her one-shouldered dress to a reporter, was Caterina's friend Heather.

He was beginning to realize he'd made a very serious mistake.

It was easy (or at least, it wasn't panic-inducing) to be confident and suave in a hotel room when it was just him and Caterina, who wanted this to work as much as he did. It was an entirely different matter to be here, at the actual gala, and see the sheer scope of the thing. These were not his people. This was not his place. And all of this going through without so much as a tiny wrinkle hinged on his ability to be a handsome, debonair *prince*. Rahul Chopra was an avid collector of facts, and this one fact he knew to be unassailably true: he was no prince.

"We're here. Ready?" Caterina asked as their limo inched along to the pull-off point. There, they'd get out and walk along an actual, literal red carpet to stand in front of the Hindman Foundation logo-plastered wall to get their pictures taken. She turned to look at him, her brow furrowed, when he didn't answer. "Are you all right?"

"Fine," Rahul said, his voice stronger than usual. He perked up. Wearing the outfit, it seemed, was bringing out a side of him he didn't know he had. Maybe he could just fake it all night. Just pretend he was someone who swanned around drinking $60,000 bottles of water in limousines. "I'll be fine. I *am* fine."

"Good." Caterina ran her gaze over his face. "Because it's our turn now. Come on."

The chauffeur was opening the door on her side then, and she was climbing out, immediately waving at someone and smiling her put-together, modelesque, Caterina smile. Rahul scooted out after her as she'd trained him, acting confident and graceful, feeling like he might throw up a little. Would they even notice? They were all probably staring at Caterina, anyway. *He* would, if he were them. She was radiant tonight, as she was every night. They should host an entire gala just for her.

And then he was following her on feet that felt like they were wrapped in cotton and numbing agent to the wall with the Hindman logos, smiling, smiling, smiling, without showing his teeth, as he'd been instructed. His hand had found its way back into the pocket of his trousers, and as far as he could tell, he was standing up straight.

But was he fooling them?

Rahul squinted a bit, trying to make out the expressions on the faces of the journalists and the camera people and other gala attendees, but it was hard to see anything, standing under the barrage of lights trained on him and Caterina.

"Caterina!" a woman in a yellow pantsuit holding a microphone called. "Who are you wearing?"

"This is a custom Balenciaga," she said, smiling, doing a little twirl. The cameras went nuts.

"Ms. LaValle!" someone else shouted. Rahul couldn't even see who it was. "What size do you wear?"

Caterina looked coldly into the teeming crowd and waited, silently, for the next question. It came soon after, and then another one after it, and another one, like a series of popping corn, pop-pop-pop. "Is indigo blue your favorite color? Is that why you chose that dress?" "Are you excited for your fifth time at the Hindman Gala?" "Which charities are you enthused to support this year?" "Will your father be joining you?" And finally, Rahul heard, "Who is that handsome young man beside you?"

There was a brief, infinitesimal moment when he and Caterina turned to each other, their eyes meeting, their eyebrows just slightly raised. Just a moment of, *Oh my God, is it working?* where Rahul felt, just like last year at the winter formal, that he and

Caterina were in on something together, just the two of them. And then Caterina turned back to the crowd and said, into a bouquet of different microphones, "This is my dear friend, and he's here to escort me tonight."

"And does Prince Charming have a name?" someone called out, and the crowd laughed.

And then all the microphones were suddenly under Rahul's nose. Right. A name. *Rahul Chopra* was out of the question. Why hadn't he and Caterina practiced a name?? But obviously they hadn't. They'd expected Rahul to fade into the background, as he usually did.

He opened his mouth, afraid his voice was going to crack and wheeze and deflate and humiliate the goddess next to him. Instead, he heard that confident, tux-wearing part of him take over again. A smooth, mellifluous voice said with a surety that silenced the teeming crowd for an instant, "You may call me RC. I am the crown prince of the district of Anandgarh in Rajasthan."

That was total horseshit, of course. There was no "district of Anandgarh" in Rajasthan. And he was *definitely, definitely* not a crown prince. But the reporter sharks seemed to eat it up. He guessed none of them were serious political reporters and probably wouldn't know how to spell "Anandgarh," let alone fact-check it later.

"How did you two meet?" "Are you officially dating?" "What does Alaric think?" "Will you accompany Caterina to other events in the future?"

But Caterina held up a hand. She was doing her faint smile thing, but Rahul could tell she was brimming with pleasure at the interest. "Please," she said. "We're going to be late."

Then she grabbed Rahul's hand in her soft, cool one and tugged him around the side and up the stairs of the Four Seasons Hotel.

CATERINA

That had gone better than she could've ever hoped. They swept up the stone stairs and into the quiet, cool interior of the hotel, where a much quieter crowd milled. Everyone was dressed in their glittering, bespoke best, and the hairdos on the women were more elaborate than some sculptures at the Louvre.

Caterina glanced sideways at Rahul. He looked . . . like he belonged. Not a hair out of place, no feverishly tapping hands or feet, no nervous tongue darting out to lick his dry lips. His lips, in fact, looked very well moisturized. Very . . . shapely. And soft.

"Hmm?" he asked, looking at her as if he'd heard her thoughts.

Caterina blinked and looked away as they walked up to a woman in a black suit who was checking guests off a list as they approached her. "You did well," she said, inclining her head at Rahul. At RC. She had to get in the habit of calling him that tonight. "The name was—"

"Impulsive," he said quietly. "Sorry. We didn't discuss it before, and—"

"No, I like it." She smiled a little.

"Really?" He seemed inordinately pleased by this fact.

"Yes. RC is . . . modern. It's chic. And it's just mysterious enough to keep them guessing." She nodded once, firmly. "I really like it."

"Caterina!"

They turned to see a girl catapulting herself at them. She was dressed in a black dress with a tulle-skirt overlay, and it took Caterina about 2.2 seconds to place her. "Bella!" she said, remembering just as the girl reached her and leaned in for an air-kiss. Bella Livingstone was dating Jason Ypez, whose father was one of Caterina's father's old business partners. "It's so nice to see you again! You must tell me where you got that handbag. Allow me to introduce RC, my date for tonight."

Rahul—RC—executed a perfect air-kiss, and Bella looked up at him, obviously starstruck. So she could see it too. They could all see Rahul's transformation. "I heard you say you're the crown prince of Adnan . . . Adamson . . . um, sorry." Bella giggled, her cheeks staining pink, and Caterina felt a tug of irritation.

"It's all right, I can barely pronounce it myself," RC said, and Bella laughed again.

Then, refocusing on Caterina, Bella moved half a step closer. Caterina immediately felt her walls fly up, a sure sign that her brain had interpreted something in Bella's expression or stance as a favor waiting to be asked. Then Bella opened her mouth and there it was. "I hate to ask," she said, speaking quietly. "But I heard that you went to the Hiltons' vacation resort over Christmas break."

"Really?" Caterina kept her face blank. "Where did you hear that?" Rahul, she could see in her peripheral vision, was watching this whole exchange, agog.

"I'm not sure." But Bella's blue eyes wouldn't meet Caterina's. It had to have been Jason, her boyfriend, who probably heard it from his dad. "Anyway, I would really, really love the chance to pitch Paris my ideas for a new fashion line. You know how it can be; it's just so hard to get traction unless you know the right people. . . ." She grinned, bright as a light bulb. "And that's why I'm *so* lucky we're practically sisters-in-law, according to Jason!"

Sisters-in-law? Caterina had barely seen Jason over the last two years, let alone said more than twenty words to him. And Bella . . . she wasn't even sure *who* Bella's parents were or what they did. She smiled, but made sure to keep her eyes remote to get her message across. "I'm not sure what I can do to help. The Hiltons are so very busy and hard to track down. . . ." She looked over her shoulder and then back. "Well, I don't mean to be rude," she continued, hoping she was being a *little* rude, "but we can't hold up the line anymore." She pointed to the woman in the black suit, who was waiting patiently for her and RC to check in.

"Of course, of course!" Bella leaned in to air-kiss Caterina again. "We'll catch up later!" And she rushed off to talk to someone farther down in line.

"Well . . ." Caterina raised an eyebrow at RC. "I think she was pretty impressed with you, RC. I suppose we can call tonight a success without ever having sat down."

He grinned back at her, and something in her chest hitched just a bit. "Yes," he said, winking. "I suppose we can."

CHAPTER 9

RAHUL

He had no idea where all this confidence was coming from. The wink, the easy laugh, the witty repartees . . . Never in his life had he ever behaved this way. Never in his life had he ever *thought* he could behave this way and get away with it. It was as if he'd injected himself with charm juice or something. It was all just coming together.

They were sitting at a table with Paul and Amelia Hindman now, both of whom had been utterly taken with RC, as had everyone else. He'd heard three of Caterina's girlfriends ask about his and Caterina's relationship status in what he was sure they thought was a subtle way. And another one of them was fearlessly attempting to play footsie with him under the table, though he kept moving his foot out of the way.

"Ooh, it's time for dancing!" one of the girls (not Footsie Girl, but the one in a purple-feathered headband thing who'd been complimented numerous times on her twenties attire) said to her date as the DJ struck up some fast song Rahul had never heard of. She had a head full of voluminous black curls and an infectious smile—Rahul thought Caterina had introduced her as Morgan Stokes. "Come on, Jaden. Let's go!"

As they made their way to the dance floor, Amelia Hindman turned to Caterina and Rahul and smiled, the skin around her mouth wrinkled and papery. "Don't you want to ask your date to dance, RC?" She gestured with one bejeweled hand toward the dance floor, where other young couples were congregating.

One thing Caterina had already instructed him on: if the Hindmans said they wanted something, if they so much as *hinted* that they wanted it, it didn't matter what it was—your watch, your movie tickets, your pancreas—you just gave it to them. So Rahul smiled. "You read my mind, Mrs. Hindman." He stood and turned to Caterina, holding out one hand. "Will you do me the absolute honor of this dance?"

As Amelia Hindman beamed at them, Caterina smiled, put her hand in his, and rose gracefully from her chair, letting RC lead her out to the dance floor.

It was almost exactly like the winter dance. Caterina was ensconced in his arms, her soft, clear rose perfume washing over him like a cool wave. But this time, he didn't feel so out of place. This time, he wasn't wearing a tux that hung off him like a sack or shoes that were too tight in the toes. This time, he wasn't worried that his hair was hanging limply in his eyes or that everyone was staring at them, thinking, *Why the hell is* Rahul Chopra *dancing with Caterina LaValle?*

This time, Rahul was sure that everyone was gazing at them in wonder and envy, wondering who he was and how they could get to know him. They were seeing them together as the beautiful cake-topper couple, the wealthy, handsome prince with the perfect, poised princess.

"What?" Caterina asked, studying his expression. "What's that smile about?"

Rahul shook his head. "I feel good. I feel *right.*"

She smiled a little then and squeezed his biceps. "You do feel right."

Rahul raised his eyebrows at the compliment, his words deserting him. Had . . . had she just complimented his body? Did Caterina find him *sexy* in a tux with his hair done?

Apparently realizing what she'd said, Caterina flushed a pale pink. "I mean, you're definitely wearing this new identity well. I've been getting compliments on my new boyfriend all night. Everyone's talking about us."

Rahul gazed into her eyes and watched in pleasure as her cheeks flushed even deeper. He'd never had this effect on her before. Not even close. Without even thinking about it, he spun her around, as if the moves were just coiled in him, waiting for this moment to come out. As Caterina laughed, he dipped her down, his hand supporting her weight, his fingers pressed into the bare skin like warm silk on her back. "Then let's give them something to talk about."

Right on cue, Alaric materialized beside them, faint spots of red on his pale cheeks. Rahul had been waiting for this. And the way Caterina stood and squared her shoulders, smiling a cat-that-got-the-cream smile, so had she.

CATERINA

This was the *perfect* time for Alaric to make his entrance. Rahul had just danced with her like he belonged on *Dancing with the Stars*, everyone was staring at them, and a few had even clapped when Rahul dipped her. Caterina had seen Alaric from her upside-down vantage. Though he'd ostensibly been dancing with Lizel Falk, he'd really been glaring at them. She could tell it took every last egotistical bone in his body to not rush over and rip them apart. Not because he was jealous, obviously. He just didn't want Caterina to move on in a more spectacular fashion than he had.

"Hello, Alaric." She made sure to keep her voice supercilious and frosty. Then she turned back to Rahul and laughed. "I just can't believe you said that to the princess of Sweden! You're just too much, RC."

Rahul, thankfully, played along. "Oh, Victoria and I are old friends," he replied, grinning dashingly. "She's used to it by now."

"So you're RC," Alaric said, attempting a casual tone. Of course, his teeth were clamped together so hard, his jaw muscle protruded. "I'm Alaric Konig."

He held out a hand and Caterina saw Rahul clamp it, his own hand above Alaric's. She bit on the inside of her cheek to keep from laughing. Rahul had had no problem remembering how to properly shake everyone else's hand tonight. "Nice to meet you, Rick," Rahul said dismissively, ignoring Alaric's dagger-like glare. And then, as the next song started up, he wrapped his arms around Caterina and swept her away again.

She laughed. "Rick? I don't think anyone's ever called him that before."

"There's a first time for everything." Rahul's eyes sparkled in the golden lights of the room. "And I quite like Rick. He seemed like a nice fella."

Caterina shook her head, still laughing. Rahul was so . . .

different. So completely someone new. He really had become RC tonight.

RAHUL

As he danced with Caterina, Rahul couldn't believe how high, how on top of everything, he felt. *This* was what people like Alaric felt like all the time? It was like he'd swallowed a pink cloud and drunk a few gallons of unicorn juice. Everything felt magical. *He* felt magical.

He looked at Caterina, at her beautiful smile that was all for him. She was happy, genuinely happy, in this moment, and it was because he'd made her happy. His fingers pressed gently on her waist, the silk of her dress luxuriously soft against his skin. He couldn't help but think again of the last time he'd held her this way, after the winter formal.

But tonight Caterina wasn't hurting; she wasn't in his arms as a last resort. Tonight he *belonged* with her. They were, for all intents and purposes, a couple. She was dancing with him now because she wanted to, he knew. He wasn't just a consolation prize anymore.

"Do you want to go out on the balcony?" he asked her as the song drew to a close. He gestured toward the exit, which led down a hallway that ended in a giant balcony, all done up in lights and decorations for the event.

Caterina tucked a lock of hair behind her ear and looked at him through her lashes. "I'd love to."

He led her through the crowd and into the hallway, where it was quieter and cooler. There were a few older people out here, talking business, but they didn't glance up at Rahul or Caterina as they passed. He was exquisitely aware of her presence as they

walked down the hall; the swish of her silk dress, the quiet clicking of her heels, the soft rose scent of her perfume. If he listened
really hard, he thought he could hear his own heartbeat.

Soon, Rahul pushed open the French doors at the end of the
hallway and stepped through. There were heaters on the balcony,
but it was still relatively cold. He glanced at Caterina's dress. It
had long sleeves, but the material seemed thin and the back was
low. "We could go inside, if you want."

"No, it feels good being out here after dancing for so long."
She stepped forward to the thick stone railing and looked out at
the carefully decorated patio garden below. There were net lights
over the bushes and wrapped around the trunks of pine trees. A
small stone fountain tinkled to the right side, shimmering with
underwater lights. Rahul could see that people had thrown in
pennies, hoping their wishes would come true.

"It's beautiful here," he said, glancing at Caterina, hoping at least
a small part of her knew he wasn't just talking about the view below.

She turned to him, pressing her back against the railing, her
face serious. "Thank you, Rahul."

He cocked his head slightly. "For . . . ?"

"For tonight. Thank you. This was really important to me
and you delivered. I feel okay again. About Alaric and everything,
I mean. I feel like . . . myself again, a little bit."

"You're welcome. I'm glad I could help. But, I mean, you don't
need to impress Alaric, you know. You're already so much above
him. Like, in a different stratosphere above him."

But Caterina shook her head, as if she didn't buy that. "You
were really amazing tonight. I hope you know that. You've completely blown me away." Her eyes were sincere, solemn.

"Really?" Rahul wasn't able to keep the smile off his face. "*I've*
blown *you* away?"

"Absolutely." She smiled in response to the expression on his face. There was a pause; he could see her hesitating. And then Caterina LaValle walked forward a step and wrapped her arms around him in a hug.

CATERINA

No one was more shocked than Caterina LaValle that she was actually physically hugging Rahul Chopra, feeling her hands pressing into his shoulders, the hard planes of his body against hers.

It could be the overwhelming relief she felt, flowing like liquid medicine through her veins, that they'd actually pulled it off. Or maybe it was the surety of knowing that without Rahul, she never could've gotten back at Alaric in such a satisfying manner. Or perhaps she was still feeling a little lost, after the callous way Alaric had left her last year.

But if she were being completely honest, Caterina knew she was mostly hugging Rahul because he seemed to see through the ice to the girl trapped underneath its surface. As if, in fact, he had never seen the ice at all. Something about being looked at like Rahul looked at her made her think she could be a different person—softer, gentler, kinder. Someone more like Rahul Chopra.

RAHUL

To say that Rahul was shocked would be a laughable understatement akin to saying Alan Turing had a passable talent in cryptology. After a moment of utter disbelief, he wrapped his arms around her, tentatively, making sure he wasn't overstepping. It was one thing to dance with her on Amelia Hindman's insistence, or to piss Alaric off. It was completely another to hug her "off-stage." When she didn't immediately move away, he closed his eyes and let himself revel in the feeling of being held in Caterina's arms, even in the completely platonic way he was sure she meant it.

She pulled back and studied him. "You're a good friend."

And he smiled a smile from the bottom of his soul because even if this was the last time he'd spend so much one-on-one time with Caterina, at least she thought of them as friends now. That was something he knew he'd hold dear forever.

CATERINA

Once they were back in the ballroom, Rahul left to visit the bathroom. Caterina watched the couples on the dance floor, smiling over her champagne flute at Alaric and Lizel, who appeared to be stumbling together in an attempt to dance. He stepped on her shoe and she pushed him away, looking irritated. Never had there been a less compatible partnership—except, of course, for Caterina and Alaric.

"Hi! You must be Caterina!"

Caterina turned at the fluty, female, Italian-accented voice.

A girl with long blond hair wearing a slinky crimson dress was standing by the empty chair next to Caterina. She wore last season's Prada pumps, slightly scuffed at the heel, and had one of those faces that seemed to be 75 percent smile—big and bold and unapologetic. As Caterina took her proffered hand, she racked her brain for where she might have met this girl before. She looked vaguely familiar. At some event, surely . . . maybe the yacht gala a few months ago? That night was still such a blur for so many reasons. Or maybe she was the star of some show Caterina had watched in passing.

"Hello," she said carefully, smiling back. "It's so nice to see you."

"My name is Mia. Mia Mazzanti." Mia, who obviously knew Caterina had no idea who she was and seemed to be okay with that, took a seat in the empty chair, crossing her hands neatly on the tabletop.

"Mazzanti," Caterina mused as she took a sip of her champagne. "And your accent. Are you Italian?"

"I am!" Mia beamed as she reached for a glass of mint water from a passing waiter. "And I'm so excited to meet a famous Italian American like you. I've heard so much about the beautiful Caterina LaValle. And of course, recently you've been splashed across every magazine's website." Mia's catlike amber eyes darted to Rahul, who had come back into the ballroom and been accosted by the Woodmoors, who were big in construction.

Caterina smiled slowly. "Yes, I suppose I have," she said airily, wondering if Mia was here only to snake her way into Rahul's good books.

But Mia immediately turned back to Caterina. "You go to Rosetta Academy, don't you?" she asked, propping her chin on her hand. Two slim gold bracelets clinked together; one of them had a starfish charm.

"I do," Caterina replied. "Where do you go?"

"I'm not in high school anymore, thank God." Mia laughed, sipping at her water. "I graduated last year."

"Oh. So where will you go to college in the fall?"

Mia smiled and shrugged. "I'm not sure yet." She studied Caterina over her frosted glass. "What about you? One of the Ivies, I assume?"

"Harvard," Caterina replied. "Early acceptance. It was really the only option. My father wouldn't have it any other way."

Mia's amber eyes held hers. "Indeed. I wouldn't expect anything less."

Then Rahul was back, and Mia got to her feet, slow and languid like a cat. "Well, I should go," she said to Caterina once she and Rahul had been introduced. "But I'm sure I'll see you around at some event or other before too long!"

Caterina smiled and raised her champagne flute. "Yes, I'm sure you will." She wasn't sure at all, but it seemed the polite thing to say. She watched Mia sashay away, her glass held close to her body. She was confident, in spite of her slightly shoddier clothing. Caterina wondered how she knew the Hindmans.

Rahul sat down and turned to her. "So. Are you ready to dazzle everyone with another dance?"

Caterina laughed, and was then immediately surprised at how often she seemed to laugh around Rahul. Shaking her head a little, she set her champagne down and stood up.

Heather was staring at the image on her phone in the dining hall between classes. "I still can't believe how *beautiful* you looked! We barely got to talk, but wow. These *pictures*."

It was an article on *Us Weekly* online about the Hindman Gala. Caterina couldn't keep up with them all; it seemed her phone had been dinging with notifications since she got home on Sunday and now into Monday morning. Her friends were all happy and clinging to her starshine once more like they used to. With her comeback with RC, Caterina knew she'd reclaimed her crown. She was, once again, Queen Cat. Looking at Heather's and Ava's faces, she felt a smug sense of victory. Whatever damage Alaric and DE had done to her reputation, she and RC had papered over it thoroughly Saturday night.

"Mm, thanks, babe," she said languidly, looking at a message from Sara Hindman, the Hindmans' daughter, on her phone.

Heather continued. "Seriously, where did you find him?"

Caterina looked up from her phone to see both her friends staring at her, agog. She felt a small thrill. They hadn't looked at her this way since she'd announced that Alaric had told her he loved her, and that had been years—far too long—ago. She felt the power tipping back onto her side of the scale, and she liked it. She liked it very much.

Caterina waved a hand, her glossy manicure shining under the recessed lighting in the dining hall. "Oh, RC's just a family friend. You know, one of those connections you don't think twice about until something just . . . clicks." She smiled wide and batted her eyelashes twice, just enough so she looked like someone falling in love. "He really lives up to his title—he's such a prince to me. And he treats me like a princess."

Both Heather and Ava "aww"ed and sighed, and Caterina smiled as she took a sip of her Evian.

"So will you see him again?" Ava asked. Her shiny hair was in two buns on either side of her head today, immaculate as usual.

"You *have* to," Heather added, folding her hands on the table. Her black diamond ring winked in the light. "He's amazing. Everyone was talking about him." She leaned forward, lowering her voice. "I heard Alaric was so furious after seeing you two dance that he tried to get them to turn off the music."

Caterina took a slow swallow of water before responding, so as not to sound overeager. But inside, her heart thumped in dark pleasure. "Really?"

"Really." Heather sat back. "RC's good."

"I'm sure we'll be seen together before too long," Caterina said casually, even though she was already mentally sorting through her schedule, wondering when she could fit him in again. There were a few options.

Changing the subject before they could begin asking too many more questions, she said, "By the way, are you both going to Harper's thing in a few weeks?"

"The party?" Ava asked, taking a bite of her portobello mushroom burger. "Yep, I'll be there."

"Me too," Heather said, texting someone on her phone. "It's going to be so nice to just chill in her heated pool and eat snacks and not worry about a thing."

"Her house in Aspen." Ava sighed. "Is there anything more perfect? Do you think we can ski afterward?"

"Of course," Caterina replied. "Harper said her mother's promised a weekend trip to the Aspen Ski Resort for all of us."

There was so much happy exclamation then that Caterina almost missed hearing her phone ring. The name looked vaguely familiar, so she swiped to answer and held the phone up to her ear. "Yes?"

"Caterina, this is Roubeeni, with *Glitz* magazine. We spoke last year when I covered your yacht gala."

"Oh yes, hello," Caterina said, trying *not* to remember when they'd last spoken. Roubeeni had tried her best to get Caterina to comment on the "upset on the yacht with Alaric," as she'd called it. "I assume you want a quote about the Hindman Gala?" That's what every journalist had called her for so far.

"Well, yes," Roubeeni said, a smile in her voice, "and I'm also delighted to say I've been extended an invitation to Harper Ingall's party in Aspen. I'm working on a who's-who list of young adults everyone in America needs to know. I know your schedule gets busy, but you'll make time for me then, won't you?"

This wasn't anything new. Reporters always tried to pencil in time with her at big events; a few of them had done that at the Hindman Gala event, too, even though that one was more about the adults than their heirs and heiresses. But what was throwing her off was that Harper's party was meant to be a casual thing, just a few good friends getting together to blow off steam. And then Caterina remembered—Harper's mom, who was a world-famous photographer, had a new collection coming out around then. She must've changed her mind and asked Harper to allow the press into their home for the publicity.

Caterina took a breath. She'd been looking forward to letting her hair down a bit, and that would be impossible with reporters around. Once, Heather had gotten lipstick on her teeth at a party and hadn't realized it, and the photos of her looking slightly disheveled (or, as one magazine put it, "like a junkie on the streets") had run for months, with everyone zooming in on her teeth and speculating about the color of her lipstick and why Heather didn't care about her parents' luxury cookware empire enough to take better care with her appearance.

But this was the life Caterina was born into, and this was the price tag on it. It had to be paid. "You must be psychic. We were just talking about that. And of course I will," she said in her most gracious voice. The publicity would be good for her dad's businesses and his upcoming political campaign, too.

"Great! Well, I'm sure I'll run into you before then. Take care now, Caterina."

"You too, Roubeeni." She ended the call and looked around at her friends, her smile never slipping once as she broke the news to them.

Crown on, lipstick perfect, shoulders back. Those were the rules that kept her in power, and she was more than willing to play by them.

CHAPTER 10

RAHUL

The next Saturday, Rahul peered over his shoulder into the hallway of the senior floor as he entered his dorm room, carrying a paper bag tucked under his arm. Closing the door behind him, he walked over to his desk and set the bag down, blowing out a slow breath. Then, very carefully, he extracted his purchase from the bag: three magazines. *GQ*, *Esquire*, and something he'd never heard of before called *Polished*. It was ridiculously thick and shiny and had cost him almost twenty bucks, likely due to the premium-quality paper thickness and full-page, full-color photographs inside. A quick Google search had assured him it was a great magazine for "men who wanted to be more." *More what?* Rahul had thought. More polished, probably. Which wasn't a bad thing when you were Caterina LaValle's faux romantic partner.

It had been only a week since the Hindman Gala, and she'd told him that his reception had been spectacular—way better than she had even hoped, apparently. She hadn't asked him to accompany her anywhere else yet, but now that things had gone so well, it was probably only a matter of time before she did, right? Rahul was feeling optimistic. He was *letting* himself feel optimistic because, for the first time in his life, he hadn't been an extraordinary social failure.

Now, at his desk, Rahul glanced quickly at his dresser, where the hair gel sat in its little jar. What had happened last week . . . The nicely fitted tux, the contacts, and the makeup probably had a lot to do with his transformation. And by "a lot" he meant, like, 95 percent. But if he was being completely honest with himself— as any logical person and citizen scientist should be—he had to admit at least 5 percent of RC's . . . "RC-ness" had come from the gel.

Rahul didn't know *how* he knew that, but once the gel was in his hair, something had changed. It had given him a boost of confidence, of *je ne sais quoi* (to use one of Leo's phrases), that had seemed to come out of nowhere. Maybe the gel had chemicals in it that contributed to a dopamine rush. Hmm. Maybe he'd make some time later to research it.

Turning back to his desk, Rahul opened up *Polished* to an article about the top luxury sports cars all polished men under twenty-five should know and be comfortable talking about. Very carefully, Rahul ripped out the three pages that comprised the article and taped them up to his wall, papering over his "120 Chess Openings" poster. He'd see them every day when he woke up and went to bed, thus allowing his subconscious to truly absorb the material. Plus, seeing the poster would remind him that he was capable of what he'd previously considered impossible—i.e., fitting into Caterina's circle.

There was a knock at his door, and Rahul shoved the magazines back into their paper bag. Hopefully, Leo or Grey, whoever was on the other side of that door, wouldn't notice the article on his wall among all the other clutter already present. He didn't want to have to explain this with a lie; Rahul was famously bad at thinking on his feet (except, of course, when he was RC). He strode to the door and opened it.

It was Caterina. She looked mind-paralyzingly stunning as usual in her weekend clothes, a loose blue sweater that looked soft as a cloud and slightly sparkling dark jeans that looked like they'd been poured onto her legs. She wore ankle boots with spindly gold heels that made her significantly taller than him, but Rahul didn't mind gazing up at her. It might be hard to explain her presence to his friends, if they happened to see her, but Rahul was so happy to have her here that he didn't particularly care in that moment.

"H-hi," he managed to say once he realized he'd been staring at her without speaking for five whole seconds. Her left eyebrow had risen incrementally that entire time, an escalation from DEFCON 5 to DEFCON 1: missile incoming. "Do you want to come in?"

"Please." She waited for him to move aside and then breezed in, wafting that beautiful, clear perfume of hers. Rahul closed his eyes and breathed it in—just for a half second, in case she turned around and caught him.

He left the door ajar, but Caterina reached over and pushed it closed with her fingertips. Oh shit. He realized her back was to his wall—his wall that was papered with nerdy chess posters and, now, also that article from *Polished*. What if she saw it and thought he was pathetic? What if she saw all his chess posters and thought he was too nerdy to ever ask to be her fake date again? He was just beginning to hyperventilate, his eyeballs hurting from the effort of not looking behind her at his wall, when Caterina's smooth, cool voice interrupted his runaway train of thought.

"How do you feel about being my date yet again?" she asked, folding her arms across her chest. Her thin gold bracelets clinked faintly.

"Yes," Rahul replied quickly and in relief, before his brain had fully registered that she hadn't asked him a yes-or-no question. "Um, I mean, I—I geel food about it."

Caterina narrowed her eyes. "You . . . geel food?" she said slowly, as if trying to decipher a language with which she was only passingly familiar.

"Yes. Um, no, wait. I feel good," Rahul corrected hastily. "I'm down for that. Whatever. You have going on." Now he sounded like a robot. It had been a few days since they'd spoken, and somehow, that was enough to hit the reset button on his comfort with Caterina. He was back to feeling like he had a wooden tongue in a mouth spun of dry cotton.

Thankfully, Caterina didn't renege her invitation and rush out of his room. Instead, there was a small, mysterious smile on her lips. "Good. We really made a splash with all the media that were there last weekend, so I figured it'd be wise for us to keep that streak going. You know, be seen publicly in a few high-profile spots—restaurants, clubs, more society events, that kind of thing."

It was like being paid to do the thing you'd wanted to do your entire life. He would get to go on dates with Caterina—even if they weren't real in the strictest sense of the word—and he'd get to do it not as himself but as RC, a smooth, debonair, handsome royal who fit right into her world. It was what he'd wanted for a long time. It was what he'd daydreamed of when he had the flu and was running a temperature of 104 degrees. Only now it was being handed to him on a shiny princely platter, and all he had to do was say yes.

"Yes," he said. "That sounds perfect. What's our first event?" The small smile on Caterina's face morphed into a big one.

That Friday Night: Outing Number 1

RAHUL

Rahul looked at himself in the mirror in his quiet Denver hotel room. He was back in the tux he'd worn to the Hindman Gala, and it still fit just as perfectly as it had that night. He'd also smoothed on some of the foundation that Caterina had bought for him, designed to hide his blemishes. And naturally, he was wearing his contacts. But he wasn't done yet. He reached into the small pot of hair gel on the vanity and smoothed it back into his hair, crinkling his nose slightly at the odd smell wafting from the paste. Lilies and metal and almonds and dirt. So weird.

He met Caterina downstairs, right outside the ballroom where they were attending a wedding reception for the older sister of one of her friends. His palms were damp; he kept wiping them on his pants, but they just instantly got wet again. He wasn't feeling it tonight, not like he had on the night of the Hindman Gala. That night, he'd felt something sweep through him as he entered the building. He'd felt different. Now, in the bright lights of the hotel, he just felt . . . stupid. Like someone way too old to be playing dress-up playing dress-up anyway.

Then he caught sight of Caterina. She stood with her back to him, her thick hair in an elaborate updo. Tendrils of silky straight hair fell in wisps down her neck and caressed her bare back. As if she could feel his gaze on her, she turned, smiling the instant she saw him, her brown eyes lighting up like fireworks on the Fourth of July.

Almost instantly, Rahul felt RC emerge. He strode up to her and offered an arm, which she took without hesitation. *This* was it. This was why being RC meant so much to him. As RC, he could offer a woman like Caterina his arm and she would take it, no questions asked. Rahul couldn't help but feel that this was who he'd been meant to be all along. That being born as Rahul Chopra had been a cosmic mistake, and this, here, was his chance to remedy it, to make it right.

"Ready, RC?" Caterina asked as they walked into the glittering ballroom, festooned with pink and silver balloons and filled with people in elegant evening wear. "I'm pretty sure there's a reporter from the lifestyle pages of the *Times* here."

RC grinned. "Then let's go say hi."

CATERINA

She glanced at him sidelong as they walked up to the *Times* reporter. His suit fit just right, his shoulders appeared broad and strong under the jacket, and his arm under her hand was completely steady. RC seemed to be glowing with good health and confidence in a way Rahul never had before. Caterina shook her head slightly and smoothed down the skirt of her gold-and-crimson cocktail dress with her free hand. What was *in* that hair gel Oliver had given them?

The reporter—a slight white man with a wicked widow's peak, whose name she remembered just in time: Bruce Amos—was smiling at her slightly wolfishly. "Caterina!" he said in faux-hearty tones. "You're looking well!"

He said it with so much surprise that Caterina frowned a little. "Thank you, Bruce. But did you think I was sick?"

Bruce chuckled and stuck his hands in his pockets. She didn't miss the way his eyes darted over to the side. A quick glance told her two things: who he was looking at—Alaric, who was here with supermodel Lizel—and that whatever was going to come out of Bruce's mouth next would be unpleasant. He didn't disappoint. "Well . . ." He stretched the word out into forty-four syllables. "I *did* hear from certain sources that you were so torn up by Alaric breaking up with you that you lost twenty-seven pounds and had to be hospitalized to be force-fed." Bruce leaned in close, his eyebrows knitted together in fake concern. "Was it hard to recover?"

Caterina drew herself up to her full height of five feet ten inches. In heels, she was much taller than Bruce. Looking down her nose at him, she said, "I didn't *need* to recover because I wasn't 'torn up.' Really, Bruce, you need to check your sources before you end up offending the wrong people." She let the threat sink in slowly and watched the smile fade from Bruce's shiny face before adding, "I've never been better."

"Hi." RC spoke up from beside her, his voice jaunty and self-assured. She'd almost forgotten he was there. He held out his hand, let Bruce take it, and said, "I'm Caterina's date, RC. Crown prince of Anandgarh." Letting go of Bruce's hand, RC put his hand lightly on Caterina's back, his palm hot against her bare skin. "I can confirm that Caterina's *quite* well. In fact, we were vacationing on the Italian Riviera together not too long ago. A far cry from the hospital, if you ask me." He laughed heartily and, after a pause, Bruce joined in.

He looked from Caterina to RC and back again. "You certainly do seem well. I saw the pictures from the Hindman Gala, of course, but I was led to believe that was just a farce. You know, to throw people off your trail."

Caterina shook her head, her chandelier earrings tinkling with the motion. "As I said, Bruce, you really should check your sources. And in the meantime, if you have any *worthwhile* questions for the crown prince and me, we'll be at our table."

"I'll take you up on that." Bruce watched them walk away.

Caterina smiled up at RC and took his arm again as they walked to their table. "You were good. Very good."

"Thank you."

Her mood darkening, she looked over at Alaric and Lizel as RC held back her chair. They were at a different table, chatting with someone who looked like he might be related to Leonardo DiCaprio. "I can't believe him." She took a seat as RC went around to sit next to her. "How *dare* he spread such nasty rumors?"

"But you held your own. Don't give him the satisfaction of getting under your skin."

"You're right," Caterina replied as a waiter in tails walked up to take her drinks order, "I shouldn't." She didn't say it aloud, but the truth was, Alaric still very much got under her skin. And she didn't know what to do about that.

Sunday Afternoon: Outing Number 3

RAHUL

Rahul leaned back in his padded velvet chair, a glass of bubbly in one hand that he was just holding for show. "And that's when I said, 'Martin, I think he said *Bugatti*, not Bogota.'"

There was a swell of laughter around the circular table, which was set with a cut-glass vase of taupe-colored roses. All of Caterina's friends and their parents were drinking in his every word, their eyes sparkling with mirth. They glanced at one another as if to say, *Where did she find this* gem *of a young man?* He caught her eye and Caterina grinned—actually grinned—and then he felt her hand find his under the table and squeeze once before letting go.

Rahul's breath stuttered for just a moment at this physical contact that was meant *just* for him, not for anyone else's eyes, not as a performance. It was all his, to keep and cherish. Then he blinked, catching himself, and cleared his throat. "Did I tell you all about the time I got stranded at an overwater bungalow in Tahiti?" And all their faces turned eagerly toward him again, like flowers seeking the sun.

The Following Saturday Night: Outing Number 6

RAHUL

He barely had to look at himself in the mirror anymore when he got dressed; he knew precisely at what angle to lace his shoes, how much foundation to apply to that divot on his nose. Rahul opened up the hair gel—the last part of his dressing-up routine—and frowned. The gel was more than halfway down the small jar. He'd have to remind Caterina to go with him to get more from Oliver. As he smoothed it into his hair, he considered his reflection, thinking, *Almost there.* The gel would take him all the way.

It was funny, but he couldn't smell its distinct scent anymore. He was getting used to it.

In his pocket, his phone buzzed with a text from Leo.

come watch endgame in the movie room with us, it said. grey jaya and de are all here

Thinking for a moment, Rahul wrote back, Sorry, on my way out to a thing. Next time!

you're a busy man, Leo wrote, and Rahul knew it was a question he was expected to answer.

It's just tonight, he typed back, even though he really didn't have the time to get into a discussion with Leo.

but it is not, came the response. you are busy all the time now

If only he could explain to Leo *why* he was busy. It would make things so much easier. But of course, that was completely out of the question. He'd made a promise, and he intended to keep it. Don't know what to say, he typed. I have things I need to do.

we all have things we need to do. but we make time for our friends. or at least we should

He could tell Leo was getting mad. But to be honest, so was he. Why was Leo acting so self-righteous? Didn't he know that Rahul had always, always made a point to hang out with him? Couldn't he deduce that if Rahul was off doing other things now, they had to be important? Life-changingly important, even?

Don't remember you being so righteous when you blew me off to chase Lila around at the spring ball last year, he typed back. On principle, Rahul made it a point to never bring up old hurts. There was no point. But Leo was annoying him with his condescending bullshit.

Before he could get an answer back, knowing it'd just be something that would irritate him even more, Rahul slipped his phone back into his pocket and went to find Caterina at the usual

Denver hotel where they stayed when they had events to attend. He couldn't afford to be in a bad mood tonight.

His phone rang with a different chime than the one used for his text messages. He pulled it out to see a Google alert he'd set up for the terms "Caterina LaValle and RC." Yet another picture of him and Caterina, this one with his arm around her waist as they exited the Ritz after that celebrity auction event a few days ago. More speculation about their relationship, where they'd met, whether RC had dated Taylor Swift at one point and whether her latest breakup song was about him. Smiling, he put his phone away once again. It was all finally working.

CATERINA

"And this is an *underground* celebrity club?" Rahul asked as Pietro, her driver, pulled up into the side street and parallel parked seamlessly.

Pietro had been a racecar driver in Italy once upon a time; Papa had poached him to come work for him when he was close to retirement, and he spent his days now shuttling Caterina around wherever she wanted to go. In Italy, his nickname had been "El Furio" or "The Fury." But he'd vowed to Caterina's father that El Furio would never make an appearance when he was carting Caterina around, and he'd kept his word. In some ways, Pietro was like a nanny she actually liked.

"Yes," Caterina explained patiently. Then, narrowing her eyes, she added, "But it's not literally under the ground. You do know that, don't you?"

"Um, yeah, of course I know that," Rahul said after a

suspiciously long pause, studiously adjusting the sleeve of the mint-colored cashmere sweater she'd bought him at Ralph Lauren when she was shopping for a dress.

Pietro caught Caterina's eye in the mirror and she saw laughter there.

She sighed. Pietro was always judging her dates, although he said he was "Team RC" if the options were him or Alaric. Caterina turned back to Rahul. "It's a club that regular people don't know about. Celebrities frequent it a lot. It's a place to hang where they aren't going to be bothered for autographs or photographed."

Rahul's eyes lit up. "And it's called Evanescence?"

He was incredibly attractive, she realized again. It couldn't *all* be the hair gel, could it? There was something about the essence of him that was undergoing a metamorphosis, as if he were shifting and broadening and growing. Becoming something that was always inside him, coiled up and waiting for someone to come along with air and water and sunlight, to allow it to blossom.

"Correct. So just remember, no matter how famous the celebrity you see, don't gawk. And don't act nervous. Just be—" She'd almost said "just be yourself." But that wouldn't work at all.

"Just be RC," Rahul said, meeting her eye. He understood.

Caterina nodded, feeling very slightly bad. Rahul was a good person. And he was changing who he was for her, to fit in with her social circle better. Pietro, who had an instinctual grasp of when conversations were over (or rather, when *Caterina* considered them to be over), was opening up her door to the icy night air.

"I'll be back for you at one," he said quietly in Italian, and she nodded. It was one of the things she liked best about having an Italian driver—those touches of home, of her language.

Once Pietro had gone, she walked forward, toward a little alley between two squat brick buildings that were overcome with dead ivy.

"Where are we going?" Rahul looked around, his hands curled into fists as if he might need to suddenly jump at a mugger and defend Caterina. Caterina smiled inwardly; she appreciated the display of chivalry even if she knew she had a better chance of fighting off a mugger using just her words than Rahul did using any weapon at his disposal.

"It's down this alley." She walked quickly forward, looking for the battered wooden door that would never cause a raised eyebrow unless you knew what you were looking for. About ten yards into the alley, she stopped. There it was, peeling blue paint and all, just as she remembered it. She'd only been here once before, after Oliver at CdT had told her about it. He was terrifically adept at keeping his finger on the pulse of high society, and Caterina appreciated it. Good help, when you could find it, was truly invaluable. "This is it."

"Are you sure?" Rahul sounded nervous. A brisk wind picked up, kicking brittle leaves and a glass bottle down the alley, a sonorous nighttime melody.

Caterina knocked on the door, three sharp raps. A moment later it opened a crack, and a tall, pale man dressed in a black suit appeared. She could hear the music in the distance, thumping and moving against her eardrums like a living thing.

The man waited, not saying a thing. Rahul glanced at Caterina, obviously confused.

"It's a fine night for stargazing," Caterina said, and the man nodded and stepped aside.

"Wait." Rahul walked behind her down a dark hallway with

deep burgundy carpeting and paintings of people vanishing into smoke on the walls. "Was that a code phrase? Like in *Kingsman?*"

Caterina eyed him. "I never watched that movie. I don't like Colin Firth."

"You don't? I thought all girls liked him. Mr. Darcy and stuff."

They came to a heavy wooden door with an elaborate brass handle, and Caterina grasped it. "The one time we spoke, he had bad breath," she said, and then pushed the door open.

Rahul's—RC's—eyes went wide.

"Don't gawk." Caterina spoke sharply but quietly, and his eyes returned to their normal width.

She tried to see the club from RC's perspective. She'd taken him to a few upper-class events these past couple of weeks, but this was different. Here, they were in the league of their peers, rather than their peers' parents. There was no stuffiness here, no gaudiness or display of old wealth. Perhaps that made it slightly more intimidating. RC would have to fit in with people who were more his age, something, she knew, Rahul had historically found impossible.

"It'll be all right," she said as they looked around at the low-slung tables that were shaped like hammered copper drums and old weathered wood barrels. The seating was all floor cushions and low divans studded with sequins and bright threads of color. From the ceiling hung mismatched crystal and gold chandeliers in jewel tones. At the far corner was an enormous bar, its countertop made of an uncut natural gray stone that sparkled with embedded fibers of gold and copper. There were five bartenders of different genders and ethnicities, all of them supermodel-level beautiful.

"Seven," RC breathed into her ear, and Caterina felt goose

bumps rise on her arms, her pulse picking up. That hadn't happened since the beginning of her and Alaric's relationship. Interesting. Perhaps she'd missed male company more than she'd realized. "I see seven different A-list celebrities, and I haven't even scanned the entire room yet."

She glanced at him over her shoulder, eager not to show him the effect he had on her. "Act naturally," she said, emphasizing each syllable. "That's the key." She gestured to an empty divan. "Let's sit here and catch our breath for a moment."

They sat, RC hesitating a moment before remembering her lessons on how to sit on a low chair and still look poised. He got it in one try, though, and Caterina was pleased.

"Wow," he said, shaking his head. "This is . . . I had no idea places like this even existed." A slow smile spread across his face as his eyes darted from chandelier to bar counter to the cluster of trust-fund celebrities' kids who'd be making their way over here in a few moments. Caterina knew nearly all the people in that group. "I like it."

"That's different," Caterina remarked, taking in his well-coiffed hair that she didn't even have to help him with anymore. "Do you remember how you felt about the Hindman Gala?"

RC waved an airy hand. "I was an amateur then. I still have a long way to go, but I'm getting used to this. And I'm really liking it." He turned to her, his eyes glittering. "I'm good at it, aren't I? Do you think I fit in well?"

"You know the answer to that." Caterina raised her eyebrows. "You've read the same articles I have."

He sat back against a peacock-blue cushion and smirked. "Yeah, I guess I have. You know, Rahul could *never* cut it in a place like this. But RC . . . he was made for this. No, scratch that.

This place was made for *him*." Raising a hand, he gestured to a waitress with a move as fluidly practiced as if he'd been doing it his whole life.

Caterina studied his profile as the waitress approached to take his order. His chiseled jaw, his long eyelashes, his thick, silky hair, the easy, confident manner with which he occupied his space. It was exactly what she'd wanted him to be; it was precisely what she needed to show Alaric up. Everything was working perfectly. It was like a flawless windup world she'd created from scratch. And yet . . . the way he'd said Rahul's name so disparagingly, as if he were speaking of someone else entirely. The way he was so quick to want to discard Rahul, like an old skin he was molting off. Something about it felt wrong, somehow. Yes, she'd wanted RC to fit in here. But that didn't mean she thought Rahul was *bad*. But was that what he was thinking? She opened her mouth to say something—*what*, she didn't know—when she was interrupted.

"Caterina. So nice to see you again!"

CHAPTER 11

CATERINA

Caterina turned to see Mia Mazzanti, whom she'd met the night of the Hindman Gala, standing by her table. Tonight she wore an off-the-shoulder cream dress, probably from a department store, with a gold belt cinching in the waist. A small gold Coach purse hung off her shoulder.

"Mia." Caterina smiled, surprised to see the other girl again, and gestured to an unoccupied floor pillow next to her. "Will you join us?"

"I think I have a better idea." Turning to RC, Mia said, "Do you know Everett McCabe?" She gestured to a Black boy in the group she'd left, the same group Caterina had noted before. "He's David McCabe's son, and he was pretty interested in meeting you." She turned to Caterina. "We can all go over there if you want? I know a bunch of them wanted to say hi to you, too, Caterina."

RC's eyes widened. "Wait. David McCabe? As in the director of the Firestar movies?" His voice squeaked on the word "Firestar."

Caterina gave him a warning look. The Firestar movies

grossed hundreds of millions of dollars every time they came out, but that was information that should be marveled at only internally, if at all.

Rearranging his face, RC adjusted his sweater. "Sure," he said much more calmly. "We could go say hi. If you guys want, I mean."

"Oh, if *we* want. Of course." Caterina tried to keep the smile out of her voice but wasn't sure she completely succeeded. "Well, I certainly do want." She turned to Mia. "Shall we?"

She stood and was followed by Mia. The three of them made their way to the group, where immediately there was happy shrieking.

"Cat!" Harper Ingall broke off from the group and gathered her in a hug. She was wearing her red curly hair pinned to one side, and her pink chiffon dress made her look like a chic cupcake, in the best way. Her eyes were shining with genuine joy. "I'm so happy you're here! It's turning into this big impromptu reunion of the Riviera crowd!" She giggled. "Remember that vacation?"

A waitress came by, handing Caterina her usual honey lavender gin cocktail and Rahul the lemonade he'd ordered. Mia ordered a ginger beer.

"Oh, I remember." Caterina smiled once the waitress was gone. She glanced at Mia, remembering her manners. "About two years ago, all of our social circle ended up at the Italian Riviera over the summer. It wasn't planned that way; it was like all our parents had the same idea and wanted us out of their hair at the same time."

Harper laughed. "All I remember is drinking my weight in strawberry juice. Those villas were to die for too. The views!"

Mia's eyes sparkled. "It sounds exciting."

"All *I* remember is that I lost my bracelet at that restaurant, remember? We looked everywhere and it had just . . . vanished. I was so sure Papa would kill me—it had been a sixteenth birthday present—but he was so sweet about it." It was something that surprised her constantly about her father; he was endlessly forgiving of her mistakes.

"Oh, I do remember that!" Harper said. "We all felt so bad for you. And the manager helped you look for such a long time, poor man." Then, realizing at the same time as Caterina that Mia wasn't part of the conversation anymore, she turned to her. "Have you been to the Riviera?" Harper asked her kindly. "It's one of my favorite places in the world."

"A time or two," Mia replied. They waited, but she didn't supply any more information. Perhaps she was shy about talking about herself—or even intimidated. Her attire seemed to suggest she wasn't at all at the level of most of Caterina's social circle.

"How do you two know each other?" Caterina gestured between Harper and Mia, hoping to draw Mia out a bit more.

"Oh, we don't!" Harper chirped as the waitress returned and handed Mia a copper mug of ginger beer. "We just met tonight, but I can tell Mia's going to fit into the group *so* well. She was an absolute *life*saver when I lost my phone earlier. Apparently, I dropped it and didn't even realize it. She brought it over to me!"

"Really? That's so nice of you, Mia." Caterina took a slow sip of her honey lavender cocktail, studying the girl over her glass. "So, are you taking a gap year from college now?"

"Oh yes. I'm not ready to dive back into school just yet," Mia replied, waving a free hand. The other was cupped loosely around her drink. "I moved so much for my dad's career that I want to call the shots for a little while."

There was a tap at Caterina's shoulder, and she turned to see a short Indian woman in a cream silk shirt, black pants, and square spectacles smiling at her.

"Roubeeni." Caterina bent to air-kiss the reporter. "How wonderful to see you."

"And you!" Roubeeni beamed at the three of them. "Harper, I'm so excited to be able to talk to you at your Aspen home soon. I'm sure it's going to be fun."

"Me too," Harper replied, a bright smile on her face. "I can't wait. Grace says she'll have a sneak peek of her new collection there if you want to look at it." Grace Ingall, the famous photographer, was Harper's mother. *Time* had called her this generation's Ansel Adams, though according to Harper, Grace had managed to take that as an insult.

"That would be fabulous," Roubeeni said, raising her hand, which had a buzzing cell phone in it. "Well, I'm off the clock now, as I know you all are, so I'll leave you to it. Talk soon!"

Harper turned to Caterina when she was gone and pulled an apologetic face. "I'm sorry. I know the party was supposed to be just us all hanging out, but Grace really wants as much publicity as she can get." Lowering her voice, she added, "There's a rumor going around that her Paris showing isn't even going to sell out this year. She's freaking out."

Caterina patted Harper's arm. "Oh, you poor thing. I imagine she's being unbearable about it."

Harper rolled her eyes. "You know how she is when her ego gets hurt."

"Well, I'll be sure to talk it up to everyone I meet," Caterina promised. Off to the side, the guys—RC included—guffawed at something Everett had just said.

Mia cleared her throat. "So you're having a party soon, Harper?"

Harper nodded and then understanding rushed into her eyes. "Oh yes! And I hope you'll come, Mia. I was just about to invite you! I can give you the deets if you text me so I have your cell number."

"Great." Mia smiled happily, pulling her phone out of her bag. There was a text message on the screen that she quickly swiped away. Caterina understood; she was just as private.

"Hey." RC was by Caterina's side then, and by the flush in his cheeks and the smile on his face, things were going well for him. "Everett and the others wanted to start a poker game in the back. You ladies want to join?"

"Yes," Mia said immediately. "But *you* might not want me to join. I was the best poker player at my high school in Rome."

Caterina smiled, surprised. "You went to high school in Rome? That's where my family's from. *Ammazza!*"

Mia linked her arm with Caterina's. "*Ammazza aò!* See? I knew we were going to be friends."

They walked with the rest of the group to the back, chatting about the best places to find gelato in the ancient city.

Mia wasn't overstating things. In just one hour, she'd absolutely decimated all the boys in the group. Harper and Caterina, who didn't play poker (Harper was morally opposed to gambling, owing to an addicted uncle, and Caterina found the game moved her to tears of boredom rather than passion), were seated off to the side in studded armchairs with ornate brass feet.

Mia clapped her hands, collecting money from all the guys at the table with absolutely no remorse. Caterina laughed. "I like your style," she called, enjoying her second honey lavender cocktail of the evening. "Show no mercy."

"Oh, I don't intend to." Grinning, Mia stuffed the money into her black sequined clutch and sashayed away from the table, over to the girls.

"Wait," Everett called. "You're done? We could go another round! I bet I could take you down!"

The other guys cheered him on, including RC, who had lost the least, from what Caterina could see. He seemed to have a pretty good poker face.

Mia tinkled a laugh as she sank into the empty armchair next to Caterina's. "I'm done beating you poor boys up tonight. Maybe another time."

They went back to their game, trash-talking each other in that way boys think they're so good at.

Caterina cocked her head. "So how much did you make tonight?"

"A cool thousand, mostly from Everett." Mia laughed and took a swig of her ginger beer. She was the only one of them, besides RC, who hadn't had any alcohol that night. "You would think he'd be more cautious since he's such a poor player, but—"

"I heard that," Everett called. "I'm going to take you down next time, Mia, you mark my words!"

Mia just laughed harder and waved her bulging clutch at him. She had an easy confidence about her that Caterina liked.

It was clear she wasn't like the rest of them. She hadn't shared much of herself with the group, but from what Caterina could tell—and she was pretty good at guessing these things—Mia was not nearly in the same social league as the LaValles or the

McCabes. Her clothes and shoes were older and shabbier than anything Caterina had seen anyone besides Rahul wear, and the school she'd attended in Rome wasn't one Caterina had heard of. It was probably a public school, which said a lot.

It was possible, of course, that Mia was someone who'd managed to slip past the gilded curtains looking for an in with Caterina's crowd. It happened sometimes, in spite of safeguards—people looking for information they could sell to the tabloids or money or something to bribe you with. But her gut told her Mia wasn't after any of those things. There was a fierce dignity about her that said she wasn't here for anyone but herself.

There was a chiming from her purse, and Mia stopped to pull out her cell phone. She answered the call, holding the phone up to her ear. "Darling, this is not a good time," she said, a smile at her lips. "Call me later." Then she ended the call and put the phone away.

"Ooh," Harper said, her eyes shining. Her bare legs were swung over the tufted arm of the armchair, and her hair had come half-undone, though she didn't seem to notice. "Who was *that*?"

"A boy." Mia looked at them frankly. "And he can wait."

Caterina felt a slow smile spread across her face. "Really? How long have you two been . . . ?"

"Just a short time. But when my last boyfriend left me, I decided I was never going to give any boy more than two percent of the space in my life." She paused, sipping on her ginger beer. "Imagine a pie chart of your time. Boys should take up a sliver you can't even see."

Harper let out a very loud "Hell yeah!" but Caterina just nodded slowly. "I feel the same way," she replied, thinking of Alaric. Wasn't that exactly what she'd thought when he'd broken her heart? Of course, more recently, she'd begun hanging out with Rahul, but that was different. *Rahul* was different.

"Well, that doesn't surprise me." Mia smiled that big, no-holds-barred smile of hers. "Two Italian girls. What else would you expect?"

And Caterina couldn't help but smile back.

RC

They were still laughing when they got into the car, thanks to the parting joke that Everett had told. Pietro watched them like a hawk, obviously concerned about Caterina's state of mind and RC's intentions for her.

Once they were in the back seat, RC said quietly, "Do you mind if I raise the privacy screen? I just don't want"—here he made a meaningful gesture with his head—"you-know-who judging our mirth."

Caterina laughed, a beautiful silver-bell-peal he'd never heard before. It infused him with warmth. "Sure."

He pressed the button for the privacy screen, giving Pietro a tight-lipped smile as the driver glared darkly at him in the rearview mirror. "Pietro's not, like, your dad's muscle, is he?" RC asked, wondering if the dude was really that big or just *looked* it, thanks to the bulk of his driving coat.

The car began to move. Caterina shook her head, smiling. "Are you afraid of him, RC? A crown prince like you?"

RC pretended to buff his nails and study his reflection in them. "Of course not." Then he looked up at her, grinning. "Tonight was fun. Thanks."

"I take it Everett McCabe and you are best friends now; at least, that's what I heard him say to one of the other guys."

Caterina raised her eyebrows. "That's really high praise. He's not impressed too easily."

RC felt pride in himself in a social context for the first time in his life. "Wow. That's good to know." He paused, thinking, the rumbling of the car's tires the only sound.

"What?" Caterina asked.

. He met her eye in the darkened back seat. "It's just interesting, isn't it? These guys wouldn't give Rahul the time of day. But as RC, I'm unlocking my truest potential. I have Rahul's brains and RC's social prowess. I feel . . . I don't know, invincible."

A small frown creased Caterina's brow. "Well, if they wouldn't give Rahul the time of day, that's not on you. That's on them. And more than anything, it's the way we're raised. There's always someone looking to take advantage of us or our families or our money. We have to be guarded. They're not guarded with you because they think you're a prince. If Rahul were a prince, maybe they—"

RC brushed her off, knowing in his bones that she wasn't right. He felt bubbly, his skin thrumming with excitement. It was like he'd just unlocked the secret door to Narnia—only, instead of Narnia, he'd found a world that was tailor-made for him. A world where RC was king of all he purveyed, a world where he didn't have to worry about looking wrong or speaking wrong. There was a rush of the new, a thrill of finding something that had been hidden from him for all his life but lay there in the open now, a glittering golden key to a new life. "Nah, they still wouldn't be as comfortable with Rahul as they are with me. Everett invited me to go play poker at his house, can you believe it? I actually have his number in my cell right now."

Caterina smiled and put a hand on his knee. "Well, then. I'm happy for you."

His heart thumped at the physical contact. "Thanks. I'm

happy for me too. Hey, what about that girl Mia? You seemed to really get along with her, too."

"I did. It was kind of nice to talk to someone from Italy. I mean, I left there when I was just a toddler, but still. And she and I appear to think the same in a lot of ways, which is always refreshing. She's got this powerful self-respect that I . . ." She laughed a little. "I'm going on and on about it, aren't I?"

"No. You're perfect."

She raised her eyebrows, a smile still at her lips. "Perfect?"

He studied her in the near dark, her shining eyes, her cut-glass cheekbones, the scent of her rosewater perfume swirling in the air around him. Suddenly it felt imperative that he tell her how he felt about everything she'd done for him. They were here, ensconced in this car, in this little metal bubble for only a few minutes. And right now, it felt like he could say anything, do anything, and not be judged for it. "All of this never would've happened without you. This gift you've given me, Caterina . . . I don't know how to say thank you. It's been life-changing."

She let out a small breath. "You didn't need me to change your life."

"Yes, I did. I do." He leaned forward, his heart beating faster than it ever had in his life, even counting the presidential fitness test he'd miserably failed. He was going to do it. He was going to kiss Caterina LaValle.

CATERINA

What was happening? Caterina didn't fully understand the chemical reactions taking place in her brain or her body, but there was an invisible hand pressing into her back, pushing her closer and closer toward RC. Toward Rahul.

She looked into those kind brown eyes, the same ones that had looked at her without pity or judgment all those weeks ago at the winter dance. He'd simply accepted her for who she was then, and even seeing her bent and broken, he'd wanted to dance with her.

"I'd dance with you any day," she said quietly now, realizing too late that it probably sounded like a non sequitur to him.

But it didn't seem to matter. His eyes were laser-focused on her, his every breath syncopated to hers. She had the feeling he knew exactly what she'd been trying to say, that he knew exactly how she was feeling because he was feeling it too.

Caterina's pulse began thrumming at her throat as RC bridged the gap between them, his big hand cradling her jawbone tenderly, as if it might shatter. His lips brushed against hers, softly, gently, as if he were basking in every sensation. Caterina wrapped her arms around his waist, deepening the kiss, her tongue darting out to taste him. His breathing quickened, quickening hers in response, the feel of his stubble so delicious on her own skin. She moved closer still, wanting to slip her hands under his shirt, to feel the heat of his skin against her palms.

The door opened and a chill wind swept in. Pietro leaned down, a deep frown marring his face. "We are here at the school."

RC pulled himself straight and Caterina wiped her lips, hiding a smile behind her hand. She'd been so caught up in the kiss, she hadn't even felt the car slowing down. In fact, she'd forgotten where she was completely. "Thank you, Pietro."

They climbed out of the car in silence, Pietro staring straight ahead as if he didn't know either of them.

Once he'd pulled away, RC and Caterina stood outside the main dorms, smiling at each other. The lights were on in the lobby inside and in most of the dorm rooms, lighting the building up like a pillar candle. There was a large stone fountain a few yards away, but it was silent, heavy with ice and snow this time of year. The stars above them sat like ice chips in the black sky, and Caterina didn't think there had ever been a more perfect night. Perhaps it had been handcrafted for this moment, for RC and Caterina.

I can't stop smiling, she thought in wonder. She couldn't remember the last time that had happened.

"I had a good time," she said somewhat demurely, and then worried he'd think she was acting like a movie star from the fifties.

But RC only draped his jacket over her shoulders as they began to walk toward the entrance. She hadn't even realized until then that she'd been cold. "So did I." His hand brushed hers, and the most delicious shiver went up her arms. That touch felt like a promise, like a breath before a kiss. "I can't wait to do it again, Ms. LaValle." His brown eyes, so dark they were nearly as black as the sky above them, shone.

"Neither can I." And, she found, she meant it more than she'd meant anything in her life.

CHAPTER 12

CATERINA

The next morning, Caterina opened the car door—she'd told Pietro not to bother getting out—and swung both legs out, feeling the winter morning air rush at them. Pausing, she turned to speak to him. "You'll come pick me up in two hours, won't you? I just have a bit of shopping to do."

Pietro grunted a reply.

Caterina cocked her head and let a smile touch her lips. "Are you angry at me about last night?"

"No, Miss Caterina. It is not my place to feel anything about the choices you make. Even when they are clearly not in your best interest and wear shiny hair gel."

Caterina smothered a laugh. "Do you not like Rahul?"

"I like him just fine," Pietro replied shortly. "It is the other one I do not care for."

Caterina frowned. "The other—oh. You mean RC. You do know they're the same person, don't you?"

"I am not so sure," Pietro grumbled.

Caterina thought about that for a minute, feeling a seed of unease. Pietro's comment brought back the memory of RC talking about Rahul as if he were a slightly repulsive species of insect. Caterina remembered feeling uncomfortable, as if she were watching something wrong, something that should be corrected.

She took a breath; she'd have to return to these thoughts later. Right now, she had an errand to run. She got out on the sidewalk outside Cassa del Tesoro, Oliver's shop, and firmly shut the door behind her.

In the cool interior, Caterina handed her coat and gloves to Oliver's assistant, who scurried away with them with a squeaky promise to tell Oliver that Caterina was there.

While she waited, Caterina ran her hands over a shimmering feather scarf that hung from a branch suspended from the ceiling before moving away to study the contents of a wooden shelf nearby. It held a collection of glass perfume bottles that appeared to move and wink in a patch of weak winter sunlight as if out of free will.

Oliver had an innate talent for finding rare treasures, things both tangible and intangible that most people would overlook or not see at all. It was why Caterina had made sure to nurture the relationship with him; besides being a delight, he was also tremendously useful, and Caterina appreciated useful people. So many in her life were frivolous.

Her cell phone chimed with a group text from Ava.

Can't decide between these two for Harper's party!!!! Please help!!!!

Attached were two pictures of her in a dressing room at Kate Spade, one in a long-sleeved purple dress, the other in a polka-dotted maxi dress.

Before Caterina could answer, Heather did.

Def the polka dots.

Ava didn't respond. She wouldn't, Caterina knew, until

Caterina had. Neither she nor Heather made major decisions without Caterina's input. It was a pattern she'd very carefully cultivated over the years, both with confidence and through her quick and decisive action when either of them acted without consulting her. Knowledge was power, after all.

Neither, she said. Chanel has a red jumpsuit you'd look stunning in.

OMG thank you!!!!! Heading there now

"Caterina!"

She turned, slipping her phone back into her purse, to see Oliver striding toward her.

"I'm so sorry to keep you waiting. I had an important phone call I couldn't postpone. How are you? I trust the hair gel for your friend is working out well?" He clasped one of her hands in both of his and smiled warmly.

"It is, thank you, Oliver. Remarkably well, in fact."

Oliver's eyes shone with mirth. "I knew it would."

"Oh, actually," she said, remembering, "Rahul says he's running low. He'll be coming in soon to get some from you. You'll make sure to have another shipment ready, won't you?"

"Indeed I will. It might be a couple of weeks until I can get it, but it will be here for him. Is that why you're here today?"

"No. I'm here about another matter entirely. Do you remember about three years ago, when you helped me locate Pietro's Uncle Berto in Italy?"

"Of course! His last remaining relative, in a small fishing village. Eighty-six years old." Oliver smiled fondly at the memory. "Do they still keep in touch?"

"Oh yes," Caterina assured him. "Pietro flies out for Christmas and Pasqua—Easter—every year. He's still very grateful to you, you know."

"It was your idea. I was just the vehicle."

Caterina waved a hand. "Pietro deserves all that and more. In any case, I have a similar task for you that involves someone else with Italian roots. Except this time, I have the name, and I need you to find everything you can about her. Do you think you could do that?"

"Certainly." Oliver studied her face, as if searching for clues about this new task. "Is this person giving you trouble, Caterina?"

"Oh no, nothing of the sort." Caterina considered how to phrase her next thought. "If anything, it's the opposite. I quite like her, but I need to be comfortable before I let her into my circle."

A look of understanding bloomed across Oliver's face. "Ah, I see. Well, if you follow me to the back, I can take down some details."

"Excellent." Reaching into her purse, Caterina retrieved a check. "A little to get you started. I'll have the rest when you find the information."

Oliver took the check and bowed in his usual gentlemanly way. "Thank you."

They walked together to the back of the shop, into what Oliver referred to as his "sanctum." It was a surprisingly spacious room, considering the size of the rest of the shop, and filled with aesthetically pleasing statues and one-of-a-kind finds that Oliver didn't want to sell. Caterina took a seat on a burgundy couch, across from Oliver's velvet paisley-patterned armchair. Between them was an oblong coffee table made of repurposed mango wood.

"Tell me who we're looking for." Oliver retrieved a large padded notebook with gold-edged pages from his desk before taking a seat in his armchair. His pen was poised at the ready. "You said you knew her name?"

"Yes. Her name is Mia Mazzanti. I don't know much about her except that she went to high school in Rome." Caterina could see him writing from the angle she was at; he spelled everything correctly, thanks probably to his travels. "She's about nineteen years old and graduated high school last year. Amber eyes, blond hair, though it's probably been colored. And here's her cell phone number."

Oliver looked up and copied the phone number into his book. "I see. Is there a particular angle I'm looking for that might assist you the most?"

"I want to know if she has a history of running scams, bribing people, changing her name often, that kind of thing. She said she moved around a lot; is there anything I should be concerned with there? Has she been involved in anything scandalous?"

Nodding, Oliver jotted down a few more notes in his careful hand. Then, capping his pen, he looked up at her. "Will that be all?"

Caterina smiled thinly. "That's all." She stood.

He stood too. "Shall I call you when the dossier is ready?"

"Please. And don't wait till business hours. I want to know the minute you have something. Oh, and will you charge me for that feather scarf you have in the main room? I think it'll be perfect with a dress I just bought."

Oliver spread his arms. "Certainly, Caterina. Anything you see is yours."

Turning, Caterina swept out of the room to find Oliver's assistant waiting with her coat and gloves. Donning them, she waited while the assistant wrapped up the feather scarf, then stepped out of the shop back into the cold. She felt . . . optimistic, almost *cheerful*, for the first time in a long time. It felt like things had finally changed for the better. Above her, the sun shone like a bright penny in the sky.

She was on her way to her favorite tea shop when the door to the smoothie place opened and Alaric stepped directly into her path. Caterina moved back involuntarily before she caught herself and forced herself to maintain her position. But if she were being completely honest, seeing him like this was still like an anvil to her chest.

He smiled nonchalantly down at her, dressed impeccably as usual in a black wool peacoat, under which he'd layered a cobalt-blue scarf that brought out the teal tones in his eyes. His hair was high and thick, and his skin glowed with good health and the brisk winter morning. His gloved hands were wrapped around a cup of coffee. "Caterina." Her name on his lips always sounded like poetry. Caterina steeled her heart against it. "How funny, seeing you here."

"It's not that funny." She arched an eyebrow. "We both go to the same school, which lies less than a mile that way." Very deliberately, as if he needed all the help he could get, she pointed up the sloping hill to their right.

Alaric chuckled and shook his head. "No, I mean it's funny because I was talking about you in there." He nodded toward A-caf-demy Bistro to his left, the store he'd just exited. "Lamar was asking about you. Do you remember Lamar?"

Caterina blinked and looked away at a pair of bicyclists on the road. "Of course I remember Lamar." A couple of years ago, when she and Alaric had been friends, Lamar, the owner of A-caf-demy Bistro, had predicted they were going to fall in love. They'd laughed at the time and told him not to be silly, but after Caterina had said yes when Alaric *did* finally ask her out later that year, they'd waltzed into A-caf-demy Bistro, all flushed and giddy, and told him he was right. They'd even bought him a toy crystal ball as a gift.

"Those were happy times," Alaric said quietly, as if reading her mind. When she turned to look at him, he was gazing at her with an intensity that made her breath catch.

Caterina straightened her shoulders. "Where's Lizel?" she asked, making her voice as cold as ice.

Alaric looked away and cleared his throat. "In Milan, on a shoot."

Smirking, Caterina began to walk around him. "Goodbye, Alaric."

"Caterina."

She turned, in spite of not wanting to. It was like her body was still attuned to Alaric, to his needs. It was like whatever he wanted to say, she wanted to hear. She hated that.

"It's not like it was with us." His deep voice held a thrum of sincerity. "It'll never be like that."

Tears sprang to Caterina's eyes and she blinked them away, furious. That was her fear, exactly what he'd verbalized. What if she never found something like that again? What if Alaric had been the peak? What if all that was left for her was an endless valley?

"I know," she found herself whispering. Before he could say anything else, Caterina turned and walked quickly away, leaving Alaric looking after her at the empty sidewalk, glittering in the sun.

RAHUL

"I should get a hammock for my room also, don't you think?" Leo was lying in the hammock that Owen, Rahul's roommate, had erected in the corner of the room but rarely used. Leo and Rahul had come to an uneasy truce after their heated text exchange just a few days ago. Rahul hadn't felt like apologizing—he hadn't done anything wrong, and Leo had been jumping to conclusions—and apparently, Leo hadn't either. Neither of them was prone to passive-aggressiveness, so by mutual non-agreement, they'd moved past it. Things weren't fully back to normal, though. It was like a broken bone that had healed but still hurt on cold, damp days. But Rahul didn't know what to do about that—or even *if* he wanted to do anything about it. "If I got a hammock, Samantha and I could lie in it and look at the stars." Leo glanced at Rahul. "The glow-in-the-dark stars on my ceiling."

"I got your meaning." Rahul opened the pot of hair gel on his dresser and frowned. It was as he'd suspected; he was beginning to run a little low. He'd need to be more careful with it until Oliver could get him more. Caterina said it'd be a couple of weeks.

"I wonder where Owen got this one," Leo continued.

Rahul's cell beeped with a text, and he walked to his bed to check who it was. Everett McCabe, the director's son he'd met at Evanescence a few days ago. Everett wanted to set up a redo of the poker game at his parents' Aspen mansion, and Rahul knew RC would definitely want to be there. Grinning, he began to text back. "Or you could just use that one," he said to Leo, realizing a little belatedly that he hadn't answered him. "Owen's never here anyway."

"What is this under the pillow?" Leo reached under the small square pillow he was lying on. "It is very poky."

"You can say 'sharp.'" Rahul looked up from his cell phone, knowing Leo appreciated help with his English. "According to

Merriam-Webster, 'poky' doesn't mean 'sharp.'"

Leo cocked his head. "'You do the Hokey Pokey and you turn yourself around.' Didn't anyone tell you?" He held up an unopened bag of almonds and a magazine that had apparently been wedged under the pillow. "Ahh!" He tossed the almonds to the ground. "Someone is trying to assassinate me."

Rahul looked over again at the offending almonds. "The package is made of hermetically sealed plastic. You're probably safe."

"My allergy of tree nuts is severe enough that I do not want to take that chance, *mon ami*." He turned his attention to the magazine still in his hand. "Is this Owen's? He doesn't seem like the *GQ* type to me."

Setting his phone down on his bed, Rahul hopped up and snatched the magazine away, setting it safely away from Leo's grasp on his desk. "No. That's, um, mine, actually."

Leo shot upright, as if someone had rammed a vial of caffeine into his veins. The hammock bounced exuberantly, as if caught up in the moment too. "*Yours?*"

"You don't need to shout." Rahul pushed his glasses up on his nose. He attempted to roll his eyes, but that was something he could only pull off as RC. It kind of hurt his head and felt weird when he did it as Rahul.

Leo squinted at him. "Is there a mote of dust in your eye? Would you like some saline solution?"

"No, I just—never mind." Blinking, Rahul sat back down on his bed again. "You don't have to sound so surprised. Why can't I read *GQ*?"

"Well, you can," Leo allowed. "You have just never expressed an interest in it before." He paused, appearing to think. When he spoke again, it was with hesitation, as if he were afraid Rahul might be offended. "I have seen you talking to Caterina. . . . Is this why you're reading *GQ*? And why you have no more new issues of *Make* and *New In Chess*?" Without waiting for a response, he continued. "You do not have to change who you are to get the girl, Rahul. She will like you more if you are . . . how do you say . . ." He snapped his fingers and the hammock swayed a bit. "Authentic."

Ha. If only he knew. "Right. Because that was working so well for me." Rahul shook his head and adjusted his glasses again. Ever since he'd begun wearing contacts as RC, his glasses felt cumbersome to him, pinching the bridge of his nose and behind his ears, giving him headaches with how heavy they were. How had he never noticed before? "Someone like me doesn't belong in her circle, Leo."

Leo played with the netting of the hammock, not looking at Rahul. "But you danced with her at the winter formal. . . ."

"Yeah, and then she pretended like that didn't happen and didn't speak to me for weeks and weeks. And when she did, she told me it was *just* a dance." Rahul paused, wondering how much to say. He definitely couldn't come clean about RC. He'd promised Caterina that the press (and Alaric) wouldn't get wind of who RC really was. But maybe there were certain things he *could* say. Because, let's face it, he needed some serious advice after what had happened the night of the underground club. "Whereas recently, after I've begun to change some of my interests, she, ah . . . we kissed." He hugged a pillow to his chest, feeling ridiculous saying that. It was like saying, *I won the $400-million Powerball lottery.* Or, *A lovely family of voles has taken up residence in my chest hair.* It felt completely fantastical and patently untrue. And yet. It *had* happened.

Leo jumped out of the hammock in a feat of athleticism Rahul had never seen before except on TV. "You are not serious!" he yelled, rushing forward and taking Rahul by the shoulders.

"I'm extremely serious," Rahul replied, once his ears had stopped ringing.

"She kissed you back?"

Rahul nodded.

"Was she drunk?"

Rahul shook his head.

"Was it a dare?"

Rahul shook his head again.

"Dude!" Leo threw his hands up in the air and began walking around in quick circles, as if he couldn't contain himself. "What about Alaric? Are you and Caterina a couple now?"

Rahul rubbed the back of his neck and looked away. "Ah no. We're definitely not a couple." Not *Rahul* and Caterina, anyway. "And I don't think she's interested in getting back with Alaric anymore. But I could use your advice." He looked frankly at Leo. Maybe things weren't 100 percent back to normal between them, but he could ask Leo for advice, right? Yes, he could. Besides, he didn't really have any other options. Everett McCabe and the other guys thought RC was a player, and he didn't want to ruin that illusion. "After we kissed, we sort of got interrupted and then we . . . we haven't talked about it since." They'd talked about other stuff—social outings, Everett, Harper, etc. But not the one thing he really, really wanted to talk about.

Leo stopped walking and frowned. "She hasn't talked about it?"

"No."

"And have *you* talked about it?"

"No. I've just been, like, letting her have her space."

Leo was shaking his head emphatically before Rahul was done talking. "*Non, non, non.* You do not be coy, Rahul. You have to take charge!" He held up a fist.

Rahul frowned. "Do you know me? Or Caterina? If I 'take charge,' she'll take my testicles. By force."

"Hmm." Leo appeared to consider this. "You might be right. I have heard she has a collection of them in her room."

"Yeah." Rahul looked away, embarrassed once again by his inability to do something as simple as bringing up a kiss that had already happened. It was easy for someone like Leo to tell him to "take charge" and be brave, but that was the whole problem. Rahul wasn't like Leo. RC might be . . . but Rahul was afraid to have RC bring it up without any planning. Planning was good. Planning kept tricky social things from going off the rails, like they so frequently did for Rahul.

Leo continued, unaware of Rahul's internal dialogue. "You don't want to bring up the kiss, as you will seem desperate and cloying and as if you have been thinking of nothing else." Rahul flinched at the words "desperate and cloying," but Leo didn't seem to notice. "You want to seem aloof but confident. Like a . . . a panther."

"A panther," Rahul repeated, thinking it over. Panthers were lithe, confident, even a little arrogant. He could do panther. "Right, okay."

"Okay. Let's see it, then." Leo crossed his arms.

"See . . . what?" Rahul asked, confused.

"Your panther impersonation. I do not think you can pull this off without a lot of practice."

Rahul smirked and set his pillow down before standing. "I appreciate your concern, but I've changed a lot since school started, believe me. I can do panther. Pretty easily, in fact."

Leo didn't say anything, only spread his hand out in invitation.

Rahul took a few breaths, imagining himself in RC's head. It was easier when he was wearing the clothes, the cologne, the contacts. The hair gel. But this would have to do for now. He channeled RC, but more than RC—who was more fox than panther—he tried to channel Grey. What was Grey's most alpha-male attribute? Probably his walk. It was powerful, confident, masculine. "Okay." Rahul shook out his hands, rolled his neck a few times. And then he began to walk.

Leo watched him, his mouth popping open. Rahul tried to hold back a smile as he made sure he used his hips more to convey his pantherlike stature. Leo was obviously not used to this side of him; he was probably wondering where Rahul had disappeared to. If only he could tell him about RC!

The door opened on Rahul's second circuit around the room, and Grey walked in, stopping short and eyes widening at the sight of Rahul. Probably equally impressed and dazed at this transformation. "What are you doing?"

"Being a panther," Rahul explained. *Being you*, he thought.

"I told him the way to impress Caterina was to behave like a panther," Leo added, looking lost. "And . . ." He gestured to Rahul, letting Grey take it all in again.

"I'm powerful," Rahul said. "And masculine. And alpha. Alpha males all have a certain walk. A certain confidence that immediately draws mates in—"

"You should probably stop smiling like that," Grey said mildly.

"Really?" Rahul didn't stop smiling. "I'm just afraid without it, she'll be too intimidated to be attracted to me."

"*I'm* just afraid with it, she will run far away from you," Leo retorted, pushing a hand through his hair as if in exasperation.

"And maybe drop your hands from your hips too," Grey added, crossing his arms and leaning against Rahul's dresser. "You know, maybe have your hands by your sides?"

Rahul did as he suggested. "Hmm, that does feel more relaxed. But do I still look pantherlike?"

"You're definitely reminding me of an animal," Grey allowed. "Maybe just be yourself? I'm sure Caterina likes what she's already seen."

"They kissed," Leo explained, one hand on his hip. How come Leo could stand like that and not get called out by Grey? *Because the rules are different for them*, Rahul thought, feeling a twinge of resentment. *They'll never see my potential. To them, I'm just awkward, ridiculous Rahul.*

Grey's blue eyes widened, as if this were the most astounding thing he could ever conceive of hearing. "You guys kissed? When?"

"Saturday. But we haven't really talked about it since." Rahul stopped walking and stuck his hands in his pockets, his hair falling limply over his glasses and obscuring half his vision. Suddenly he wanted this conversation to be over. Talking to Leo and Grey was agitating him; there was no comfort in it like there used to be.

"So the plan is . . . ?"

"The plan is to get her to bring it up so I don't seem desperate and cloying. According to Leo."

Grey made a "probably a good idea" face. His gaze drifted over to Rahul's walls. "Hey. What happened to all your chess posters? Like half of them are gone."

Rahul felt his cheeks warm as defensiveness settled over

him like a mist. Grey, with his height and muscles and naturally brooding nature that attracted girls like Jaya, would never know the feeling of being chronically one step behind everyone else. Of wanting so badly to fit into the world of the one you love but never being able to.

Grey had been an outsider all these years by *choice*, a luxury that Rahul wasn't familiar with at all. And now, just as RC was working as the key to all those impenetrable social locks he'd contended with all his life, he was supposed to go back to being himself? "I'm just changing things up. Nothing wrong with that, is there?"

Grey and Leo exchanged a look, and Rahul knew—just *knew*—that they'd been talking about him behind his back. The thought stung more than it should have. It was pretty obvious to him now that Grey and Leo belonged together as friends, whereas Rahul never had. "There might be," Grey said finally, his voice mild and even. "Depending on why you're doing it and whom you're hurting to get there."

Huffing a disbelieving laugh, Rahul walked to the chair at his desk, sat down in it, and crossed his arms. "I have to say, you guys are being a little selfish right now."

Leo's jaw hardened, his fists clenching and unclenching. "'Selfish'? By telling you we are worried about you? That we miss hanging out with you?"

"I've never made a big deal about you guys changing." Rahul uncrossed his arms and picked up a pencil, tapping the eraser side against the desk. "When you began to go out with Jaya, Grey, everyone saw a big difference in you. We didn't needle you about it. And, Leo, when you and Sam began going out, you couldn't stop talking about her. It was nearly incessant. That was irritating as hell, but I didn't say a word to you."

Leo's face closed off. "I am sorry I was so irritating by being in love," he said, and Grey patted his shoulder once, as if in sol-idarity.

"When I changed," Grey put in when Leo didn't continue, "I think everyone saw it was for the best. But this"—he gestured around Rahul's room and then at Rahul himself—"doesn't seem to be the same thing."

Rahul narrowed his eyes, his pencil pausing in its frenzied tapping. "What are you saying? That I'm—"

"That you have become a big asshole!" Leo snapped, his accent twisting the word into something uglier, harsher. "And you have forgotten who your friends are. You have forgotten who *you* are."

They waited, staring at him, Leo breathing fast, Grey's blue eyes implacable, watchful.

Rahul tossed his pencil down. If they were waiting for an apology, they were going to be waiting a long time. He'd done nothing wrong. *Nothing.* He was finally seeing new possibilities for his life, and he wasn't about to apologize for it. "Sorry you feel that way," he said, making an effort to keep his voice level.

Leo shook his head, turned on his heel, and stalked off, leaving Rahul's door wide open.

Grey lingered a moment longer, studying Rahul's face. "Yeah," he said finally. "Me too." Then he left too, closing Rahul's door softly behind him.

Rahul clenched his fists and took a few deep breaths. When he felt calmer, he picked up his cell and texted Everett McCabe.

What can I bring to the poker game?

nothing just yourself brother, the response came.

Rahul read the message over. With his new friend group, he didn't have to explain himself. They accepted RC fully. He'd never had that—complete acceptance—before, not with his friends at school, not with his family at home, who had a stand-in because Rahul wasn't good enough. He'd floated along all his life, desperate for a social connection that he never got, feeling adrift, a ship without an anchor.

Now RC was his anchor. RC was his chance to right all the wrongs in his life. And if his friends couldn't see that, then . . . He glanced at Everett's message again. Maybe it was time for new friends.

CHAPTER 13

CATERINA

She got the voicemail just as her AP Calculus class got out.

"Caterina," Oliver's smooth voice traveled down the line, "I have the report."

Caterina went still.

"Mia Mazzanti has moved a lot, as her father is a diplomat for the UN. Her mother is a homemaker. Her parents live in the Netherlands at the moment, but Mia herself has an apartment in the town of Rosetta. No scandals, no history of bribery, nothing of note. Please let me know if you have any other questions."

Caterina let out the breath that had built in her chest. Mia was clean. A diplomat's daughter—that explained last season's shoes and the slightly shoddier clothing than Caterina was used to. She should have no reservations in pursuing this friendship with the girl from her home city. She smiled to herself.

Feeling buoyant, she sent a text to her dad she'd been meaning to send since yesterday.

Papa! Pietro showed me the new Bugatti! Custom?? You didn't have to do that!

The reply pinged back a minute later as she was packing her

books into her bag. I was missing my little topolina. I can't be there, but maybe the car will make things a little happier.

Laughing lightly, Caterina picked up her cell phone and perched on the edge of her desk for just a moment as she texted him back. Her dad's love language was definitely gifts, and if she were being honest, it wasn't one she minded at all. This one, though, was a little profligate, even for him. There are other ways to do that than buying me a custom Bugatti :)

Ah, but I heard Geoff Lodge talking about how he couldn't afford one for his son. Then I knew I had to get one for you.

Caterina's smile dimmed. So he'd gotten her the car because of his decades-old rivalry with some stuffy businessman? Her dad had just wanted to parade his wealth. The gift had almost nothing to do with her at all. She typed out a quick reply—I have to get to class, talk later <3—and got to her feet, slinging her bag onto her shoulder. *So what?* she told herself. *He still loves you. He was still thinking of you.* There was a pit in her stomach, though, that she didn't much like.

"Caterina. Hi."

One foot out of the classroom door and shrugging into her coat, she turned to see Rahul at her side, nervously twisting his tie around his bony fist. Her heart lifted, both at his familiar face and at the somewhat endearing anxiety she'd missed seeing lately, since he'd become RC. Strange, that.

Then, remembering the kiss they'd shared in the car and hadn't spoken of since, her cheeks went warm. She hadn't really known what to say about it. To be completely honest, she wasn't sure if she wanted it to happen again. On the one hand, it was all she could think about. But on the other . . . she'd just gotten over Alaric. Was she really ready to be diving back into those waters again? "Hi." She kept walking, knowing he'd follow her as everyone always did.

"Are you—where are you going? Do you want to grab dinner in the dining hall later and talk about the next event? I'm game for whatever else you want to do. To give the media something to talk about." He cleared his throat as he did when he was nervous and fiddled with his wire-frame glasses.

"Actually, I have a better idea," Caterina replied as they went around a group of seniors, all of whom called out to her. She nodded at them as she went, not wanting to get stopped. She smiled at Rahul over her shoulder. "I just got a new car, and I've been dying to take it out for a drive. Would you like to keep me company? I want to get used to it." A drive in the Bugatti—even if she didn't love it nearly as much anymore, after her chat with her dad—was harmless, wasn't it? They'd be talking. They'd plan the next event. There definitely wouldn't be any kissing; she'd need to keep her eyes on the road, after all.

Rahul smiled in that beguiling way that made her heart beat a little bit faster than was completely normal. "That sounds awesome. I—I can't wait."

"Wonderful. I have to get to my next class, but I'll text you."

"Yeah." Rahul nodded several times. "Sure. Okay."

Caterina flounced down the stairs and out into the cold, knowing he was watching her as she went.

RAHUL

He checked his hair in the mirror, grimacing. It looked awful, limp and flat. Picking the hair gel jar off his desk, Rahul unscrewed the lid and peeked inside, considering his options. No. There was barely enough left. He couldn't risk using it now and not having any for an actual big event. He adjusted his sweater collar, wanting to rip it off his body. Being in this body, being Rahul 98 percent of the time, just wasn't cutting it anymore. Not when he knew he could be RC, the guy he'd always wanted to be, the guy the world liked so much better.

It was the day of his drive with Caterina in her new car, and while he was ecstatic to be spending time with her, he was also uneasy. Maybe even a little afraid. She was so used to seeing RC, to having RC's witty repartee in her ear all night. What if going as himself just made her realize how little she liked the real him?

His phone dinged with a text from Caterina.

Outside, was all it said.

Well, there was no time to think about that anymore. Grabbing his wallet and stuffing it into his ill-fitting jeans, Rahul sighed and walked out of his room.

"Wow." Rahul was unable to keep the sheer awe and wonder from imbuing his voice.

Caterina was pulled up to the curb outside the main building in her new car, a glossy, duo-chrome lime-green and gold Bugatti with a vanity plate that said QUEENCAT4. The paint job was obviously custom. Rahul ran a reverent hand over the hood as he walked to the passenger side.

"Do you like?" Caterina asked through the open window, her eyes shining. She was wearing a car coat, a pine-green turtleneck sweater, and black pants, looking absolutely like someone who'd drive a car like this.

Rahul sank into the cream leather seats, taking care not to sigh in absolute blissful pleasure. "It's pretty nice," he said in what he hoped was an offhand way, to make up for his very uncool impressed air from just a few moments before. And because he couldn't help himself: "Did you know Ettore Bugatti, the founder of Bugatti cars, comes from a family of artists? His dad is a jewelry designer."

Caterina gave him an amused smile. Her face was perfect as always, her makeup of professional quality. He caught sight of himself in the rearview mirror and tried not to frown. The difference between the two of them was stark enough to be funny. "I did know that, actually. My father is good friends with Herbert Diess, the CEO of the Volkswagen group; they own Bugatti now. But the Bugatti family was cursed, in a way. It's a really interesting story. I'll tell it to you sometime."

"Oh, right. Sure. Of course." It wasn't surprising she knew way more about all of this than he did. Bugatti was a Caterina thing like chess was a Rahul thing. He should've known that.

Caterina continued to smile. "But thanks for the compliment, and the fact. Buckled in?"

He nodded, not able to speak for a moment. He was so massively underdressed, underprepared, and underequipped to be out and about with Caterina LaValle.

"Good." She put the car in drive, oblivious to his thoughts. "You're going to need that seat belt." And then she squealed out into the road, leaving Rosetta Academy in their dust.

They'd been going for about forty minutes, leaving behind the town of Rosetta, driving in the wilderness between it and Aspen. As they wound up into the surrounding hills, the air turned positively chilly and they rolled up their windows.

"I have no idea where we are," Caterina said, glancing at her GPS. "But I'm having so much fun driving that I don't even care."

Rahul grinned at her as the world flashed by outside his window. So far, she didn't seem to mind him so much. They hadn't talked a whole lot, both of them engrossed in the drive and Caterina's playlist. "Was this a Christmas present?"

"More like a just-because present. My father likes to surprise me with gifts when he's traveling and misses me. It's his way of saying he's thinking of me even if he's not there wi . . ." She drifted off as giant snowflakes began blowing against the windshield of the car. "What the hell?"

Rahul suppressed a chuckle; it was the first time he'd ever heard her say that. It was so . . . human and un-goddesslike, somehow. "It's snowing." He glanced up at the sky, which was rapidly turning into a solid wall of dove gray. "And those are nimbostratus clouds. It looks like it's going to be snowing for a while."

As if the weather had an ear pressed to his car window, the wind began to buffet the car, snow covering the windshield and windows until visibility was nearly nil.

"Shit!" Caterina's hands were clamped around the heated steering wheel, her face white. "I need to get off the road!"

"Yes," Rahul agreed, glancing into the rearview mirror. There was almost a solid wall of white all around them. "Visibility is poor enough that other drivers likely can't see you, just as you can't see them. It's probable that we'll plow into someone else or vice versa. Seventeen percent of all vehicle crashes happen in winter conditions."

Caterina gave him a withering look, just for a second, before returning her eyes to the invisible road. "And what do you propose?"

Rahul squinted out the window, trying to catch a glimpse through the flying snow. "There," he said, pointing. "I think there's a small road about three hundred meters ahead to your right, and it looks like there's a cabin down there. I'm not sure if it's empty, but it might be worth checking out."

He'd barely finished the thought before Caterina had swung her steering wheel around and they were making their way down the small road to the right.

"I just want to get off this godforsaken road and out of the car," Caterina muttered as they bounced down the road. "I love my Bugatti, but I can already tell she's awful in adverse weather."

Rahul saw he'd been right; there was a small log cabin tucked away in a nest of pine trees. Its dark wood stood out, stark against the white curtains of snow. Caterina put the car in park and they both got out, hunkering against the blowing, roaring wind. "Should we just knock on their door and ask to be let in?" Rahul yelled.

"Yes!" Caterina shouted back, her steps long and lithe as she crossed to the front door. Even hunkered down into her coat, she had an easy confidence to her that Rahul could never muster, except as RC. She reached the door first and authoritatively knocked twice.

Rahul came to stand beside her, under the eaves of the roof, somewhat sheltered from the snow. His hair was wet and hung over his forehead in limp strands. He tried not to fidget, but he'd kill for a mirror, just to make himself a little more presentable. At least in the car, Caterina was focused on driving her new car. But here, in this cabin, they'd be face-to-face. There'd be no distractions.

Rahul realized his hands were freezing; he hadn't thought to bring gloves. He tried peeking in the window next to the door, but the curtains were drawn tight. "What if a murderer lives here?" he asked, the thought occurring to him suddenly and rather unpleasantly. "Don't they usually live in rural areas like this, away from civilization, so they can chop people up in peace?"

Caterina raised her hand and knocked again. "A murderer wouldn't dare murder me."

She said it with such serious conviction that Rahul laughed in spite of his uneasiness. "Because you're Caterina LaValle?"

She cocked an eyebrow at him. "Precisely," she said before reaching out and twisting the doorknob.

The door opened silently inward.

CATERINA

"What are you *doing*?" Rahul asked, his eyes wide behind glasses that were coated in melted snow. "This is someone's house."

Caterina wanted to laugh at his outraged, shocked expression. Rahul was obviously someone who was very used to following the rules. Whereas Caterina had learned from a very young age that the rules were only meant for certain people and that the LaValles were not certain people.

"Hello?" she called, stepping into the dim, cold interior, which was still dozens of degrees warmer than outside. Caterina felt instantly drier, protected from the wind.

The sun-bleached drapes had been drawn on every window, and the house had a smell of disrepair and abandonment about it. Every surface was coated with dust; there was no furniture in the minuscule main room or the attached kitchen. On the kitchen counter, there was a butane lighter and an old cup containing brown sludge that Caterina didn't want to examine too closely.

"Well." Rahul closed the door behind him and stood in the middle of the room. "Doesn't look like anyone lives here, at least. We can probably rule out the serial killer. Unless he only drops in occasionally."

He wasn't entirely joking, Caterina could tell. He seemed uneasy, uncomfortable somehow. Was it just the idea of a lurking murderer or something else? Maybe something to do with her? Surprising herself, Caterina found she didn't like that thought; she wanted Rahul to feel comfortable in her presence. She pulled her cell out of her pocket and looked at the screen. "Signal's non-existent, probably thanks to the storm."

Rahul checked his phone too. "Yeah. Same here."

"I guess we'll just wait it out in here until the storm passes. The Bugatti won't be able to make it back, so Pietro'll have to come pick us up." She looked around, squinting in the gloom. "There's a fireplace. Do you know how to build a fire?"

Something very much like relief passed along his features as he put his phone away. "I do. I know six ways, in fact." He strode across the tiny room to the fireplace. He was bundled into his too-big black coat, and his jeans were baggy at the knees, but there was a determined set to his jaw. "I'll take care of it, don't worry."

Caterina bit her lip to hide a smile. Something told her he was trying to play the part of the protector, the one who could take care of her when things got dicey. She didn't need it, of course, but . . . but she had to admit it was nice. Being here, stuck in a snowstorm with Rahul, felt like a salve for a pain she hadn't realized she had. Which was nonsense, obviously. She was being sentimental and ridiculous, and the thought alarmed her.

She turned to him as the fire suddenly bloomed and said, in the bossiest tone she could muster, "That fire better not go out anytime soon."

Rahul glanced at her, his eyebrows raised. "I'm sure. I took this wilderness training course a couple years ago, and fire building was one thing I always aced."

Caterina sighed and spread out her coat on the floor before sitting on it. He was always so levelheaded and good-natured. "Is it hard?" she asked, looking at him in the flickering firelight.

He walked to where she sat, spread out his own jacket, and sat beside her, his legs stretched out in front of him. From up close, she saw the knees of his jeans were faded and nearly threadbare, as if he'd had the pants for years. "Is what hard?"

"Being nice. Being a kind person. Doesn't the world take advantage of you at every opportunity?"

Rahul appeared to consider this as he looked into the crackling flames, the lenses of his glasses dancing with firelight. "I guess there are people out there who'd like to take advantage of that. But I try to surround myself with people I trust. Like Leo and Grey or Jaya and DE." Something very much like sadness passed across his features as he said those words. Caterina waited, but he didn't add anything else.

Feeling the heat of the fire on her skin, Caterina said softly, "I was taught never to trust anyone. Everyone has the capacity to hurt you."

Rahul studied her expression. "I guess that's technically true. But statistically, certain people have a lower chance of hurting you than others." He cleared his throat, and Caterina could tell he was wondering whether to say whatever thought was on his mind.

"Just say it," she said, looking straight ahead.

He didn't ask her what she meant. "Alaric, for instance. I wouldn't have advised you to, ah, embark on a two-year-long relationship with him. His heart was never in the right place. Not like yours is."

Caterina smiled thinly and glanced at him. "Most people say I don't have a heart, you know."

"Most people are wrong," Rahul said simply, holding out his hands to absorb the warmth of the fire.

"I always took it as a compliment. When people said that, I mean. It was evidence that I was doing what I'd always been taught to do—look out for number one, be ruthless, be cunning, never let anyone too close. That nickname I have? Queen Cat? I love it."

"Why?" Rahul looked genuinely curious.

Caterina adjusted her legs, tucking them to one side. The cabin shuddered a little as the wind howled, poking at the windows, looking for a way in. "Cats are the ultimate narcissists, a study in being heartless. They're cold, and yet people live to serve them. Put a cat and a bear together, and the bear's going to run away when the cat hits it on the nose. Why? Because cats have the don't-fuck-with-me attitude that can put something twenty times their size in its place. That's what I've always coveted."

"Cats also poop in a box and murder things just because." Rahul's face turned bright crimson a moment after he uttered the words. "S-sorry. I just, I have a problem saying things without thinking them through first. Not when I'm RC, obviously. But i-it's . . . Sorry."

Caterina allowed herself a little laugh. Her shoulders relaxed as they often did around Rahul. "It's okay. You're right.

I guess I don't want to be *all* cat. I enjoy modern plumbing."

Rahul grinned, looking relieved. A knot in one of the logs in the fireplace popped, and they both turned to watch the fire again, silent for a few moments. There was a smell of damp and rot in the cabin, but Caterina didn't mind. At this moment, she'd rather be here than on the Italian Riviera.

RAHUL

He glanced at her sidelong, her strong profile looking more delicate than it ever had. Her eyes were soft, almost unguarded. Rahul plunged forward with his thought, even though alarm bells in his head told him not to. "Do you . . . do you remember the winter formal?"

She looked at him, tilted her head a little, her long wavy hair brushing the tops of her thighs. "Of course I do. It wasn't that long ago."

Rahul swallowed. "Right, yeah. But I mean . . . do you ever think about it? About you and me dancing together?" He ran his fingers over a soft, worn patch of denim at his knees.

Caterina studied him, the firelight playing in her brown hair. "Sometimes," she said quietly, and Rahul's heart battered against his chest. "Do you?"

"Yes. Yeah. I do. That was when I—" He stopped short. He'd been about to say, *That's when I fell in love with you.* Disastrous. "When I saw you in a completely different light."

A half smile tugged at her lips, but her eyes were cool. "And what light was that? The 'Caterina's not perfect like she makes herself out to be' light?"

Rahul rushed to speak, his fingers clenched together on his lap. "No, not at all. Before that night, I'd always noticed you from afar. How pretty you were"—here, his cheeks heated; he probably shouldn't have said that, but it was too late now, so he continued—"how many friends you had, that kind of thing. But you were also just one of the ultrarich kids, always surrounded by other ultrarich kids. But that night . . ." Rahul shrugged and ran a hand through his hair. "You looked so young, somehow. So exposed.

"When you were watching Alaric, I could see the heartbreak on your face so plainly. I knew I couldn't undo the things that had happened, but I wanted to stay anyway and take your mind off them, even if for just a few minutes. When you danced with me, it felt like you might break in my arms. I still remember how you looked up at me at one point and said, 'Isn't it funny how all the pieces of your heart can still love the person who broke it in the first place?' We talked so much that night; hours passed like seconds. And when we were done, I felt the tears on the lapel of my tux. You'd been crying while we were dancing. I don't think I'd ever even thought about you crying before that."

He cleared his throat, wondering if she thought he was weird for saying all that out loud. And then it occurred to him that he'd felt *comfortable* enough to say all that out loud to Caterina. Whoa.

Caterina was staring at him, unreadable. Even if she *did* think he was weird, he needed to say this next bit.

"And after that, every time I looked at you in the hallways or on social media, surrounded by your friends, looking hard and sphinxlike, like nothing could touch you, I knew the truth. I felt like I'd gotten a glimpse into the kind of person you *really* are, when no one else had."

Caterina played with a wooden button on the jacket under her. "Dancing with you felt . . . safe. I felt protected for the first time in forever. Experience has taught me that new people are almost always on the brink of hurting me, of taking what they want and not caring what they leave behind." She looked at him from underneath her long, fake eyelashes, and his heart melted a little. "But I didn't feel that way with you."

Rahul held her eyes. "I would never hurt you. Not knowingly."

Caterina nibbled her lip for a second, as if weighing what she was about to say next. The fire crackled in the space between her words. "I was so afraid I was being gauche, that you'd run off and tell everyone that Caterina LaValle was a sad, soggy mess. But you didn't. You just held me and danced with me. Why?"

Rahul listened to the insistent tapping of snow at the windows for a moment before responding. "You were more beautiful—rawer and truer—that night than ever before," he said simply.

A ghost of a smile hovered on Caterina's lips. "Even with smudged mascara and a red nose?"

"Especially with smudged mascara and a red nose. You were hurting. I wanted to be there for you."

Caterina looked down at her silk pants–clad thighs. "I . . . I was worried for the longest time that you'd tell someone. But the days passed into weeks and then into months and you never did."

"You asked me not to." He didn't say that he'd fallen in love with her that day with a helpless thud, and he'd do anything from that point on to keep her safe. That's what he'd learned that day in the ballroom—although Caterina LaValle seemed like the toughest, most independent girl in the entire school, she might be the one who needed protecting the most.

She looked up at him, shaking her head a little, oblivious to his thoughts. "And Rahul Chopra always keeps his word."

He couldn't decipher the look in her eyes, a flickering emotion that she was trying to bury. "I do." He paused, not wanting her to take his next statement as pity, but wanting to say it anyway. "I'm sorry people have hurt you so much."

Caterina's look changed into something icy smooth, and his heart seized. But then she sighed, deflating, and Rahul sighed too in relief. "That's life for a LaValle, I guess. I can't tell you the number of times I thought someone was my friend, only to find out they were after something else I had—money or connections, usually. That's why I run a background check on almost everyone I let into my life now."

Rahul glanced sharply at her. "You ran one on me?"

She nodded, studying his reaction. "Yes. A quick one. Just to be sure. Well, Oliver did; he's the one who helps me with things like that."

He considered this. "And what did you find?"

She smiled a little. "My three favorite words: nothing of note."

"My life in a nutshell," Rahul mumbled.

Caterina frowned. "That's not true at all."

Rahul shrugged, feeling that kernel of embarrassment he seemed to feel so often now in his own skin.

They sat in silence for a moment, letting the fire's heat wrap them up in its arms. Then Rahul said quietly, "Not being able to trust people sounds really lonely." Rahul didn't have many friends, and the friends he *had* he'd fallen out with, which felt bad enough. But to make the decision to have *no* friends, to trust no one . . . It would be like being stranded.

"I'm surrounded by people," Caterina replied, which really

didn't address what he'd said. But Rahul decided to let it go. Another minute passed in silence as they listened to the snowstorm building around them. Caterina glanced sidelong at him. "You're very easy to talk to."

"Am I?" Rahul quirked his lips to one side. "I don't think most people would say that about me." RC, maybe. But Rahul? No way. Most people didn't even notice his existence.

"Most people wouldn't say I have a heart, and most people wouldn't say you're easy to talk to," Caterina mused. Her brown eyes glittered. "It sounds like most people don't know us."

"No, they don't." He studied her expression, understanding that she was telling him something important. She'd let him have a little piece of herself; she'd shared something with him that no one else knew.

"What about your parents?" Caterina asked suddenly, as if she wasn't able to contain herself any longer. "You hardly ever speak about your family, either, I've noticed."

Rahul leaned over, picked up the lighter off the floor, and flicked it on. Watching the flame dance, he said, "It's not a very interesting story."

"You don't want to talk about it." Caterina looked a little disappointed, Rahul realized in astonishment. She *wanted* to know about him. Maybe she wanted to know about RC, though. He and Rahul had the same history, after all, in spite of what most people thought.

"N-no, it's not that," he amended in a hurry. "I mean . . . my mom's a politician, like I said before. And politicians need perfect families to appeal to their constituents. I get that."

"Still." Caterina adjusted her body so she was facing him more. A thin, delicate necklace with a crown pendant hung at her throat and caught the light from the lighter that Rahul was still playing with. "It can't be easy."

Rahul's cheeks burned. He focused intently on flicking the lighter on and off. "I understand, though."

Caterina placed a cool, dry hand on the back of his hand, just for a moment. His heart juddered and jumped in his chest, as if she had electricity flowing through her veins. "You understand because you're a kind, sweet person, Rahul."

He looked into her eyes over the flame and slowly let his finger off the button. Setting the lighter to the side, he turned back to Caterina. "Thank you," he said, not looking away even though his pulse was hopping wildly.

She hesitated for just a moment before leaning into him. Putting his hands against her cheeks, Rahul let his head dip until his lips found hers.

CHAPTER 14

CATERINA

And once again, they were kissing. Caterina knew she should give it more thought. Was it wise to kiss Rahul, when *RC* was the one who was boyfriend material and the media darling—and oh, who happened to not be real? That had been a big draw for her, the idea of not having to please yet another shallow, uncaring guy while still having the satisfaction of showing the media a suitable boyfriend.

But the thing was, she *wanted* to kiss Rahul. His warm lips, just the right amount of soft and firm, the slight stubble at his jaw, the way he cradled her face with the utmost care as if she might break—all of those things were what she wanted, needed, in this moment. She'd been more vulnerable with him in the last ten minutes than she'd been with anyone her entire life, and yet she didn't feel that familiar sense of panic at the thought that she'd let her mask slip, that she'd said too much. Instead, it felt . . . good. It felt right that Rahul should be the one to hold everything she'd said.

And the fact that he thought she was most beautiful at the winter formal—that he'd seen her red-faced and crying and kept that memory locked inside a box—what did that mean? Caterina thought it meant something important, something big, something she was a little afraid to look at right then. But she could kiss him. *That* she could manage.

She moved even closer to him, close enough that his hand slipped from her cheek to her waist, and he pulled her into him, bathing her in his soft warmth. He was wiry, not as tall as the boys she usually dated, but he was safer, too. In Rahul's arms, she felt protected from the world, shielded in a way she'd never been with Alaric or any of the boys before him. In Rahul's arms, she felt cherished for who she was, not what she brought to the table or the newest business deal her father had made. There were no expectations with him except that she be exactly who she was. And in this moment, knowing she was accepted for everything she was, Caterina felt forgiveness. For Alaric, for all he'd done to her, for everyone who'd ever wronged her. She felt forgiveness and she felt forgiven, and that, too, was the magic of Rahul Chopra.

After a moment, her heart beating wildly, Caterina pulled back and rested her forehead against his. She'd told herself she wasn't ready to date so soon after Alaric, but that was untrue, she realized. She just wasn't ready to date someone like the boys she'd always dated. But if Rahul asked her out, she'd say yes in a heartbeat. She smiled at the realization, her heart singing. She'd say yes.

RAHUL

There was no way she'd say yes.

Rahul pulled back and gazed into her shining brown eyes.

She was smiling, her lips red and swollen in an incredibly sexy way. He wanted to ask her if she would be his girlfriend, for real. The question he'd wanted to ask her since they'd first danced together.

But how could he just blurt it out now? He was sitting here with Caterina LaValle in an abandoned cabin in the middle of a snowstorm with a fire going; it didn't get more romantic than this, at least not in his limited experience watching rom-coms when he couldn't get out of it. But there was the problem—it was *him* here with Caterina. Rahul, not RC. And she deserved someone like RC to ask her out. Not Rahul in his awkward—what were the words Leo had used?—oh yes, "desperate and cloying" way. He couldn't ask her; she'd say no. But RC would come up with something spectacular, something she *couldn't* say no to.

Rahul smoothed her hair back from her face and began to rise to his feet. "Uh, I should add another log to that before it goes out."

CATERINA

Caterina grabbed his elbow, stopping him. Oh no, he didn't. "Rahul," she said carefully. "There's something you should know about me."

"Okay . . ."

"I never ask boys out. Ever." She raised a meaningful eyebrow. "Boys ask *me* out. Not the other way around."

Her heart raced in her chest. This was the closest she'd ever come to putting herself out there with a boy she liked. Normally, she liked to sit back and wait for it to happen. You couldn't get rejected if you didn't ask a yes-or-no question.

But she couldn't let Rahul take his time. Graduation would roll around and he still wouldn't have asked her; she knew this in her heart. So, yes, she was probably being domineering and commanding, and someone less patient than Rahul wouldn't have put up with it. But the truth was, she had no idea how people openly talked about their feelings for each other. Weren't they afraid? Didn't it feel horrible to be that vulnerable, to leave your throat exposed in that way? Caterina had no desire for that.

Rahul swallowed, his Adam's apple moving in his throat. "Um . . . Are you . . . ? That is, are you saying . . . ?" He trailed off. His forehead was damp, his expression anxious and complicated.

"If you asked me, I'd say yes," she said gently, wanting him to get it so badly it hurt. *Just* do *it, Rahul,* she tried to beam directly into his head. *Ask me out right now.*

He turned more fully to her and sat on his folded knees. "Caterina," he said, looking deep into her eyes. "Will you do me the great honor of going out with me?"

The smile burst onto her face without her permission. "Rahul, I'd love to." And then she found herself in his arms again.

Mia walked in the door, and Caterina raised a hand to get her attention.

"Caterina!" Mia bustled over in her yellow puffer jacket and dark jeans, her hair pulled back in a high ponytail. "I'm so glad you texted."

They air-kissed, and Caterina went back to pouring her white pear tea. "I'm glad you were free to meet up. I hope you don't mind the surroundings. They're not much to look at, but Hospitalitea is my favorite teahouse in Rosetta." She gestured around them to the tiny, dim tea shop. Shelves of repurposed lumber, brimming with tins of custom-mixed loose-leaf tea, were stacked against its colorful walls. Flavors like "Tranquilitea" and "TEArs of the Patriarchy" had become staples in Caterina's private suite in the dorms.

Today Caterina had snagged a small table for two by the window, though it wasn't the warmest spot in the shop. There were a few other people around, mostly older, huddled into their coats and hogging tables by the rickety radiator in the corner.

"Oh, I love it!" Mia looked around appreciatively as she took off her jacket and draped it along the back of her chair. She was wearing a plain white sweater underneath. "I haven't had a chance to check this out yet."

"How long have you been in town?" Caterina poured Mia a bit of tea from the teapot and then returned it to its tea-light heater. "I hope you don't mind that I already ordered something for us. This one's 'Pearish the Thought.' It's got a nice, subtle pear flavor."

Mia's nose wrinkled with a smile. "That's a cute name. And to answer your question, just a few months." She sipped carefully at her tea. "Mm, this is very good. Good choice."

Caterina smiled, glad that Mia liked her tea. "Will you be staying a while, then?"

"I'm not sure yet." Mia set her cup down and traced a finger along the top edge. "That all really depends on how things go here. I might not like it enough to stay."

Caterina played with the crown pendant at her throat. "Or you might love it. You never know."

Mia shrugged. "Maybe. I'm still getting a handle on everything." She brushed a hand through the air, as if brushing away her words. "But what *I* really want to hear about is RC, the man of the hour. That journalist could not stop singing his praises before you came to Evanescence the other night."

Joy bloomed in Caterina's chest simply at Rahul's mention. It was ridiculous. "Really? Well, he does seem to have that effect on people. They just . . . I don't know, *gravitate* toward him."

Mia smiled a teasing half smile. "Is that what happened to you? Did he suck you in with his gravitational force?"

Caterina looked down into her steaming tea. "Kind of. We've just been keeping it casual so far, but he asked me out yesterday."

Mia cheered and clapped her hands. The other patrons glanced their way, but she didn't seem to notice. "That's exciting! So you're a couple now?"

"It would seem that way." Caterina shook her head slowly. "I can't believe it. It's just so . . ."

"Why can't you believe it?" Mia asked, cocking her head. "He's no frog. And you're exactly the kind of girl the dashing, handsome, rich crown prince of some small kingdom would date."

Caterina studied Mia, trying not to smile.

"What?" Mia leaned forward, the steam from the tea cloaking her olive-toned face.

"It's just funny you used a Frog Prince analogy. That's all."

Mia's amber eyes glittered, as if she sensed gossip. "Why?"

Caterina took a breath, running her fingernail into a groove in the table. She'd said too much. The only people who knew about Rahul/RC were Pietro and Oliver, and somehow, Caterina sensed that she could trust Mia, too. She wasn't involved in all the social politics like Caterina's other friends were. But old habits were hard to break, and Caterina knew she couldn't divulge the truth about Rahul, not even to Mia. Not yet.

"No reason." She smiled. "I'm just happy to be with RC, that's all. He really is the prince of my heart, as it were."

After the slightest pause, Mia put a hand to her heart. "That's the sweetest thing I've ever heard. So what drew you to him? Was it just the debonair charm?"

Caterina sipped her tea and considered the question. One of the old ladies at a nearby table laughed, her voice high-pitched and honeyed.

"Well," Caterina said finally. "That's hard to explain. RC's just . . . different. He doesn't play games the way the other boys I know do, the way Alaric did. He's forthright and honest and"—she laughed a little—"I don't know. When I'm with him, I don't feel the need to be anything except myself. Oh, and do you know what he did? When Alaric cheated on me last year, when I had nobody to turn to who wasn't more interested in 'the scoop' than how I was feeling, RC asked me to dance. At the winter formal last year." She felt a stinging behind her eyes and blinked them forcefully, rapidly. Her period must be on its way. That was the only explanation. "Anyway." She stopped and took a bolstering sip of tea, feeling thrown by all she'd said. She shouldn't have said the part about the winter formal—RC didn't go to Rosetta Academy, and it was a specific truth that could easily be pulled at.

But Mia didn't seem to be interested in that. She was watching Caterina closely. "Sounds like you had no problem explaining that at all." She paused, drumming her fingers on the table in slow motion. "It sounds to me like you're in love."

If not for her rigorous etiquette classes, Caterina would've sputtered her tea all over the table. "*Love?*" she said finally, her voice just a touch too loud for the space. Gaining control over herself, she added more quietly, "Let's not get carried away, shall we?"

"I think you've already been carried away in RC's manly arms," Mia countered, laughing.

And Caterina couldn't help it; she actually pictured Rahul picking her up and swinging her around, her hair trailing behind her. Feeling her cheeks warm, she shook her head. "Stop."

Mia leaned back, tipping her chair. "So what does RC think about you, then? Do you suppose his feelings run as deep as yours?"

Caterina sipped her tea to buy herself some time. "I think so. . . ." Biting her lip, she looked out the window on her left, watching as a biker whizzed by across the street, his face red from the cold. She looked back at Mia, who was watching her closely. "I *hope* so," she amended. "I really, really hope so."

Mia appeared to consider this. "I'll bet he does. You have that effect on people, don't you? You draw them in with your charm and your beauty and your air of royalty."

Caterina raised her eyebrows. "My goodness. Thanks for the compliment."

Mia hadn't touched her tea in some time. "Where's RC's family from? He said Anandgarh, right?"

Caterina laughed a little and refilled her mug. "Are we playing twenty questions now? Why do you want to know about his family?"

"No reason," Mia said easily. "Just wondering is all." She held her mug up. "A toast. To new love and new beginnings. And new friendships."

Caterina clinked her cup against Mia's, her cheeks warm and her heart singing. "To new beginnings."

They walked outside once they were done with their tea, both of them bundled into their coats, thick scarves covering their necks and chins. Caterina detested wearing hats, but she'd made an exception for this crystal-cold day. She led Mia down the street, each of them stopping to look in the different shops as they went.

"This one's an actual psychic." Mia pressed her hands against the glass window of one shop and peered in. "But they're closed. Blast. I would have loved to know what they saw in my future."

Caterina laughed as they continued to walk. "Why? Is your future in question in some way?"

Mia tossed her a half smile. "The future is *always* in question. Nothing is ever set in stone. Things can change in an instant."

"Hmm. I've always felt secure about my future, but perhaps that was my upbringing."

"My family moved a lot, sometimes at a moment's notice," Mia said a little wistfully. "I suppose that's what being a diplomat's daughter will do for you."

Caterina glanced at her, glad Mia had finally revealed a bit about her family. Now she wouldn't have to pretend to not know that her father was a diplomat. "Do you have any siblings?"

Mia looked at her. "No. I was all alone growing up. You?"

Caterina shook her head and stopped to look in the window of Bookingham Palace, a bookstore she knew Jaya liked to frequent. "No, it's just me and my father. My mother died when I was very young. I have no memory of her at all."

"How unspeakably sad," Mia said, coming to stand beside her as they looked at the travel books on display. "Growing up without a parent. It must feel like you've lost a limb."

"Oh, I don't know about that," Caterina countered. "I never knew my mother." They began to walk again. "I suppose I never felt like I was missing anything. My father gave me all I needed. And I always had friends."

"Friends." Mia smiled. "You know, I was going to ask you if any of your school friends would be joining us at the tea shop. Harper, perhaps?"

A couple walking hand in hand passed them by, laughing at something.

"No, Harper doesn't go to Rosetta," Caterina explained. "She goes to another private school in Aspen, one her mother attended. As for my other friends . . ." She thought of Heather and Ava. She had no idea what they were up to this weekend. "I suppose I'm at a point where I'm reevaluating my friendships."

"Really?" Mia sounded genuinely curious. "Why?"

Caterina waved a gloved hand in the air. "I'm not sure they really understand me. Or that I understand them, if I'm being honest." She shrugged and then glanced sideways at Mia. "What about you? Have you made friends here in Rosetta yet?"

Mia smiled. "I think I have now." Stuffing her hands in her jacket pockets, she turned to Caterina. "I want to thank you for being so welcoming to me. I know it can't be easy for someone like you. You probably always have to be on the lookout."

Caterina nodded, allowing that. Maybe someday she'd tell Mia about the background check she'd run on her and they'd laugh. "It does get tiresome sometimes. But there was something about you that I connected with. I like to think I have a sense about people."

Mia smiled at her words.

They got to the end of the street, and Caterina saw Pietro parked in the SUV. "There's my driver. Would you like a ride home?"

Mia tipped her head back, enjoying the sun on her face. "No, thank you. I prefer the walk."

"Well, thanks for coming out today. Let's do it again soon."

Mia opened her eyes and grinned. "I'll expect a full report on your date with RC then."

Laughing, Caterina began to walk toward her car. "You can count on it."

CHAPTER 15

RAHUL

"Apparently, a new student's supposed to start at Rosetta in a couple of weeks," DE was saying as Rahul rushed into the restaurant, his heart beating wildly with the knowledge of how things had changed between him and Caterina. DE stirred her Coke with a straw, looking pretty . . . flat. Usually, rumors of someone new would have DE all sparkly and breathless and conjecturing. But that thing with Alaric last year had diminished something vital in her. Asshole had done a number on two women Rahul cared about. "A senior."

Rahul slid into the restaurant booth beside Jaya and held his own news carefully in his hands, waiting for DE to finish her story.

They were at So Sushi Me, a restaurant that Grey and Jaya loved for reasons unknown to him. In spite of the vinyl seating that appeared to have gotten into a series of fights with a herd of cats, perplexingly sticky *and* greasy floors, and sweeping views of a dirty parking lot, the food was actually delicious, so none of the rest of them minded too much.

Leo and Grey and he had never fully talked about their fight.

Their meals together in the dining hall were stiff and awkward, the girls carrying on most of the conversation. Was this optimal? No. But to be honest, Rahul couldn't ask for anything else: he wasn't willing to give up his friendship with Jaya and DE, and Caterina's group still didn't know, as far as he could tell, that they were going to be dating.

"It's weird, right?" DE continued, a tiny bit of her former curious self poking through. "I mean, we have, like, two or three months of school left. Why is he transferring now?"

"Definitely weird," Leo replied, folding his paper napkin into a swan. He'd taken an origami elective last semester. "And I heard he comes from an old mob family."

"Really?" DE asked. "Because I heard they were all spies for some elite government agency."

"I'm sure none of that's true!" Jaya laughed, snuggling closer to Grey, who put a big, solid arm around her shoulders. He probably didn't even realize he was smiling. That's what Rahul wanted: unnoticed, casual happiness. "He's probably just your average nice guy who has a perfectly good reason for transferring so late in the year. I think people are just bored. There's not enough juicy news this close to graduation or something."

That was it. Rahul couldn't have asked for a more perfect entrance. "What about this? I did it. I asked Caterina out."

The chorus of exclamations at his news was immediate and deafening.

"Oh my God!" (Jaya.)

"What did she say?" (Grey, in a somber tone.)

"Are you fucking serious?" (DE, whose green eyes were bugging out of her head.)

"Congratulations." (Leo, who barely glanced up at him.)

Rahul looked at Leo and Grey, feeling irritation spark. He didn't appreciate the vibe he was getting from them.

Things were becoming clearer to him. Now that he was pulling away from the back of the pack, now that he had his own life—an *enviable* life—Grey and Leo were beginning to resent him for it. By being the screwup, the one they could laugh at, the one who was always there to remind them that at least their lives weren't as bad as his, Rahul had provided a boost to their egos. Now he was refusing to play that role anymore. And instead of being happy for him, this was their thought process: How dare he imagine something better for himself?

But this was big news, and they weren't going to ruin it for him. Maybe this conversation would just be between him, Jaya, and DE. He turned to the girls, putting the guys out of his mind completely. "Yes, I'm serious. I actually asked her on a date. And . . . she said . . ." He shook his head slowly, mournfully, and both their faces fell as one collective, forlorn mass of gloom. Then Rahul grinned. "She said yes!"

"Oh my God!" Jaya clapped her hands to her mouth.

"Holy shit, Rahul." DE was staring at him, shaking her head back and forth. "Holy fucking shit. You tamed the beast."

The guys didn't say anything, but Grey gave Jaya a smile.

Rahul laughed and addressed the girls. "I know." Then, his smile slipping, "But seriously, don't call her a beast."

DE held up her hands as if in surrender. "Sure. I'm the last person who should be passing judgment, anyway." Breaking eye contact, she took a sip of her Coke, her cheeks faintly flushed.

Leaning forward, Rahul put a hand on hers and held her surprised gaze. "Hey. If you're guilty of anything, it's that you loved too freely and too hard. You gave your heart to someone who didn't deserve it. Yes, you hurt Caterina in the process, but that wasn't intentional. And I don't think you'll ever do it again. So you should forgive yourself."

DE stared at him, going completely still. He noticed in his peripheral vision that the others were having a similar reaction. "Who are you and what have you done with my friend?" DE asked finally.

Rahul laughed, secretly pleased that RC was beginning to push his way into Rahul's life too. He shook his head. "Same person, DE. Just learning to be a little more connected, I guess."

"Wow." Jaya's brown eyes sparkled. "That's really good, Rahul. I can see Caterina's been good for you."

At the mention of her name, Rahul breathed out and laid his head on the laminate tabletop that smelled faintly of vinegar. "Yeah, but now I have to figure out where to take her. This is really hard. I've been thinking for, like, twenty hours straight and I have no ideas. Nothing seems good enough."

"We'll help you," Jaya said immediately. "Won't we?"

"Yep." DE sipped at her Coke again. "'Course we will. It's Rahul's big day out. We have to make it special." She paused. "Wait a minute. Does this mean she's, like, going to be hanging out with us and stuff?" She looked fearfully at the door. "She's not on her way over right now, is she?"

"Relax," Rahul said. "I don't think she'd be caught dead in a place like So Sushi Me anyway."

"Good point. Let's just make a pact to hang out in janky restaurants from now on, okay?"

"I thought you said you were not afraid of Caterina anymore," Leo put in, speaking only to DE. His body was angled slightly away from Rahul. "That since she feeds on fear particles like a demoness, you would not give her the satisfaction of having any of yours."

Rahul raised an eyebrow at this admission, and DE flushed scarlet. She was always cursing her extremely pale skin that gave away her emotions so easily. "I said nothing of the kind." But she attempted to hide behind her gigantic glass of Coke.

Rahul mock-glared at her.

"Okay, I'm sorry," DE said, reemerging. "What's the big deal, though, about the date? She said yes, right? That's, like, more than half the battle right there."

"Not really. I don't have any idea where one takes Caterina LaValle out on a date."

Except he did, and that was the problem. Over the past weeks, he'd seen the kind of places she frequented, the kind of thing Caterina was used to. Underground celebrity clubs, galas held in expensive hotels, restaurants that shut down *just* to serve her crowd. How was Rahul supposed to compete with that? His budget was more Ritz crackers than Ritz-Carlton. He didn't think Caterina had really considered that part when she'd said yes. He sighed, old insecurities pushing up to the surface like toxic seedlings. "Maybe this was all a big mistake. I should tell her the date's not going to happen."

"No!" Jaya and DE chorused. The guys were still ignoring him or pretending that this wasn't earth-shattering news he was sharing with them. It irritated him, it angered him—and, if he was being honest, it saddened him. This was what it had come to, after all their years of friendship. Well, let them pout. Whenever they were ready to see reason, he'd accept an apology.

Rahul looked at DE's and Jaya's faces, both shocked and

aghast. "Guys, let's face it. I'm not rich. And Caterina's used to dating rich guys. Guys like Alaric."

DE snorted. "Really, Alaric? You're comparing yourself to *that* douchebag?"

"Look at it this way," Jaya put in. "Every rich boy she's dated, she's also ended things with."

Rahul considered this. It appealed to his logical side. "That's true. . . ."

"You have so much more to offer her than money," Jaya continued, her hand entwined with Grey's on the table. "You're sweet, you're nice, you're a good listener. She probably said yes because she can see all those things, Rahul. Not because she mistook you for a millionaire."

That was true too. Rahul had never told Caterina he had money, and she knew what his parents did. She knew he had nothing, compared to her. And she'd still said yes, hadn't she? Feeling a little better, Rahul took a gulp of his ice water. "Thanks, ladies."

"I know. You should take her to the Four Seasons," DE said. "It's expensive and you'll probably spend your entire entertainment budget on it, but at least it's something Caterina'll appreciate."

"Bad financial decision." Grey, who'd recently become independent from his father's estate, shook his head, apparently moved enough by a suggestion he considered so awful to finally speak up in spite of his irritation at Rahul. "Take her somewhere that's meaningful, but free. We're surrounded by natural beauty. There are mountains and lakes and national forests—"

"And hypothermia. It's, like, twenty degrees this time of year," DE countered. "She'll freeze to death; even the Ice Queen has a limit. Okay, so forget the Four Seasons. Take her dancing at some club. The lights will be low and the music will be thumping and she'll be too distracted by all that to think about how inexpensive it is."

"I don't think Caterina's really the nightclub type," Rahul said. And neither was he.

They were all quiet as the waitress came up and took their orders. He looked at Jaya and DE, stumped. "Why is dating so hard?"

"Because maybe we're all meant to be alone and dating is this farcical scheme concocted in the medieval ages by people who had too much time on their hands." DE took a morose sip of her Coke. She was obviously having problems adapting to being single.

Jaya and Grey looked at each other. "It's not hard once you're over that initial hump," Jaya said finally. "You're at the most difficult place right now, the place where you need to be your best self, to impress her with the dazzle of it all."

Rahul held his tongue. What he wanted to say was, *My best self is not me at all. My best self is RC.* And then he had an idea.

"What you need is somewhere entertaining but unique," Jaya continued, breaking into his thoughts. When he looked at her, she was smiling kindly at him. "It doesn't have to be fancy; it just has to have personality. Somewhere she hasn't been yet, but somewhere she'd love. And I have just the place." She pulled out her phone and began tapping away at the screen.

CATERINA

For the first time ever, Caterina had butterflies in her stomach at the thought of seeing a boy. It wasn't an unpleasant sensation, as she'd always imagined it being. It was, in fact, pretty nice. It signaled to her that things had changed, that she had something to look forward to. That she had hopes for this thing, whatever it was.

She was on her way to her AP Psychology class, which she shared with Rahul. Smiling as she walked across the sunlit campus, past pine trees laden with snow and groups of students who stood out like flowers in their maroon uniforms against a landscape of white, Caterina shook her head, marveling at how things were changing. She'd never imagined that she'd have said yes to Rahul at the beginning of all this. She'd never have thought he'd fit into her world so seamlessly.

Her phone rang in her pocket, and she pulled it out with a gloved hand to see her dad's name on the screen. Sliding to answer, she held the phone up to her ear, frowning lightly. He never called her when she had class unless it was important. "Papa?"

"Caterina." Another sign this was serious; he was calling her Caterina, not *topolina*. "Do you have a moment to talk?"

"Yes, of course." She kept walking, watching her boots sinking into the fresh dusting of snow on the sidewalk that had fallen after the groundskeepers had shoveled. The brisk air nipped at her nose and the tips of her ears.

"I have seen quite a few articles about you and this boy RC popping up everywhere, and people have begun to ask about him. My private investigator did a cursory search, but was unable to find anything about the crown prince of Anandgarh."

Caterina laughed quietly to herself as she passed a group of bundled-up juniors, including Jaya's sister, Isha, who waved at her. She waved back before answering, "That's because he doesn't exist."

Her dad didn't sound amused. "Pardon?"

Caterina glanced around her at the nearly empty surroundings before answering. The closest people were already at the humanities building, at least ten yards away. Caterina was running a little late. "RC doesn't exist, Papa. He's my friend Rahul, whom I gave a makeover and some social training classes to. He's not the crown prince of anywhere. He's just my . . . friend." That wasn't quite right, not anymore, but she didn't have the words or inclination to explain to her dad exactly who Rahul was or what he'd grown to mean to her.

"Caterina." There was a crackling sound as her dad blew out a big breath. "That is completely unwise. Reporters are more than capable of cracking this wide open, and then you'll—*we'll*—be the subject of scandal."

Caterina felt a twinge of disappointment and irritation at his words. "We won't be the subject of anything," she said. "I've been careful. Somehow, whether through the magic of makeup or just simply magic"—here she laughed to show she was at least half joking—"Rahul looks absolutely nothing like himself when he dresses up. And if they can't find anything on RC, well, it'll just add to the mystery." A few snowflakes landed on her eyelashes, and she blinked them away as she walked on.

"I disagree. Eventually they're going to want to know what's going on. And more than that, Caterina, why would you do this when there are so many more eligible boys at your school?"

"Like who?" She narrowed her eyes, feeling the sparks at the edges of her words. "Alaric? The Konig boy who treated me so well?"

Her dad made a sound of exasperation. "Well, then choose someone else! What about Vanya Petrovic? You've always been friendly with him!"

Caterina's hand tightened around her phone as she got closer to the humanities building, with its grand pillars and inscribed Latin saying—*In Knowledge, Power*—above the wide oak double doors. The final bell would ring in another minute or two. "I don't want to go out with Vanya. I want to take Rahul."

"The LaValle name is on the line, Caterina." Her father's voice was dangerously low but still controlled. "This is not about some schoolgirl crush. This is about knowing your station and respecting it."

Caterina stomped up the stairs. What he was saying, without saying it, was that Rahul wasn't good enough for her. For them. The precious LaValles with their custom Bugattis that they purchased out of spite. "I have to go," she said, yanking on one of the double doors to pull it open.

"Think about what I said. I trust you'll make the right decision for our family." And then her father was gone.

She stood still for a moment in the hallway, staring down at her phone's blank screen. Disappointment and anger crashed together in her head, twin beats of the same song. Why couldn't her father see what she saw—how happy she was in each one of those photographs, how she smiled with abandon when her arm was entwined with Rahul's, as she'd never done with Alaric?

In her AP Psychology class, looking behind her across the rows of students, Caterina caught Rahul's eye. Seeing the warmth in his brown eyes, his gentle smile, thawed her. Her shoulders, still rigid from her call with her father a few moments ago, relaxed. Her dad could say whatever he wanted. There was no way in hell Caterina was going out with anyone else besides Rahul—RC.

She smiled, wiggling her fingers at him, and he promptly dropped his pen. Giggling to herself, she turned back around.

"All right, guys," Ms. Rivard said from the front of the class, reading a sheet of paper at the same time. Teachers were always multitasking experts, Caterina had noticed. "Your big test is next week, so it's going to be a review period today. Get together in groups of two and study chapters two and three, please. I'll let you pick your partner, since you're all adults or nearly adults now and will choose wisely, I presume." She looked over the top of the paper at all of them, as if checking to see if anyone disagreed. "Okay, get to it."

Caterina stood and was immediately swarmed by four different people. She smiled. "Thank you for asking," she said to all of them, "but I . . . need to visit the restroom. Why don't you partner with each other?"

The four wandered away, grouping off among themselves, and the moment they'd left, she saw Rahul standing by his table, looking right at her. Trying to contain her smile, Caterina walked to him and cocked her head as all around them, people moved their desks together and began riffling through the psychology textbook. "Why, Mr. Chopra, I couldn't help but notice you're partner-less."

He dipped his head. "Ms. LaValle, it is a travesty. I couldn't find one person who wanted to be my partner." Looking up at her, he added, "You, meanwhile, seemed to have your pick of the litter."

Caterina waved a hand in the air. "Oh, I didn't see anyone who caught my eye. Until now."

Rahul beamed. "You want to work with me?"

She was a little surprised that he even had to ask. She'd agreed to go out with him, hadn't she? Maybe if he'd been privy to her phone call with her dad, he'd understand better. But of course, she wouldn't share that with him. It wasn't even worth repeating.

In answer to Rahul's question, Caterina dragged a nearby desk over to his and sat down. "What are you waiting for?" she asked, looking up at him innocently. "We've got a test next week."

Laughing a little, Rahul sat in his desk next to her. They reached for his textbook at the same time, their fingers grazing. Caterina's heart skipped a beat at the unexpected contact.

"You take it," she murmured, tucking a lock of hair behind her ear, suddenly unable to meet his eye.

"No, go ahead," Rahul said, his voice deep. She could feel his gaze on her, warm and heavy. "Hey."

She looked at him finally, her cheeks heating at the intensity of emotion on his face. He was looking at her like she was a woodland nymph who'd stepped out of the forest and into his life.

"I'm really excited about our date this weekend." His voice was shaky, and she knew it had taken all his courage to say that out loud. "I'm going to make sure you have a good time."

She smiled, at the sheer goodness of him. "I know you will, Rahul." Reaching over, she placed her hand on his, feeling the warmth from his skin seep into hers. Neither of them pulled away this time. "I really can't wait."

RAHUL

How was this his life? How was any of this real? He was sitting in a classroom surrounded by students immersed in their work, and somehow, he was having a grand romance. And it really said something about his feelings for Caterina that sitting in AP Psych during a review period qualified as a "grand romance."

He glanced around at everyone, really quickly. No one had noticed the seismic shift that had just occurred, even though every bone, every nerve ending, every blood vessel in Rahul's body, was alerting him to the fact that something truly life-changing was happening. Looking back at Caterina, he put his free hand on top of hers. "Me too. You can't know how long I've waited for this." Was it totally uncool to say that to her? Probably. Would Leo ever say anything like that? Not in a quadrillion years. But it had felt wrong not to say it when she was putting herself out there like that. Rahul knew it wasn't in her nature to emote. To be honest, it wasn't in his, either. He supposed they were both changing for each other, and the thought was wonderful and unbelievable all at once.

"Really?" Caterina's voice was just a whisper. Ms. Rivard was saying something about multiple-choice questions, but neither of them seemed to care.

"Really," Rahul replied, thinking, *God, I could sink into her eyes and never come out. Forget the hallucination I had during Ms. Rivard's ten-minute eye contact experiment. This would be serious mind-breaking shit.*

"Caterina and Rahul!" Ms. Rivard called from the front of the room, and they both immediately pulled their hands away from each other, Rahul feeling completely bereft. "Are you guys working on what you're supposed to be working on?"

A few students craned their necks to see the two of them in the corner.

"Yes," Rahul answered in as normal a voice as he could muster.

"Thought so," Ms. Rivard replied, but her raised eyebrow said otherwise.

Caterina caught Rahul's eye over the textbook and laughed a little, shaking her head. His heart bloomed with a thousand feelings. This date was going to be the most epic thing ever.

CHAPTER 16

CATERINA

It had been a week since the snowstorm and the cabin, a week since Rahul had asked her out. And now here she was, walking toward the green in the icy darkness of a winter evening. Rahul had asked her to meet him there, at the grand wooden gazebo in the center. As she drew closer, Caterina smiled at Rahul's silhouette inside the gazebo, which was lit with twinkling lights wrapped around its thick beams.

"Hi," he said from the shadows. "You look beautiful."

Caterina looked down at herself as she ascended the curved steps. She was dressed in her blue coat, under which she was wearing a black sheath dress and tights. She'd wanted to keep things simple for their first date. "Thank you. And you look . . ." She drew closer, able to fully see him now, bathed in the glow of the twinkle lights. There was a pause as her brain adjusted to the reality of what she was seeing versus her expectation. "Like RC."

It wasn't Rahul before her; it was RC. His hair was styled carefully, his brown eyes just slightly dulled behind the contacts he wore. He looked stunning in a greige sweater she'd picked out for him a couple of weeks ago, in a very catalog-model way. For some reason she couldn't explain, Caterina felt a disappointed lump come to her throat.

He smiled at her in that suave, confident way RC did, not a hint of apprehension or doubt anywhere on his features. "I do, indeed. I thought I'd give our date that special touch."

Caterina gave him a half-hearted smile in return and took a breath, trying for a bright tone and not quite succeeding. "So. Where are we going tonight?"

He held out an arm, and after just the slightest hesitation, she put her hand on it. "Somewhere magical," he said, his voice just a breath in her ear.

RC

For the first time in a while, RC felt comfortable in his skin. In the reflection of the car window, he saw that his thick black hair hung just so, his jaw looked chiseled, and his posture was better than it ever was when he was Rahul. He looked like someone who belonged in a car like this, someone who was meant to be chauffeured around.

RC glanced at Caterina as the car service he'd arranged with the front office sped along the glittering streets. Was she having a good time? Was she impressed that he'd put so much effort into being RC? Was she excited to see where he was taking her?

It was hard to tell with Caterina, that was the thing. She was just so used to being poised and put together, to keeping herself walled off from the rest of the world so that it didn't hurt her. As if sensing his gaze on her face, she turned to him and smiled lightly.

"Everything okay?" RC asked in as offhand a way as he could manage.

"Fine," Caterina answered, but her smile didn't broaden.

It was the PR smile she used for everyone else, he realized with a sinking feeling, not the secret Caterina smile only he knew. Why was she acting like this?

CATERINA

By the time the car had deposited them outside what looked like a very glamorous old Victorian house, Caterina had decided she couldn't do it. Not like this. If she was going to be out on a date, the first real date she'd had since Alaric, it was going to be with someone she really wanted to be with.

She turned to RC outside, on the broad porch of the house, which was decorated with twinkling lights and large potted evergreens. "I want you to do something for me. Please."

He studied her expression and then nodded. "Okay. What?"

"I want you to wash all of this off." She gestured to his hair, his makeup. "And I want you to just be Rahul on this date. Will you do that for me?"

Shock and alarm passed over RC's carefully applied face. "What? Why?"

Sighing, Caterina took his hand. It was warm, much warmer than her own. "When I said yes to the date . . . I was saying yes to Rahul," she explained gently. "Not RC. RC is for events and galas and . . . other people. *I* want Rahul. Okay?"

RC looked down at himself and then back up at her, confused. "But RC's so much better at this. At everything."

Caterina felt her heart break a little. She shook her head. "He's really not. I promise."

RC studied her for a long moment, and just when she thought he was going to refuse and break her heart even more, he nodded. "All right."

Inside, she waited in the lavender-scented hallway next to a short, wide-hipped middle-aged woman who'd introduced herself as a docent—this must be a museum of sorts, then—while RC excused himself to the bathroom. A few moments later, the door to the bathroom opened. Caterina held her breath.

Rahul appeared, glasses in place, his hair slightly damp and hanging flat. His face was completely makeup-free, and there was a big splotch of water on his collar. He looked at her, his eyebrows raised, a questioning smile on his face, and shrugged.

Caterina's heart swelled. Walking forward, she squeezed his hand and nodded. "You look beautiful," she whispered, and he smiled, just a little more confidently. "So," she said, threading her arm through his. "Where are we? I'm dying to know."

The docent looked up, ready to launch into a no-doubt-rehearsed explanation, but Rahul beat her to it. "This is a Victorian mansion, owned by one of Jaya's friends. Apparently they've turned it into a sort of fashion museum of the time."

"And, as a special twist," the docent, not to be outdone, put in, "every single one of the pieces here was directly passed on to the person who donated it, which means we have a complete history of each article of clothing. We're very lucky to have something like this here in Rosetta. And, of course, you're lucky to be able to come here before it's open to the public."

"I am," Caterina agreed, looking into Rahul's eyes. "I'm very lucky."

RAHUL

"This is incredible," Caterina breathed, bending over to read the note attached to the black-and-red silk gown in front of her. They were in what was the master bedroom of the house, a small, dark room with wooden everything—walls, ceiling, and floors. "Oh, look: This dress was worn to the wedding of this woman's ex-best friend. Apparently, the best friend married the woman's longtime beau, so she had it specially made for the wedding. It has an inside pocket for concealing a knife." Caterina laughed. "That's a woman after my own heart."

When she looked at him, Rahul forced a laugh too. "Yeah, definitely." She seemed to be having a good time. She'd thanked him twenty times for this thoughtful date. And he had to say, Jaya's friend had really knocked it out of the park with this one.

And yet . . . something about it just felt uncomfortable. Like he wasn't able to fully allow himself to relax, like there was always a hand pressing down on his shoulders, or tapping him on the temple, or a voice whispering in his ear to remind him that he was Rahul right now. This was one of the most important moments of his life, and he was his old, drab, socially incompetent self when he could be doing so much better. He could *be* so much better.

Why had she wanted him to be Rahul? It made no sense. Why would Rahul not be good enough for the galas and the events and her social circle, but good enough for their first date?

Socially inept as he was, Rahul knew these were questions he should keep to himself. He could just imagine Leo—the old Leo, the one who'd cared—wringing his hands and spewing a flurry of French words if he were to ask Caterina why she didn't want RC here at the date. So he kept her company as she walked from room to room, agog. He smiled at her exclamations of interest and happiness, and he was glad she was having fun.

But he just couldn't relax.

CATERINA

They walked into the parlor of the mansion, a room with a small brick fireplace in one wall. In the center of the room, poised on a settee, was a mannequin wearing an enormous hoop skirt. Caterina gasped quietly, every fashionista nerve in her body lighting up with interest. Walking over to the mannequin, she studied the card placed next to it, describing the origin of the dress and the details of the fabric and draping used.

The docent hung like vapor in a corner of the room, her hands folded neatly over the front of her thighs, watching Caterina with a small, self-satisfied smile on her face. It was obvious she could tell Caterina was suitably reverential toward the artifacts before her. While Caterina studied the detachable collars and cuffs, Rahul came to stand beside her. He shifted from foot to foot, fidgeting with his sweater and his glasses, as if he couldn't get comfortable. Caterina looked up at him askance. Why was he so ill at ease?

He cleared his throat. "Ah, that's a nice dress." He jerked his chin toward the mannequin. "Kind of like, ah, Marie Antoinette vibes."

Caterina bit on the inside of her cheek to keep from smiling. He'd pronounced it "An-toy-nettie" because he'd obviously only ever read the name and never heard it pronounced. Caterina opened her mouth to respond, but before she could, the docent had stepped forward and was speaking in clipped, judgmental tones.

"Marie Antoinette"—she pronounced the name with a very sharp emphasis—"is from a different era, completely. She was from the Rococo period, whereas this dress is clearly from the Victorian era, by which time Marie Antoinette was already dead." Her pale blue eyes were stern as she glared at Rahul, looking very much like a principal addressing a wayward student (not Dr. Waverly, the principal at Rosetta, obviously. Things were different at Rosetta Academy).

Rahul seemed to wither under her stare. His tan cheeks flushing red, he swallowed compulsively, his eyes darting between Caterina and the docent as he wiped his palms on his jeans. "R-right. I know. Yeah. It was just, just an observation. . . ."

Caterina stepped closer to him, straightening her shoulders and putting on her most imperious air. She didn't like the way Rahul was acting, like a chided puppy. Where was the confidence she knew he had within him? But more than that, she didn't like the docent making him feel this way. Gazing at the woman coolly, she said, "Might I remind you that Rahul and I are both here under the invitation of the *owner* of this house? I don't remember a condition of the invitation being that we must both be experts in Victorian-era fashion to visit."

The docent blinked, a hand fluttering up to pat the bun on

her head. "Oh yes, of course, of course. You're right. I'll, ah, leave you two to it, shall I?" Smiling a subservient smile now, she put-tered off toward the kitchen.

Caterina turned to Rahul in the dark, quiet parlor and put a hand on his elbow. "I'm having a lot of fun, so you know."

His expression brightened. "Really?"

She leaned in and planted a soft kiss on his cheek, feeling the muscle of his jaw under her lips. "Really."

RAHUL

Was she just being nice? Her nearness was driving him to distrac-tion, her skin soft and supple against his, the scent of her rosewa-ter perfume maddening. As Caterina straightened and smiled at him, Rahul realized he wanted her to look at him with pride and happiness and desire, the way she did when he was all decked out as RC. He wanted her to see him as someone who belonged in her world, not someone who was told off by the docent because he didn't even know how to pronounce "Antoinette" correctly. If she'd just been content to let him be RC here, he could've avoided all of this.

Frustrated, Rahul rubbed the back of his neck and followed Caterina from the room.

CATERINA

An hour or so later, Caterina sat cross-legged on a wooden chair in the kitchen, her heels discarded under the table. "This was probably the most unique first date I've ever been on, hands down."

The docent, apparently eager to make amends, had insisted that they stay for pizza when she heard Caterina mention how hungry she was, and they had accepted. She'd made them a frozen pizza, set out a pitcher of lemonade, and then melted away, muttering about accounts.

"Really?" Rahul chewed his slice of cheese pizza. His mouth was only full enough so he could still say his name, she realized, and the thought made her smile. "Even compared to Alaric? Didn't he fly you somewhere on your first date with him?"

Caterina rolled her eyes. "Yes, but I can fly anywhere anytime I want. This—" She spread her arms wide. "This is magnificent. A hidden gem in the tiny town of Rosetta. Who knew?" She smiled at Rahul because the same could be said about him.

Not getting her meaning, he raised his eyebrows. "Victorian fashion over Bora Bora or whatever. Wow. I'll have to thank Jaya."

"So this was all her idea, then?" Caterina asked. It disappointed her just the tiniest bit that Rahul hadn't thought of it himself.

But Rahul shook his head. "No, no. She wanted me to take you to her friend's ski-in, ski-out chateau in Aspen. She put me in touch with him, we got to talking, and that's when he told me about this museum. It was like an offhand, passing remark. Something about how he'd be in Rosetta anyway, getting this ready for the opening week coming up. But when he told me what the opening was for, I knew right away I needed to bring you here instead. You told me you wanted to minor in Victorian-era fashion and you have that antique ring. . . ." He paused, looking a little worried. "Did I make the right choice? Jaya and the others didn't seem to think so."

Caterina set her slice of pizza down and reached forward to put her hand on Rahul's, something inside her going still and soft. "Wait. When I did I tell you I wanted to minor in Victorian-era fashion?"

Rahul studied her for a moment before responding, as if he wasn't sure of the intent behind her question. "In the limo, on the way to the Hindman Gala."

Caterina's heart squeezed. He'd remembered. An offhand remark like that, and he'd held it close all this time. "Well. You made absolutely the right choice bringing me here." He'd chosen this for her. He'd forgone the Aspen chateau and chosen this quirky, lovely Victorian fashion museum instead because he knew it was her passion, and that was such a Rahul thing to do that Caterina wanted to wrap him up in her arms. "I would so much rather be here than in some chateau in Aspen."

"Right . . ." He frowned, as if he were trying to work out a very difficult equation in his head. "Because . . . you can visit a chateau anytime?"

Caterina chuckled at his attempt to decipher her emotions and reactions. "You got it. That makes the chateau not as special as this. This . . ." She looked around them at the fusty kitchen, which hadn't been changed much, except to update the appliances. "This is precisely what I wanted to do tonight, and I didn't even know it. Thank you, Rahul."

Rahul smiled at her. "So you're having a good time. For real."

"I'm having the *best* time. For real."

Rahul hopped up from his seat. Walking over to the slightly modified Victorian-era gramophone on the counter, he fiddled with it until it began playing an old record, the noise scratchy and still rich somehow. He smiled at Caterina and then, walking back over to her, bowed low and held out one hand in an invitation.

"Are we going to dance?" Caterina asked, surprised. "Right here?"

"Right here," Rahul said.

"I'm not putting my heels back on," she warned.

In answer, Rahul kicked off his own shoes.

Giggling, Caterina put her hand in his and let him lead her to the dance floor—aka the center of the small kitchen. She laid her head on his shoulder and he wrapped his arms around her, and they swayed gently in time to the music from another era.

Caterina closed her eyes, feeling his heart beating against her chest, not able to say where her own heartbeat ended and where his began. She felt the strength in his arms, the protective way he held her, as if he'd shield her from anything vile the world threw at her. She smelled soap on his skin, soft and warm and so Rahul. Pulling back, Caterina looked into his eyes, so much sharper behind his glasses than when he had his contacts in. "I'm really glad we're here together," she whispered.

His gaze drifted down to her lips. "I'm really glad you're with me," he whispered back. "Gladder than you could ever know."

She pressed her lips to his then, drinking him in, never wanting him to let go.

RAHUL

Maybe it wasn't exactly what he'd wanted for their first date. Maybe things would've been smoother, more fun for Caterina, had he been RC. But still, Rahul couldn't find too much fault with this moment, right here, right now.

Caterina's body, so fragile and soft under his hands, so perfectly molded to him. Her skin, silk and heat, pressed against his. Her mouth, eager and hungry and searching. She was the question and she was the answer. She was everything.

CHAPTER 17

CATERINA

Two days after her first date with Rahul, Caterina lay in bed, one arm flung over her stomach, the other bent over her eyes. She couldn't sleep, which was a sure sign that something was very awry. When she was going through the final weeks of her relationship with Alaric, the first sign, before her brain even let her acknowledge that something was wrong, was that her body stopped letting her sleep restfully. It kept her awake at night, in those inky hours when everyone else was unconscious, because it wanted her to know, to face the inevitable. And now it was happening again.

It bothered her the way Rahul had seemed slightly uncomfortable the entire night of their date, even while he laughed and joked with her, as if he were wearing a pair of shoes that were two sizes too small. At first Caterina had been worried that they lacked chemistry, that he didn't feel the same way about her as she did about him. But those fears had been erased the moment they'd danced together in the little old-fashioned kitchen. No one kissed that way if they didn't feel it in their bones, in their marrow. So what was it, then? Why had he had that discomfited edge all night?

And then it came to her, like a lightning flash in a raven-black sky: His face had fallen at the very beginning of their date, when she'd asked him to take off the hair gel, to wipe off the makeup, to just be Rahul with her. That had to be it; that was why he'd seemed so uncomfortable the rest of the evening.

Caterina moved the arm that had been covering her eyes and sat up slowly in bed, her silk covers puddling around her as she did. She stared straight ahead in the near darkness, knowing in her heart that Rahul Chopra was becoming more and more self-hating with every day that passed, with every event that he went to as RC. And it was all her fault.

Scrabbling for her phone, she checked the time. Four a.m. It was much too early to text anyone, but she knew who she had to talk to. And she knew she'd be forgiven for waking her up.

Caterina jogged along the brightly lit, Olympic-size indoor track at the athletics center, keeping pace with Jaya. Even at this hour, the track was populated by a handful of other students, all clearly more athletic than her. Caterina never ran except when it was unavoidable or a matter of emergency, and she thought this morning's conversation qualified as both.

She glanced at Jaya, who appeared moderately awake, considering it was only five a.m. Her black hair was pulled back into a high bun, and her face was devoid of makeup in a way that Caterina would never let hers be. Even now, Caterina wore foundation, eyeliner, and a touch of nude lipstick. She'd also taken the time to brush dry shampoo into her hair for volume before gathering it up into a ponytail. "Thanks for meeting with me so early. I'm sorry I woke you."

"Don't worry about it at all. I come running here nearly every morning anyway. I just moved up the time today." Jaya looked like a flower in her bright pink Lululemon leggings and tank top. "It sounds like you have some things on your mind."

Caterina didn't say anything, mostly because she didn't know what to say yet. Instead, she watched her legs, clad in plain black leggings, as they pumped up and down, carrying her along the track. With every heartbeat, she wondered if this was the right thing to do—to confide in someone else. She'd gotten closer to Jaya than other people over the last semester, and Caterina was sure she wouldn't gossip about this to anyone. Jaya would only want to help. But still . . . Was it a betrayal of Rahul?

"I heard the first date went well," Jaya prodded when Caterina still hadn't spoken. "At least, according to Rahul."

Caterina adjusted her ponytail. "It did. It was a lot of fun." She smiled, though she could tell it wasn't as bright as it should've been.

Jaya studied her expression for a moment, frowning a little. "But . . . ?"

"But . . ." Caterina shook her head, concentrating on her breathing while she got her thoughts in order. Maybe there was a way to ask the question without telling Jaya everything. "Have you or any of the others noticed anything about Rahul lately? Any changes in him?"

"Well, he's been spending more time apart from us . . . with you, I assume."

"Anything else?" Caterina pressed. "Anything with his, ah, personality?"

Jaya appeared to consider this for the next few moments as

they moved along the spongy track, their feet swallowing up the miles. "Well, I suppose so. Grey and Leo had a falling-out with Rahul, though Grey didn't want to go into the details. Oh, and also, Grey mentioned that Rahul was changing the types of things he read. And his room was looking different too. Almost as if he was trying hard to impress—" She stopped short.

Caterina looked at her. "Me. You mean he's changing who he is to impress me."

Jaya smiled apologetically, her cheeks pink from the exercise. "It's just what Leo and Grey thought. But Rahul seems to feel it's all for the better. He says he never would've landed you if he hadn't made the changes. And he's loved you since the night of the winter dance."

That word again, "love." First Mia had used it to describe how Caterina might feel, and now Jaya was using it to describe how Rahul felt. But she couldn't think of all that now; there were other, more important matters to discuss. Caterina waited until a senior boy, Langdon, passed them before she spoke. "Has he told you the extent of the changes he's made?"

Jaya shook her head, confused. "What do you mean?"

"Besides his room and his reading material. Has he said anything else about any changes?"

"No, I don't think so."

Caterina nodded. She'd figured as much. Rahul, sweet, loyal Rahul, hadn't told his friends just how much Caterina had demanded of him. He hadn't told them about the makeover or RC. He was still protecting her, keeping his word. The thought only made her feel worse. How had she been so single-minded, so selfish, so self-absorbed, that she hadn't seen all the ways she'd been hurting him?

"Caterina? Are you all right?" Jaya had slowed her pace and was looking at her in concern.

Caterina forced a smile and blew out a breath, picking up her pace again. "I'm fine."

She wasn't, but that was immaterial. She was much more worried about Rahul, about finding a solution to the thought that was haunting her.

Later that day, Caterina perched on the hood of her Bugatti, two steaming to-go coffees in her hands. The cold from the metal hood seeped through her wool pants, making her shiver. She was parked on a slight hill overlooking a valley that held a small, frozen pond in its cupped hand. The late-afternoon sunlight was obtuse; dusk wasn't far behind.

A whistle sounded behind her. She turned to see Mia, walking up the small hill, dressed in jeans, an oversize tan sweater, and a plaid scarf. "So this is it, huh? The Bugatti?"

Caterina hopped off the hood, smiling slightly, and handed Mia her coffee. "I brought you a latte. And yes, Papa got it for me a few weeks ago."

Mia ran her hand over the roof, her eyes drinking in the way the sunlight hit the duo-chrome paint. "Wow. Lucky you. He must love you a lot."

Caterina shrugged and took a sip of her cappuccino. "I'm his only daughter. Those are the perks, I suppose. I'm sure your parents showered you with the same single-minded attention."

Mia met her eye and raised an eyebrow. "No, not at all. They're far too pragmatic to do that. Though I suppose they did their best."

Caterina could hear the unspoken words. "Was it not enough?"

The wind blew, shaking the aspen grove to their left. "I'm hard to please." Mia smiled thinly. "Anyway, you said you wanted to talk? Is everything all right?"

Caterina took a breath and looked back out over the valley. The sun sparkled off her crown necklace, a little star in her peripheral vision. Mia walked closer so they were both looking at the same view. "I'm having some second thoughts about RC."

Mia glanced sharply at her. "Really? But I thought you said the first official date went well."

"It did, but . . ." She turned to look at Mia. "Sometimes doing the right thing is a lot harder than doing the wrong one."

A look passed over Mia's face, one that Caterina couldn't decipher. But before she could comment on it, Mia was speaking again. "That's very true."

Caterina looked down at the cup in her hand. "I think I'm hurting Ra—RC by being with him," she said softly, watching her breath on the chilly air. "And that's the last thing I want to do."

After a moment, she felt Mia's arm around her shoulders. "I've seen you with him, and that's not true. He looks happy when he's with you."

Caterina couldn't meet Mia's eyes. *RC looks happy to be with me,* she thought. *But Rahul doesn't.* To Mia, she said, "I suppose so."

"Caterina. He makes *you* happy, doesn't he?"

Caterina closed her eyes, just for a moment. "He does. He makes me so happy." Opening her eyes, she turned to her friend. "But it's not that simple." Dating him just because he made her happy was a selfish thing to do. She could see she was hurting him, and she couldn't just look away from it.

Mia studied her expression and then squeezed Caterina's

arm. "Well, don't rush anything. Take your time and think it through."

Caterina took a deep swallow of her drink, letting the heat bolster her. Was there another solution she wasn't thinking of? Could they continue to date somehow, without Caterina hurting him? She could ask him to stop being RC—tell him that was what she wanted. But no. Caterina knew that just as she couldn't continue hurting Rahul, she could also never tell him how to live his life. Those were his choices, and he had to make them. She could only control her part in things.

"I'll talk to him after the Musicians' Fund charity event tomorrow night," she said quietly, as much to herself as to Mia.

"There you go," Mia said, letting her arm slide down. "I'll be there too for moral support."

Caterina half smiled at the other girl as the sun dipped behind the mountains, chilling her skin. "I'm so glad you will."

She knew what she had to do now. It was the responsible thing, the right thing to do. It would hurt, but this wasn't about her. This was about saving one of the most important people in her life.

RC

He took Caterina's elbow as they walked up the big concrete stairs to the art gallery where the charity event was being held. The night sky above them was a polished black; the moon like a cold spotlight shining down on them. Caterina's long dress was the color of rust, and it pooled around her ankles. "You're stunning." He gave her his dashing RC smile.

She smiled back, but it was hesitant, not as bright as usual. "Thanks. You look . . . great."

RC stuck his hands in his pockets and did a little shimmy-twirl on the broad step, a lock of hair falling in his eye. He didn't sweep it back; he knew it looked good. But Caterina didn't look overcome with desire or adoration. In fact, she looked less impressed than she had on their date when he'd been dorky, awkward Rahul. And she looked . . . anxious. Caterina LaValle was *never* anxious.

RC frowned. "Is everything okay?"

The night air was brisk, biting even. Caterina huddled deeper into her coat and looked up toward the art museum. Her throat was long and pale in the dim light; the choker at her throat glittered like a pelt of stars. "Fine. I just think . . . we should get going. I don't want to be late. It's a big night."

"Okay." RC waited, but she didn't meet his eye as she began to climb the steps again.

His pulse picking up, he followed in silence.

CATERINA

"We can certainly all learn from the LaValles," Mr. Tannish said, beaming down at Caterina. "Thanks to your father for the donation, Caterina."

"He was just so sorry he couldn't come," Caterina replied, smiling demurely. "The Musicians Fund is a cause so dear to his heart." Truthfully, her father couldn't be bothered to come to every charity event he was invited to, and he was invited to dozens every year due to his donations. So he often sent Caterina in his stead, as so many other parents did. Case in point:

nearly all of Caterina's social circle was present here tonight.

She looked over her shoulder. The event was being hosted at the Madison Art Gallery in Aspen, a gorgeous space full of white marble and gold accents. Most of her friends were clustered in one corner, looking at someone's phone. Mia, she noticed, was talking to RC by the band, both of them deep in conversation.

Caterina felt a flurry of nerves. Seeing them talking brought to mind the conversation she herself needed to have with him later. The conversation she'd been actively avoiding by circulating around the room instead.

"Is it true that he's writing a book?" Mr. Tannish asked, pulling Caterina's attention back to him. "Your father, I mean?"

She turned, her smile at the ready. "Well, that's what the rumor mill says. It's always been a dream of Papa's, to write a memoir one day. I know it would be so inspiring to so many if he did." Her gaze slid back over to RC and Mia. She wished she could listen in on what they were saying. Was it anything about her?

RC

"Well, you look dashing tonight, RC." Mia walked over to him, her blond hair up in a fancy bun on her head. She was wearing a gold sequin dress, the kind he'd never seen Caterina wearing, likely because it was too loud for her style. Mia had paired her gold dress with a dramatic purple eye, which actually looked kind of good, even if he'd never have put the two colors together.

"Thank you. So do you."

She handed him a glass of champagne, which he surreptitiously put down on a nearby table. He never drank; it was a well-known scientific fact that alcohol was a literal toxin that attacked your brain cells.

Mia touched him lightly on the arm. "Caterina told me you took her out on a real date recently."

There was something sharp about Mia; she reminded him of glass shards wrapped in velvet. Although, to be honest, the same could be said of the vibe Caterina put out. And in her case, it wasn't true at all. (Well, maybe a little. But in a good way.)

"Yeah." RC smiled. "It was nice. Just the two of us, no event to escort her to."

Mia regarded him over her champagne flute, the lights from the giant gold chandelier overhead catching the glass and winking off it. "Really. So, are you a couple now?"

"I suppose we are," RC replied, not sure about the tone of her question. It didn't sound happy and excited, like Jaya or DE. "It's just been one date, but I'd like to think that's where we're headed."

There was a pause during which Mia continued studying him, her amber eyes intense and focused. And then she sighed. "I like you, RC," she said, shaking her head.

RC felt an unpleasant tightening in his chest. "Thank you," he forced himself to say calmly. The band began to play another song, right beside them, which felt like a thousand elephants trumpeting directly into his skull.

Noticing his expression, Mia took his elbow and led him to a quiet, empty table toward the back of the room. "Here. Is this better?"

He nodded as he took a seat across from her. "Yeah, thanks." His voice sounded hoarse, as if he'd been yelling. There was something coming; he could feel it.

Mia put her elbows on the table. Her purple eye shadow was hypnotic, lending a very surreal air to this entire interlude. "RC . . . Rahul." She paused, letting that piece of information sink in. She knew who he really was. Had Caterina told her? "She told me how sweet you were at the winter formal, dancing with her when she'd just been broken up with." Mia smiled, a little sadly. "That's why she gave you this opportunity. The chance to become someone shiny and new, the chance to become RC. The chance to rub elbows with directors' sons and actual supermodels and drive around in Bugattis. She wanted to pay you back for the kindness you showed her because she really appreciates it. But . . . love? Feelings?" Mia shook her head slowly. "I don't think she's where you are, RC. I've seen the way you look at her, and . . . I just really don't want you getting hurt."

RC sat back, his heart trip-hammering in his chest. "She told you that? That this is all just payment for what I did at the dance?"

Mia spread her pale arms and shrugged. "It was a nice gesture, wasn't it? She's a good person. She's just not in love. And I think, at least, it seems to me like maybe you . . . are?"

RC pinched the bridge of his nose, not able to look at her anymore, not able to take the pity oozing out of her. Had Caterina told everyone? Was that why they'd all wanted to hang out with him—out of some sense of obligation?

And then it hit him. That's why she didn't want him being RC at their date. Everyone had been treating him like a child, with big, bright smiles and lots of praise, and he'd been too stupid to see it. He'd internalized it as reality.

"Not everyone feels that way," Mia said, reading his mind again. She reached over and patted his hand. "I think you're great as RC. And a lot of other girls have told me they do too. They have no idea you're anyone else. It's just a few of us Caterina's confided in, and it didn't seem right to me, so I wanted to let you know. If I were in your shoes, Rahul, I'd want to know." She paused, biting her lip. "Did I do the right thing?"

RC pushed his chair back and stood. "You did the right thing," he bit out. Then he crossed the floor to where Caterina stood, deep in conversation with Mr. Tannish.

CHAPTER 18

CATERINA

RC's eyes were blazing. There was no other word for it.

"Hi." Caterina tried on a smile, knowing it wouldn't be returned. "Is everything . . . okay?"

"I need to speak with you. Now, please." He walked away, heading out of the main room.

Caterina turned with a smile. "I'm sorry, Mr. Tannish. Would you please excuse me for a few moments?"

"Of course, dear," he said, his brown eyes twinkling merrily. "Love must always come first, eh?" Laughing uproariously, he drifted off to speak with a couple by the chocolate fountain.

Caterina took a deep breath and, picking up the hem of her long, persimmon-hued dress, she walked as quickly as was physically possible in six-inch heels to find RC.

She found him sitting on a bench down a quiet hallway, away from the crowds. There was only one light on in the ceiling, casting him in shadows. He sat with his head bowed, his hands clasped loosely between his thighs, looking utterly defeated.

Caterina's heart squeezed in her chest as she walked up to him, her shoes whispering on the white-and-gold carpet. He didn't look up even when she was close, though he had to have heard her.

She sat beside him, feeling tendrils of worry wrapping around her. "Rahul? What's going on?"

He looked up at her, his eyes pink around the edges. "Am I just a big project to you?"

She blinked, uncomprehending. "I beg your pardon?"

"That's why you wanted me to change back into Rahul on our date. Because you can't bear to see me as RC when you only 'created' me because you wanted to pay me back for our dance at the winter formal."

"Rahul . . ." Caterina frowned, not sure where any of this was coming from. "I have no idea why you're—"

"It's true, right? That's why you chose *me* to be RC. But the entire time, you've been applauding me and praising me like you would a slightly unintelligent dog. You don't appreciate RC for who he is; to you, he's just a big joke."

Caterina closed her eyes for a moment. There it was. She wasn't appreciating RC enough. She wasn't giving him his due. And therefore, she must just be acting out of obligation. She opened her eyes again. "You're wrong," she said slowly, firmly. "I never felt a sense of duty toward you. But you're so consumed with RC, you don't even know who you are anymore. You've lost sight of what's important."

"Have I? And are *you* going to tell me what that is?"

Caterina felt a spark of anger at the way he was talking to her. There was no hint of Rahul there. "Stop it," she said. "You're not a jerk, so quit acting like one."

His eyes flashed as he stood and mock-saluted her. "Ma'am, yes, ma'am." Dropping his hand, he looked at her, his face full of fury. "That's what you want, isn't it? You want me to be your lapdog. You never wanted RC to have his own opinion, to become someone others might respond to. That's right, Caterina, there are people who *genuinely* like RC. Not everyone's brimming with a sense of duty like you are."

"I don't feel a sense of duty toward you!" Her voice rang out across the long, empty hallway, but she was too shocked, too mad, too outraged, to care. "Where are you getting this?"

"It doesn't matter where I'm getting it," RC said. "What matters is that it's true."

She looked at him, so resolute, so sure that he was right, that all the horrible stories he'd cooked up in his head about her were indubitably true. That was her doing, wasn't it? She'd created this. She'd refused to see the signs. She'd looked the other way when he'd said self-deprecating things. And now it was too late. Now he was taking her rejection of RC as her rejection of him. He didn't see himself as Rahul at all anymore, and the thought terrified and sickened her.

"Rahul . . . ," Caterina began, biting her lip. She'd known she had to do this; now was as good a time as any. "I can't . . ." She swallowed the lump in her throat.

He looked down at her, his dark eyes hooded and blank. "I'm done, Caterina. I'm sorry, but I can't do this anymore. Not with someone who sees me as some charity job."

She sat staring at him—at his blurry image—for a long minute before she realized her eyes had filled with tears. "Okay," she whispered.

It wasn't true, what he'd said. But perhaps this was for the best. Perhaps letting him go was the kindest thing to do, the only step she could take in maybe, one day, helping him get back to himself when all this was behind him.

A flash of something crossed his face, too quick for her to make out. Then he turned on his shiny heel and was gone.

RC

He was shaking as he walked away, every bone, muscle, and sinew in his body trembling violently like a rubber band pulled too tight. At least he'd said his piece, he thought as he hurried away, almost running. His heart pounded violently in his chest; there was a bitter taste in his mouth. At least he'd told her exactly what he thought of her payback. At least he'd had the courage to tell her to her face that he wanted no part of it.

And she'd just let him go.

RC blinked hard as he raced toward the exit, ignoring the small pockets of well-dressed people in the main hall who turned to look at him as he went flying by. There had been a part of him that had hoped she'd ask him not to break up with her, that she'd swear none of the things he'd said were true, that she'd make it okay somehow. But she hadn't. She'd basically just agreed. It was obvious now to him that she'd *wanted* him to break up with her. So why, then, had she even said in the cabin that boys always asked her out? Had he misunderstood that, too? Had she been trying to let him down easily in some conversational code that was too hard for him to decipher? Nothing made sense anymore. RC's head pounded in confusion and hurt and anger.

Out in the cold, he began walking. He'd call the school's car service in a minute, but for now, the bracing chill in the air, burning down his nose, throat, and lungs, felt good. He stuck his hands in his pockets, bent his head, and put one foot in front of the other. Somewhere down the block, a car honked, long and angry.

After a moment, RC chuckled. The funniest thing about all of this was that he'd convinced himself that he was some kind of Frog Prince, someone who'd been redeemed. That in becoming RC, he'd finally become worthy of Caterina LaValle. How hadn't he been able to see the truth? That no matter who he became, he'd never be good enough for her? That the Rahuls of the world could never be with the Caterinas, no matter how much face paint or magic paste or whatever the hell else they put on?

He turned at the light and headed up the empty road, the traffic lights swapping from red to green as he walked alone and lost in the winter night.

CATERINA

She sat on the bench in that empty hallway for so long, she lost all track of time. Finally, Mia walked down the corridor, sat next to her, and held out a small crystal bowl of vanilla ice cream with two spoons in it. She didn't say anything; good friends never needed to. Caterina couldn't do this, let herself be this vulnerable, with the girls at school; Heather and Ava wouldn't know what to do with her if she did. But with Mia, things were different. So Caterina took a spoon and ate ice cream with her friend.

Three Weeks Later . . .

RAHUL

"And that's what cognitive dissonance means," Ms. Rivard, the AP Psych teacher, said. "It *will* be on the AP exam, people. Hello?" She waved a hand in their collective faces. "Are you guys ready for spring break or what?"

There were a few whoops and cheers around the room. Ms. Rivard rolled her eyes. "Rahul?"

He was listening to her, but it took him a moment to register that she'd just said his name. That was happening more and more lately, ever since he and Caterina had broken up. It was like the world was some distance away; as if he were on a ship and the world were on the shore, yelling, trying to get his attention, but having to compete with distance and howling winds. "Hmm?" he said finally.

Frowning a little at his tepid response, Ms. Rivard said, "Tell us an example of when you've experienced cognitive dissonance— that is, when your actions didn't match up with your beliefs and it caused you psychological discomfort."

When was the last time his actions didn't match his beliefs? How about the time he broke up with the love of his life when every internal fiber had been screaming at him not to?

"Rahul? Hello? What is *up* with all of you? I swear, they need to add senioritis to the *DSM*. . . ."

He blinked and returned to the world to see Caterina looking over her shoulder at him, her brown eyes soft and sad. She gave him a small, wistful smile, but he looked away, ducking his head and pretending to read his book. The thing was, anger didn't fade as fast as he used to think it did. In fact, before Caterina LaValle, he never thought of himself as an angry person at all.

CATERINA

Ava and Heather caught up to Caterina as she walked out of the humanities building and cut across the green, heading toward the dining hall for coffee and a break.

"Caterina!"

She turned to see them crunching across the stiff grass, Ava's curly hair flying behind her as she hurried to keep up with Heather's longer steps.

Caterina waited while they caught up with her, her hands cupped around her elbows. She was cold, and felt very, very small and alone. She wasn't sure she had the energy to speak with Ava or Heather right then.

"Hey. Are you okay?" Ava's face was drawn in concern. "Where are you going?"

"I'm fine." Caterina made sure to keep her voice firm and remote. She didn't want to cry with them; that wasn't the kind of friendship they had at all. "I just wanted to get some coffee."

Ava and Heather exchanged a look.

Heather spoke next, her voice timid and unsure. "Um, Rahul kept looking at you during class, and you were looking at him . . . Is something going on there? You can tell us, you know."

They didn't know about RC because Caterina hadn't told

them. She hadn't trusted them with it, and now she supposed there was no point in telling them. All of that was over.

Caterina sighed, her breath frosting the air. "Thank you. But there's nothing going on there. It was probably just a coincidence." She looked over her shoulder at the dining hall, feeling exhaustion permeating every fiber of her body. She needed time to get away, to think, to just be. "I have to get going, though. And you guys should really get to class."

"Okay," Ava said, her mouth pulling down in disappointment. "Do you want to hang out later?"

Caterina smiled a little. "Sure. Just text me." She knew she wasn't going to hang out with them. It was like she'd had a limited amount of social energy, and the breakup with Rahul had used up all her reserves. She felt depleted, washed out, even several weeks later, which was odd. Her reaction was all out of proportion; she and Rahul had shared one ill-fated date. And yet no amount of reasoning seemed to help her shake it off.

Raising a hand in farewell, she turned and walked, alone, to the dining hall.

Holding her cup of coffee like a talisman against whatever the universe might have in store for her today, Caterina decided she'd go find her car next, though she didn't really have a plan beyond that. She just needed to get away.

Pietro saw her coming and immediately set his newspaper down, hurrying to get out of the driver's seat. She usually called when she wanted him to pick her up, but today she'd felt like the walk down to the private car lot at the edge of campus. "I'm sorry, Pietro," she said. "I should've called."

"No problem, Ms. LaValle." He opened her door for her as

she approached. "Is everything all right?"

She slid into her seat in one seamless movement. "Yes, why?"

"Ah . . . your classes?"

She waved a hand at him. "I went to psychology; that was more than enough."

There was a pause, and then he nodded. "Yes, of course." Closing her door, he got into the driver's seat and looked at her in the rearview mirror. "Where to, Ms. LaValle?"

Still staring out her window, Caterina sighed. "Anywhere, Pietro. Let's just drive around for a while."

The car purred to life and then they were pulling away, leaving the school and all its occupants behind.

They'd been driving about fifteen minutes when Pietro said tentatively, "I do not mean to tell you your business, Ms. LaValle."

Caterina smiled. "But you always do, Pietro. And that's how you always start out those sentences: 'I do not mean to tell you your business, Ms. LaValle.'"

His brows furrowed and he looked at the road again. "It is part of my duty to your father and you."

Caterina leaned forward. "I know. And I appreciate you looking out for me."

Looking at least temporarily mollified, Pietro said, "Did he hurt you? The boy?"

It usually delighted Caterina when Pietro called her ex-boyfriends "the boy" and her "the young lady." But this time, she couldn't find any joy in it. "Not especially," she said quietly, holding on to her coffee with both hands. "It's more like he hurt himself and I didn't want to stick around to watch it. Which, I suppose, makes me selfish."

"That is not selfish," Pietro replied. "Not selfish at all.

Sometimes the greatest show of love is walking away, hmm?"

Their eyes met in the rearview mirror again. And Pietro had the good grace to remain silent when Caterina blinked and turned her head to look out the window, tears blurring her vision.

RAHUL

"Rahul. Wait."

He turned to find DE striding across the green to him, her unsanctioned combat boots crunching the frozen blades of grass. There was a thick scarf around her neck and chin, but her green eyes were big and worried.

When she caught up to him, she searched his face for a long moment. "You too."

Rahul frowned and pushed his glasses up. "What?"

DE began to walk, and he turned and kept pace with her. A chilly wind wound its way under his jacket, and he clamped his teeth against the cold. "Caterina's been wandering around all pale and weird. She didn't even give me a cutting glare when I walked within ten feet of her." She darted a glance at Rahul out of the corner of her eye. "You guys broke up?"

"Yeah." His voice was tight, controlled, only because he didn't trust himself to show any emotion right now. He wasn't sure he could rein it back in if he let it out, which was . . . interesting. Rahul Chopra, unable to manage his emotions.

DE sighed. "Rahul, I know it sucks. Believe me, I know. Love is . . ." She waved her fair hand in the air. A giant pentagram ring glittered on her middle finger. "It's unrealistic for most people." As they walked, she met his eye and held it. "Love is elusive; it's the pot of gold at the end of a fucking double rainbow. Most people don't even get a glimpse of that their entire lives. And we just have to accept that."

Rahul raised an eyebrow as they passed the science building on their right, where a bunch of juniors were congregated outside the door, laughing. "Are you trying to cheer me up? Because you're doing a hell of a job."

DE slung an arm around his shoulder. "I'm sorry. But actually, I'm *not* trying to cheer you up. I'm trying to bolster you. I've been where you are. When someone you love breaks your heart, it feels like a shattering of who you thought you were."

Rahul thought about it; she was right. Caterina going out with him for payback *had* shattered his vision of who RC was. It had made him question what he believed about RC—that RC was someone who belonged, unquestionably, in her world. But there was one important distinction. RC had other friends, other people who showed him who he was meant to be. Other people who accepted—no, who *adored*—him. So what if Caterina wasn't one of them?

Turning back to DE, Rahul spoke. "Thanks. But I think I'll be okay." *Okay* was subjective, after all. *Okay* could mean *fine*, or it could mean *I'll never love again*. He didn't have to specify which *okay* he was talking about.

DE patted his arm. "Yeah. I know that. Hey, are you still going to Harper's party? Because the whole group's been invited—you know we all bonded at her mom's art gallery opening last year—so we figured we'd go skiing in Aspen first, and then get dressed at the lodge and head over to Harper's. You should come with."

Rahul thought of Leo and Grey, of their tepid reaction to

him telling them he'd asked Caterina out. What would it be like now that they'd broken up? Would Leo and Grey openly laugh at him, at the fact that he ever thought he could be with someone like Caterina?

"You know what?" he said. "I think I'll sit this one out. I have plans anyway." Nodding once, he walked off to his next class.

CHAPTER 19

CATERINA

She wasn't in a partying mood. Still, she knew she couldn't let Harper down by not showing. Caterina studied herself in the hotel mirror at the Four Seasons, where she and her friends were staying the weekend of Harper's party. She was still in her robe, her hair in a bun, her eyes dull. Definitely not ready for a party.

"Knock knock!"

Caterina turned to see Mia at the door, along with Ava and Heather, who'd walked up at the same time. They were all holding garment and makeup bags, their hair in buns. It was the first time Mia had met Heather and Ava, and there seemed to be an awkwardness in the air, all of them silent, not looking at one another.

Caterina forced a smile. "Hi. Come in." When they were inside, she said, "Mia, these are my friends Ava and Heather. Ava, Heather, meet Mia."

"*Enchantée*," Heather said, holding out her hand.

Ava smiled at Mia. "We've heard a lot about you."

"Oh, me too," Mia said, smiling sweetly and taking Heather's hand.

"Hi, Caterina." Ava bustled forward and pecked her cheek. "Zahira said she'd meet us at Harper's. That's fine, right?"

"Sure," Caterina replied, air-kissing her in return. "Where is she?"

"She's visiting her aunt who lives downtown, but she brought her clothes with her. Speaking of which, the Chanel jumpsuit you recommended is so gorgeous!" Ava flounced into the attached bathroom with her garment bag and makeup. "Seriously," she called, her voice echoing on the tile. "Thank you."

"I'm wearing a vintage DVF wrap dress." Heather hung her garment bag in Caterina's closet and unzipped it. "It's a dark purple. . . . Do you think that's my color?" She turned and surveyed Caterina, seemingly coolly. But Caterina saw just a smidgen of real anxiety there. Had that always been there? Was *she* causing it?

"It's a beautiful color on you, especially with your blue eyes," she said, and Heather immediately smiled and relaxed, following Ava into the bathroom with her own dress and makeup.

"Sorry." Caterina turned to Mia. "Only two people fit in that bathroom at once, so we're going to have to take turns."

"We have lots of time," Mia assured her. She set her garment bag on the bed and put a hand on Caterina's arm. "How are you doing?"

"I'm all right." Caterina spoke quietly; she hadn't told Ava or Heather that she and RC had broken up. "Harper said he was still going to be at the party. Apparently, Everett really wanted him there, and I didn't want her to disinvite him, so . . ." She sighed and shook her head. "It's strange, isn't it? We had exactly one official date. But somehow, I'm sadder now than I was when Alaric and I broke up. At least then, I'd seen the cracks in the foundation. I knew what was coming. Besides, I never felt safe with Alaric. There was always a part of me that was on guard, never letting him see me fully. This . . . I don't know. RC felt like someone I could be friends with. Someone who would be at my side for a while, making life colorful. You know I even thought about us being together through college? I'm going to Harvard, he's going to MIT, and it just felt . . . fated. How stupid was that?"

Caterina was alarmed to find that her voice was breaking as she finished. It was uncharacteristic for her, to make big plans with a boy she'd barely dated. But with Rahul, somehow she didn't think she needed to play those games, to act like she cared less than him. Because Rahul would never hurt her. She hadn't considered that the opposite might happen—that she'd end up hurting *him*, however unwittingly.

"You'll be fine." Mia squeezed her shoulder. In the bathroom, Ava and Heather were talking and laughing too loudly to hear this conversation. "You will," she added more forcefully when Caterina didn't look convinced. "You know why?"

Caterina shook her head.

"Because I'm going to be right there by your side. And you don't need some annoying boy when you have as fabulous a friend as me."

Caterina had to laugh. "Well, now, that's true." She paused, hesitating. "I saw you talking to him that night at the Musicians Fund gala."

Mia cocked her head, but her face was blank. "Oh yeah?"

"Yeah. Did he say anything to you about me? Because he just, he kept talking about how I feel obligated toward him and all of these outrageous things I've never even thought, let alone said. I have no idea where he got those ideas. Do you?"

Mia blinked. "I don't. I mean, when we talked, he mostly just stuck to poker and Everett and all of that. Nothing at all about you." She paused. "But obligation? Wow. That would be a hard one to come back from."

Caterina frowned. "What do you mean?"

Mia shrugged and her eyes remained on Caterina's face. "Oh, just, you know. I have a sense about people. And RC, he seems like such a proud person. Someone who really wouldn't like to think you were doing him a favor or looking down on him in some way. And if he thinks that . . . well, reconciliation seems futile." She smiled sympathetically. "I'm sorry. That's too brutally honest, maybe."

Caterina shook her head, even though Mia's words were like sharp stones. "No, it's not. You're right. And I suppose it doesn't really matter where he got it. In the end, it's for the best that we broke up. I don't want to hurt him anymore."

Mia squeezed Caterina's elbow. "Okay, now," she said in a businesslike fashion. "Let's get you polished and beautiful." She turned Caterina around so they were both facing the mirror. Caterina was surprised by how wan she looked, how washed out and tired compared to Mia.

"I don't know if that's going to be possible," she said, attempting a smile. "Even with that gorgeous black Gucci dress I was going to wear."

But Mia looked unmoved. "It *is* possible. Because you're Caterina LaValle and the LaValles own the world. Don't they?"

It was exactly what her father might say. Nodding once, Caterina picked up her makeup brush.

RC

He wasn't going to Harper's party with Caterina, so he wasn't able to afford a hotel room in Aspen. Which meant he was here, getting dressed in his own dorm room. Thankfully, it was Saturday night, and the dorms were practically empty. He knew for a fact that Leo, Sam, DE, Grey, and Jaya had all been invited to Harper's party, and had decided to make a day of it.

RC's heart felt bitter, like a stone pit in his chest rather than the living, beating, thrumming thing it used to be.

Caterina had only gone out with him out of a sense of obligation, of payback for the dance at the winter formal. The thought hurt him more than anything ever had. As logical and practical as he was, he'd really let himself be that deceived. He'd actually thought she found him charming even when he messed up, that he'd somehow been able to unlock her vulnerability, a side to her that no one else saw, that no one else *got* to see. He'd loved her, yes, but more important than that, he'd *liked* her. All of her. The "her" she kept hidden away so skillfully, so effortlessly. The "her" she was when the cameras and mics were turned off, when the journalists and photographers had turned their backs, packed their bags, and gone home. The "her" that only RC could bring out.

Yeah, right.

RC studied his reflection in the mirror. His eyes were bloodshot; he hadn't been sleeping too well. Every time he closed his eyes, he saw one of two images: him gathering Caterina into his arms in the kitchen of the Victorian mansion, or him breaking up with Caterina and the shock her face had registered for a moment before she'd conceded and let him go. It was like she'd considered arguing with him for just a moment, telling him he was wrong, and then had realized there was no point to it. There was no point to it because he was right. Everything Mia had told him was the truth.

Anyway, it was time to focus on getting dressed. He'd considered not going, but Everett had texted him to make sure he was, and RC found he couldn't say no. Everett seemed to genuinely enjoy his company. So he would go to Harper's party, because he deserved to hold his head high even if Caterina had hurt him. He deserved to be RC, the one everyone loved. One day soon, he knew, he'd want to be RC forever. Maybe once he'd graduated and gone off to college. Maybe this summer. More and more, it was becoming imperative that he leave Rahul behind like old, threadbare socks.

RC adjusted his cashmere sweater—a gift from Caterina—and smoothed his hair back. The sweater brought back memories of the day he'd gone shopping with her, how he'd made her laugh because he couldn't remember the difference between teal and mauve and kept messing those up, but he pushed the thought away. *None of that was real, Rahul,* RC thought derisively. *Stop being such an ingenue.*

He had everything in place except the hair gel that he'd begun to ration. Opening the pot now, he glanced inside, realizing there was very little left. Dammit. He could make it work for this one time if he was judicious, but he needed to go to Oliver's shop very soon. Just thinking about not having any more made RC panicky; his chest felt tight, like a big rubber band had wrapped around it and was squeezing the breath out of his lungs.

Slipping his wallet and phone into his pockets once the gel was in his hair, RC headed out the door to Harper's party.

CATERINA

Caterina had barely walked through the large wooden front doors into the bright, airy marble-tiled foyer when Harper came running, pushed her way through the crowd of guests (most of whom, Caterina noticed, were Harper's mom's friends), and slung an arm around her. "I am *so* glad you're here right now."

As if on cue, a petite Trinidadian girl with long black curly hair in a gorgeous gold paisley dress walked up to Harper, looking harassed. Caterina remembered running into her at previous parties—her name was Latesha (Tesha for short), and her father owned a few world-famous architectural firms.

"Harper, your mom's on the warpath again," Tesha said, rolling her big brown eyes. "I managed to get away, but you need to get her photographs in order before she finds you again. Consider this your warning." Without waiting for a response, Tesha disappeared into the crowd.

Harper groaned and clutched her head. "I can't even with my mother."

Caterina glanced at Mia, who raised her eyebrows. Smiling, she asked, "Uh-oh. What's Grace done now?"

"She has completely lost her mind. She keeps making me move the prints of her photographs around the table!" Harper led them through the large, open great room with the three-sided fireplace into a study that was barricaded behind French doors. The robin's-egg-blue walls of the study were covered with the various portraits and landscapes Grace had done over the years as her style evolved. The *Time* article comparing her to Ansel Adams was there too, framed and hung up on the wall over the large gray wooden desk.

Harper pointed to the surface of the desk, where a few black-and-white prints of people crossing busy streets, presumably Grace's newest work, were scattered. "She wants them to look carelessly just left there, you know, like she couldn't be bothered." Seeing Caterina's and Mia's blank looks, Harper explained, "For the journalists. It would never do for the great Grace Ingall to actually appear to *care* what people think. She's an artiste!" Harper put the back of her hand to her forehead for effect, then returned to what she was saying. "Anyway, so I just laid them across like this. Then she comes in and tells me it looks *too* messy and I need to make an effort. So I rearranged them, and then she said now it looks like I was *trying* to be careless, which ruins the entire point." Harper threw her hands up, the tiered silk skirt of her burgundy dress undulating with the motion. "Why can't she just come in here and do it herself?"

While Harper was talking, Mia had been moving the photographs around. Now she stood back, her tongue poking out from one corner of her lips. "There." She put her hands on the hips of her teal-blue tulle skirt. "How does it look now?"

Harper and Caterina turned to survey her handiwork. "Oh my God," Harper said slowly, her eyes wide. "How the hell did you do that so fast?"

The pictures were all slightly touching one another, but were haphazard enough that it looked like Grace might've just tossed them onto the table. Still, Mia had taken care to make sure each one's strongest features were prominently displayed.

"It looks really good," Caterina said, turning to her newest friend. "Well done."

Mia smiled and took a bow.

As they walked back out into the great room, Caterina ran into Jaya, Grey, DE, Leo, and Samantha, who appeared to have just wandered in.

"Oh, hello!" Jaya said, smiling at her. "And hi, Harper. Thanks so much for inviting us all!"

"You're welcome! Make yourself comfortable. There are people circulating with drinks, but just between you and me, say no to the melon milkshake. I've gotta go make sure my mom has everything she needs, but I'll catch up with you guys later, okay?" Harper waved to them all and took off toward her mother, who was speaking rather intensely to a short, gray-haired waiter.

"Whoo, I do *not* envy her," DE said, and then snagged a glass of cucumber-infused water off a waiter's tray.

"Mm. Grace can be rather difficult, especially right before a show," Caterina agreed, and tried not to laugh as DE's eyes nearly fell out of her head from the force of her surprise. It was the first time Caterina had been openly friendly to her after the Alaric debacle last year.

"I'm Mia," Mia said from Caterina's side, and Caterina felt her cheeks warm.

"Excuse me; I'm forgetting my manners. Yes, this is Mia Mazzanti, my new friend."

Mia wrapped her arms around Caterina. "Her new *best* friend."

Caterina laughed, but Jaya and the others only either smiled politely (in Jaya's, Leo's, and Samantha's cases) or appeared dubious (in DE's and Grey's cases). But never mind. They weren't used to Mia like she was. "So, ah, did Rahul come with you all?" Caterina asked, but they shook their heads.

"No," Jaya replied as she exchanged a look with DE. Clearly they'd been talking about this. "He chose to ride alone."

Caterina bit her lip and glanced at Mia before saying, "I see." After a pause, she added, "Ah . . . It might take you a moment to recognize him tonight. He looks pretty different when he comes to these things." It was just a guess, but Caterina couldn't imagine that Rahul would come as himself. This was prime RC territory. When they were still on speaking terms, she'd told him he could go as RC to Harper's party, even though his friends would be there. They'd thought then that this would be a good time for RC's official debut with his friend group. Caterina felt a pang when she thought about how she'd called him a "proper debutante" and he'd done a little twirl for her.

"Different how?" Grey asked, his brow furrowed.

Caterina shrugged. "You'll see."

And that was when he entered.

They all turned to look in his direction—how could they not?—as he yelled, "RC in the house! Where my boy Everett at?" and Everett McCabe went bounding over to him. The two of them did a strange handshake and clapped each other on the back the way boys sometimes did, and the way Caterina had never seen Rahul do.

"Ho-ly shit." DE set her cucumber water down on a nearby table. "That's *Rahul?*"

"He goes by RC at these events he's been attending with me," Caterina said. "But yes. That's him." She cut her eyes toward Mia, who was watching Rahul, her eyes wide, her eyebrows up in her hairline. She assumed Mia would have a lot to say later, when they were alone.

"He's—he's completely . . ." Jaya trailed off, her eyes, like all of theirs, glued to Rahul as he made his way through the crowd, bumping fists and winking at people as he went. He said something to Harper's mom that made her blush and smile, and then he was headed right for them.

"Different," Leo finished, shaking his head. *"Mon Dieu."*

Caterina couldn't deny that RC looked really, dashingly handsome. He was wearing the cashmere sweater she'd bought him with dark jeans and boots. His hair was styled perfectly, every lock thick and luscious and shiny. His smile, too, was just as artificial as the rest of his trappings. It didn't reach his brown eyes.

"Heyyyy," he said, holding his fist out for DE to bump, which she did, after a long, shocked pause. He caught sight of Mia, and his showman's smile dimmed just a bit. "Hey, Mia." Then he was looking at Caterina, and his smile was gone completely. A look of hurt flashed across his face, replaced quickly by a mask of cool defensiveness. The muscle in his jaw ticked. "Hi."

"Hello," Caterina replied, balling her fists by her side when all she wanted to do was wrap her arms around him and tell him how much she missed him. Did he miss her? She couldn't tell, but honestly, she didn't much care. *She* missed him like the parched earth missed the rain, whether or not he reciprocated those feelings. In that moment, Caterina was thankful for her ingrained training—show no emotion, no matter how big a reaction you were having on the inside.

"Rahul . . . ," Leo said, shaking his head. "You are so . . . You . . .

You . . ." He rubbed a hand across his face. "I do not know what to say."

"Well, firstly, it's RC, not Rahul." The smile was back, but it was strained. "And secondly, I know. I'm just . . ." He spread his arms wide and spun in a slow, confident circle. "I'm who I was always meant to be."

CHAPTER 20

RC

He was making a concentrated effort not to look at Caterina, but that last comment was 100 percent meant for her. Maybe she didn't appreciate RC, but lots of other people did. Just look at the reception he'd gotten when he walked in the door! It was like he was a mini-celebrity now. He was finally visible.

"I liked who you were before," Grey said in his characteristic impassive, unimpressed way.

RC snorted. "Right. Maybe what you enjoyed was me being even more socially inept than you."

"That's not fair," Jaya said, frowning.

RC looked around at all their faces, all of them in various states of shock or annoyance. Not a single one of them was happy, surprised, excited for him. He'd expected it; that was why he'd come to this thing alone. But still. Seeing it like this, so plainly, just made him realize how far apart they'd all drifted. How little the people he was once closest to in the world really got him. How could they not see the obvious? "Oh, come on. You have to at least admit this is pretty cool. When have I *ever* looked like this? Or gotten a reception like that?" He waved in the general direction of the front door. "Do you know who that was who came up and shook my hand? Everett McCabe. The son of David fucking McCabe. He's my buddy now."

Leo shook his head slowly. "I remember when *I* used to be your buddy." Sam took his hand and squeezed it, looking sad.

"It's not like I died!" RC laughed incredulously. "I'm right here!"

Shaking their heads, Leo, Samantha, Jaya, and Grey wandered off. DE stood looking after them with raised eyebrows. "Awkward."

RC scoffed. "Yeah."

"DE!" a girl in a golden dress called. "Come show us that Scandinavian dance move!"

"Tesha!" DE yelled. She picked up a glass of infused water and rushed away.

So that was that. All his friends dissipated into the crowd, leaving him with Caterina and Mia.

Incredible. He had almost everything he'd ever wanted, he was finally someone who could fit in seamlessly with them all—understand their jokes, make jokes of his own, get the nuances of their emotions—and they were literally turning their backs on him. They wanted the old Rahul, the bumbling, unintentionally hurtful, sad excuse for a human. Every muscle in his body seized with anger and hurt and disbelief.

He glanced at Caterina. Opened his mouth to say the thousand things he wanted to say. Mia looked at him with her eyebrows raised, pity dripping off her face. Right. Rahul shut his mouth, realizing Caterina didn't want to hear what he had to say. His heart ached so badly for a moment that he couldn't breathe. Then he walked off without looking back, though every cell in his body wanted her to call out to him.

CATERINA

She watched his retreating back. Mia squeezed her elbow. "Yikes," she said under her breath.

This was what Caterina had done. This was the mess she'd made. She'd taken someone sweet, someone kind, someone innocent and turned and twisted him into something unrecognizable.

"Well, what can you do?" Mia said into the silence. "He's going to act however he wants to act."

But the words kept echoing in Caterina's mind. *What can you do?* What *could* she do? She had a responsibility in how this had all played out; she wanted to be the one to clean it up.

Why had she wanted Rahul to become RC in the first place? Pacing to the big leather couch, she sank down on it and thought back to a few weeks ago, to the start of school.

"What are you thinking?" Mia asked, sitting down beside her, and Caterina gave her a distracted smile.

"I'm thinking . . . I'm the reason Rahul became RC in the first place."

It was because of Alaric. She'd been feeling especially hurt, especially rejected, especially alone, because of the breakup. She'd been angry, too, at his pity, at the way he'd told her he was taking a supermodel to the Hindman Gala. And she'd wanted to strike back. Instead of examining her feelings or talking about it, she'd done what she'd been trained to do from a very young age—she'd plotted revenge. She'd iced over her heart and the blood in her veins. And she'd pulled Rahul into it. All because she was so terrified of being vulnerable, of the world seeing her as anything other than an untouchable queen.

"Right . . . ," Mia said slowly. "That was a pretty big surprise."

Caterina looked at her. "I think I need to tell him how I feel about him. I think I need to put my heart out there, Mia."

Mia nodded slowly, thoughtfully. "Hmm. That might be a really good idea."

A group of older people came and sat on the couch, but Caterina hardly noticed. She was looking at RC, where he stood with Everett and a few other guys. He had one hand in his pocket, his attention focused on whatever Everett was saying. And Caterina felt a swell in her heart. Because he looked just like he had when she saw him playing that chess game on his phone. The real Rahul was still in there, waiting to be unlocked. And she was the one who could unlock him.

It was simple, really. Her extreme fear of vulnerability had made her want him to be someone else. So now she'd be as vulnerable as she possibly could. She'd tell him exactly how she felt about him, exactly how deep her love for him ran. She'd hold nothing back; she'd be more open, more raw, more able to be bruised and hurt than she ever had. But she'd do it because this was the way she could save her Rahul. This was the way to turn the impostor prince back into her beloved frog.

Giving Mia a quick smile, Caterina stood and made her way through the crowd to him.

RC

RC stood with a dozen or so people in the area right off the sunken living room, the party thrumming and buzzing with layers of conversation. The recessed lighting glittered off the polished marble floors, and rousing classical music was drowned out by swells of laughter.

Everett had his arm slung around Harper. They weren't dating, from what he'd told RC, but he was hoping that would change soon. Seeing them together, laughing and making inside jokes, poked at RC's raw, pulverized heart. That was him and Caterina not too long ago. He remembered being in absolute shock that she seemed to like him so much. But that had just been him reading all the signs wrong again.

"Ms. Ingall," a catering service staff member interrupted them, breaking into RC's sad fog of thoughts. "I'm sorry to bother you, but where would you like me to set the cake?"

Harper frowned, her pale red eyebrows knitting together. "Cake?"

"Yes, the lychee-guava cake you ordered for your mother?"

"Oh, right!" Harper looked around at them all, an apologetic smile on her face. "Sorry, guys, I totally forgot about this. Let me go sort it out really quick."

"Okay, but hurry back or I'll have to hunt you down," Everett said, faking a threatening scowl.

Giggling, Harper pranced away with the caterer close behind her.

"I love hanging out with her, man," Everett said, his eyes going all moony the moment she was gone. "I have it bad." He looked at RC, his brown eyes hopeful. "You think she likes me back?"

RC scoffed. "Dude, there is *no* way she doesn't feel the same way. She's constantly finding excuses to come talk to you."

"Definitely likes you," Carter, a bearded guy in his early twenties whom RC had met a few times, agreed.

Everett beamed. "I hope so. I think I'm going to ask her out soon. Where do you think I should take her?"

"Is she into old stuff?" RC asked, but then the short reporter from Evanescence, Roubeeni, was in their circle.

"Hey, guys. Sorry to interrupt you, but can I grab you, Everett, for a quick interview?"

"Oh, sure." Everett set his empty glass down on a passing waitress's tray.

"And, RC, Carter, I'll be back for you guys in a few?"

They nodded and she was gone.

"Whoa, incoming," Carter said quietly.

RC turned to see Caterina, her face set, her bright brown eyes fiery and determined, heading straight for him.

"Yeah, I should probably just go see what Trevor and those guys are up to," Carter said, melting away quickly. Clearly he wasn't a stranger to Caterina's wrath.

She climbed up the step that separated the sunken great room from the area RC was standing in, her black ankle boots clicking loudly on the marble floor. "Hi." Her voice was controlled, though determination shone in her eyes.

"Hey." RC nodded, trying not to let his heart break at just how beautiful she looked. Her thick hair cascaded down her shoulders in big, silken waves, and all he wanted to do was run his fingers through them.

"I need to speak with you," Caterina said softly. "Will you meet me in the conservatory in about twenty minutes? It's on the far side of the house." She pointed, her big black-and-gold bangle sliding down her arm.

"You can tell me whatever it is now," RC countered. He hated waiting for things; it just made his anxiety go haywire.

She bit her lip. "I can't. Not yet. I need some time to prepare."

RC's heart stuttered in his chest. "Is it something bad?" Though how much worse could it be? They were already broken up.

Caterina shook her head without hesitation. "No. It's something good. Very good, in fact." She allowed herself a small smile. "Life-changing good, maybe."

"Oh." He was thrown; he had no idea what this could be. Life-changing good? Did her father get some good news about his businesses or his upcoming political campaign? But why involve RC in that? And more importantly, why did he care so much? He was furious with Caterina for the way she'd treated him, and still a part of him couldn't help but be drawn to her. "Okay. I'll be there."

Nodding, Caterina went back down into the great room and disappeared into the crowd. A middle-aged man, one of Harper's mom's friends, had begun to play on the baby grand in the corner of the room, adding to the general mayhem. RC could barely hear himself think.

Someone cleared their throat delicately beside him. He turned to see Mia, in her mermaid-y skirt and a lacy top. Her mauve-painted lips were pulled up to one side, her thin arms crossed. "You look worried."

RC shifted his weight; Mia wasn't his favorite person, but he wasn't sure exactly why. Something about her reminded him of an icy lake, deceptively thin, waiting to swallow you into its depths. "I'm not worried." But he spoke too quickly.

Mia's smile broadened. "Caterina wants to talk to you, I imagine. Whatever could that be about?"

RC's breathing quickened. "Wait. Do you know what she wants to tell me?"

Mia leaned closer to him. She smelled like dark things in a forest—moss and damp wood. "Caterina and I are best friends, *Rahul.*" He tried not to flinch at her using his name here, at this party, where anyone might overhear. "Of course I know. I know just about everything there is to know about her."

He didn't like the way she said that at all, like a cat with a nearly dead bird. But he forced his distaste down. This was important. "So what? What is it?"

Mia put one hand on his upper arm, her golden cat eyes holding his. "Caterina's dad has just acquired a *huge* company. She's telling everyone, spreading the news as it were. But . . . she's worried you won't know how to respond. Think of this as a test of sorts—can you truly help her? Can you be someone who knows how to slot into her life and handle the media attention that comes with it?"

RC frowned. "Handle it? What do you mean? Why would I need to do anything about her father's business news?"

Sighing, as if RC were a particularly opaque child, Mia tugged on his arm and turned him around so they could both see Caterina.

RC watched her on the far side of the room, where she was immediately accosted by Trevor Hodges, whose parents owned some big newspaper or other. Trevor leaned in toward Caterina, smiling confidently and easily, the dimple on his cheek showing. Caterina laughed at something he said and touched him on the arm. Just then, a photographer from Trevor's newspaper paused and asked to take a picture of them. The two of them posed easily, looking very much a power couple. RC felt jealousy plant its stinger deep inside him, the metallic taste of its poison turning his mouth sour.

"Oh." Realization at what Mia was telling him began to mingle with the jealousy.

Maybe that's what he'd done wrong. Maybe, even as RC, he just hadn't been able to foster relations with the media enough for Caterina. He'd been content to follow her lead. But maybe he should've done more to show her he could fit into her world just as easily as the Trevors and the Alarics in her life. Caterina had looked determined as she walked up here, and she insisted the news she had to give him was good. Good enough to change her life, apparently. But maybe what she meant was, the news could change *their* lives together. Why else would she have brought it up to him? Maybe if he handled this well, she'd give him another shot at being her boyfriend. It wouldn't change the fact that she'd dated him out of some sense of obligation, but maybe—maybe that had been *his* fault, as usual. Maybe that had been him being awkward and clueless.

RC turned to Mia, his face flushed with possibility. "Are you saying—"

Mia held up her hands. "Do what you want. This is your decision. I'm just giving you a gentle nudge. Okay?"

"RC!" Roubeeni was back at his side, tiny and energetic. "I thought we could chat in about fifteen, twenty minutes? I'm going to interview Carter really quickly, and then I'd love to talk with you in the study."

RC studied her, his mind working overtime, and then glanced at Mia, who winked at him and slipped away into the crowd. "Roubeeni," he said slowly as a genius idea began to take root in his mind. *Thank you, Mia.* "Why don't you meet me at the conservatory instead? I think I have something for you that'll make a really interesting angle for your paper."

"Really?" She smiled. "What's that?"

"You'll have to wait and see," RC said in what he hoped was an intriguing manner. "Talk to you then." And he melted into the crowd, just as Caterina had done, smiling. Roubeeni looked after him, intrigued.

He passed by his friends from Rosetta, who were all standing around eating snacks. "This cake tastes a little funny," he heard Leo say.

"It's a little dry," Samantha agreed.

"Maybe it just needs some Wickers jam filling," Leo replied, and they kissed, to DE's protestations. Grey and Jaya just laughed.

None of them looked up at RC as he passed them. He wasn't sure if they hadn't noticed him or if they were all still feeling some kind of way about his new self. But he'd deal with that later. One thing at a time.

What he'd done with Roubeeni was good. It was perfect. When Caterina shared her news—about her dad's new business— Roubeeni would be there to get it all down for the magazine. It was exactly what Trevor would do. Maybe then Caterina would see RC could still fit into her world. Maybe then she'd give him another chance. Mia had said so. It had to be true.

CATERINA

Caterina paced the length of the conservatory, her heels clicking on the tile and driving her a little mad. Finally, she kicked off her boots and walked in her tights, just to give herself some quiet in which to think. At least the conservatory was adequately heated; it was a comfortable place to chew on her words.

In just five minutes, Rahul would be here. She paced past a grouping of hanging ferns, past the cluster of comfortable chairs to the glass wall on the far end. This time of year, she was looking out onto a mostly dormant garden lit up with landscaping lights and kissed with snow, but it was still beautiful in a way. Caterina had a sense of old things ending and new things sprouting, deep under the ground, where no one could see them yet. But in time, with enough care and light and air, they'd grow up to be beautiful, big and vital and healthy.

That was her hope, anyway.

She turned and began to pace back toward the door, rehearsing what she'd say to Rahul.

I like you? No, too trite. It sounded like something a sixth grader might say to her math class crush.

I've thought about us dating through college? Ugh. Now she sounded like a stalker.

I love you? Caterina stopped short. It was, by far, the one that felt truest. Was she . . . falling in *love* with Rahul? She blinked, her stomach in knots. Was this what love felt like? It was sickening and exhilarating at once. It was like being on a constant roller coaster. It was too much. She *definitely* couldn't just lay that on him right here.

Maybe she'd wait for him to stride through that door and see how she felt. Go with the flow, as people said. Caterina had never been a "go with the flow" kind of person, but wasn't that precisely the point? Wasn't she trying to break old, brittle habits and reset them so they could grow into stronger ones?

There was a noise behind her, at the door. Her heart beating furiously, Caterina turned. RC entered the room, smiling.

She smiled back and stepped forward, toward him, her hands

held out. It was time. She would say everything in her heart.

And then the reporter Roubeeni entered too, her cell phone at the ready.

Caterina let her hands fall, the smile vanishing off her face. "What's going on?"

RC

"I brought Roubeeni along, so she can hear what you have to say too." RC tried not to act *too* excited; he wanted to preserve at least a little bit of an air of coolness. The object was for Caterina to think he could fit right in with all the attention, just like her old boyfriends. He could be an asset, not a liability.

He had to admit, she looked way less impressed than he thought she'd be. "You . . . brought a reporter here." She looked from him to Roubeeni, who was watching their interaction closely. "Why?"

RC spread his hands like a convivial host. "If there's good news to share, the world should hear it!"

"Caterina, there you are!" Mia walked in, ending a call on her phone. "I've been looking for you. . . ." She trailed off as she took in Caterina's expression, and then RC and Roubeeni. "What's going on?"

Caterina folded her arms, her lips set in a thin line. "I had something important to say to RC. But apparently, he thought an audience was needed, because he brought Roubeeni, too."

"Oh?" Mia looked from Caterina to RC, her expression unreadable. "Everything's about the media now, is it, RC?"

He frowned. What? Why were they acting like this was a bad

thing? Mia had said . . . well, she hadn't said anything directly. Had he misunderstood? Or maybe he just wasn't being clear enough. "No, this is good. If it's something for your dad's businesses or, like, about the political campaign . . ."

Caterina shook her head. "And that's all I'd have to say, right? Something about my father or the business. Because I couldn't ever want to speak personally to you."

Was she upset? She sounded upset and she looked upset, but . . . why? Isn't this exactly what she'd wanted, for him to be more like the Trevors and the Alarics in her life? "I don't understand," RC said. "I—is this not the right magazine?" He felt bad asking that in front of Roubeeni, who obviously took great pride in her work.

"I think I may have left my keys in here earlier." Leo had appeared at the conservatory door with Sam. His eyes were red and his voice sounded a little hoarse. "I don't feel so . . ." He stopped as he took in the gathering and everyone's expressions. "What has happened?"

Picking up her boots, Caterina let out a breath and brushed past RC and then Leo, her face red. "Never mind, RC," she said in a high, tight voice that felt like a sucker punch to his gut. "I was obviously wrong."

"Nice work," Mia hissed as she walked past, following Caterina.

Confused as hell, RC rushed after them, but Caterina was practically running, her boots still held in one hand. Mia, he noticed, was keeping pace with her, speaking in her ear, her expression serious as they both turned right off the main hall. What the hell had just happened? What the hell had he done?

In his pocket, his phone buzzed. Still feeling dazed, RC pulled it out and held it to his ear. "Hello?"

"Mr. Chopra?" Oliver's smooth voice drifted down the line. "It's Oliver from CdT. I have good news. One more small pot of the Estonia gel has arrived, but I'm afraid there are three other people waiting for it. Since you are a personal friend of Ms. LaValle, I thought to offer it to you first. Are you interested?"

There was a large mirror in the great room where RC had stopped, and he happened to glance into it now, studying his reflection, the phone at his ear. Of course. It dawned on him with the suddenness of a snakebite. He'd been rationing his gel, hadn't he? And tonight there wasn't really enough for a full use, but he'd stretched it anyway. It was clear the magic of the gel wasn't as potent as it was when he used his usual generous amount. It wasn't what he'd done; it was what he *hadn't* done. He hadn't been RC enough, and now Rahul had peeked through and ruined everything.

Leo and Samantha passed by him, talking urgently, Leo's eyes meeting RC's in the mirror. RC looked away and walked a few paces into a quiet hallway; he didn't have time for Leo's questions.

Panic leaped into his chest, like flames from a quickly growing fire. He needed to go to Oliver's right now. He needed to get more of the gel; he had to rectify this situation. "Yes," he found himself saying into the phone, his voice thick with urgency. "I need it. Please hold it for me, Oliver." Rahul might be frozen with confusion, but the moment RC was all the way back in the driver's seat, this would all be taken care of. He and Caterina would have a serious talk. He'd explain himself. As angry as he was with her, as much as she'd hurt him, he still didn't want her to hate him.

"All right, Mr. Chopra. But I close in forty-five minutes. Do you think you'll be able to make it in time? I can't hold it much longer than that, I'm afraid."

RC checked his watch. "Yes, I'm coming right now. Please just—just wait." He had just enough time to hurry back to Rosetta and go to Cassa del Tesoro before it closed. And then he'd rush back here. Ending the call with Oliver and opening his Lyft app, RC hurried to the front door.

By the time he arrived at Oliver's shop, night had settled in for good. Cassa del Tesoro sat like a small glowing beacon on the side of the road, inviting him in. RC marveled at his panic, his anxiety, that had built and built with every mile he'd covered on his way here. How was he still able to function when his brain was going haywire?

He'd convinced himself on the way into town that Oliver was going to tell him he'd changed his mind and sold the hair gel to one of the three other people after all, that the gel RC had was the very last of it there was in the world. What would he do then? How could he bear to go back to being Rahul, when he knew there was such a grand, big world waiting for him on the other side? When he was this close to being the man Caterina needed him to be? It would be like sending snowflakes back into the sky once they'd fallen or pushing shed tears back into their ducts. You could never go back. The only way was forward; the only life he wanted was RC's.

He pulled the door open and rushed into CdT, waving the assistant away, not stopping until he found Oliver in the back, placing what looked like an antelope skull studded with gemstones on a shelf.

"Ah." Oliver turned with a smile when he saw RC's haunted expression. His assistant melted away. "You made it, Mr. Chopra."

"Please call me RC," he said, a little out of breath. "Where's the gel?" RC tried to say it in calm, steady tones, but was afraid it came out in a desperate rush anyway.

After the longest pause in the history of the world, Oliver nodded. "It's in this back room here. I haven't had time to put it on the floor yet."

RC nearly collapsed against a velvet chair in relief, his damp palms grabbing the curved back of it. "Oh, thank God." He took a deep breath and blew it out slowly, trying to settle his pulse.

"Why don't you come with me?" Oliver wound his way toward the checkout desk, beyond which lay a door.

RC obeyed, his heart finally slowing, his mouth finally replenishing itself with saliva. Oliver had it; he hadn't sold it to anyone else. It was all going to be fine. RC could come out now—permanently, soon enough.

As Oliver opened the door to the large back room, beyond which RC could see a wide variety of antiques and objects from different locations around the world, a worrying thought occurred to him. "I, um, probably don't have all the money up front," he said, realizing that he didn't even know how much the gel would normally cost. Oliver had been kind enough to give him the last pot for free. "But I can pay you in installments, and pay interest on it, whatever you need."

Oliver smiled at him over his shoulder as he walked to a chest of drawers with ornate brass handles. "I'm certain we can come to an arrangement, Mr. Chopra." RC stood awkwardly off to the side as Oliver looked through the drawers for a few long minutes. Finally, just when RC was beginning to lose hope, thinking that maybe Oliver had sold it after all, Oliver turned around, a small iridescent glass jar held in his spindly-fingered hands.

RC's gaze zeroed in on the gel as if it were the only sign of life on an alien planet. "I'll pay whatever your asking price."

"Let's have a seat and chat about it, then." Oliver sat gracefully in an armchair and waited for RC to sit in the couch across from him. When he had, Oliver continued. "Perhaps something besides money would work better for this deal."

"Okay," RC said, a little confused. "Like what? I don't have any jewelry or gold."

Oliver shook his head and set the jar gently down on the table between them. "I don't just trade in objects. In fact, there's something else far more valuable to a merchant like me." He smiled widely, all of his teeth perfectly even and white.

"What's that?" RC asked. A finger of uneasiness pressed along his spine.

"Information." Oliver crossed his thin legs and drummed his fingers on the one on top. "Would you be willing to part with information, RC? You strike me as someone who'd have plenty of that to go around."

"I guess I might," RC said, unsure. He glanced at the hair gel. There was definitely more going on here than met the eye, but . . . what were his options? How could he say no, when the key to his happiness, to his freedom, to his *future*, sat right there on that table? Oliver was the gatekeeper, the keeper of the keys. And if RC had something Oliver wanted, if RC had the power to barter for the gel, he would. There was no question about it.

Taking a breath, he met Oliver's dark eyes. "What kind of information are you looking for?"

Oliver cocked his head, a small smile at his lips. "Let's talk about Caterina LaValle."

CHAPTER 21

CATERINA

Tears pricked at Caterina's eyes as she walked as quickly as she could without causing a scene. She didn't want people talking about her, talking about how she was so unlucky in love, how she was alone again. She felt too raw.

Mia, ever loyal, kept pace with her. "I'm here for you. We'll get through this together."

They turned off the main hallway into a smaller one, Caterina desperately looking for somewhere she could gather herself in private. Instead, she found herself face-to-face with Alaric, who was standing with one hand braced on the teal-blue linen-wallpapered wall, the other rubbing his face. He stopped short when he saw her, just as surprised to see her as she was him.

He looked good, she noticed. He was wearing a taupe cashmere sweater with a thick black stripe along the chest, black jeans, and boots. His hair was combed just right, as always, the blond gleaming like polished gold. He had a new watch she'd never seen, probably a gift from Lizel Falk. The thought stung a little more than she wanted it to.

"Caterina." He looked at her with a slightly lost expression on his face, blinking his long eyelashes. "You . . ." He stepped forward, so much taller than her, a frown deepening between his brows. "What's wrong?"

Caterina brushed roughly at her eyes. She'd probably smeared her mascara; dammit. "What do you care?"

Mia cleared her throat and walked past them, ostensibly to look at one of Grace's framed photographs farther down the hallway. Caterina knew she was just being polite and attempting to give them some privacy while still being near enough in case Caterina needed her. Mia was such a good friend.

"Of course I care," Alaric said, stepping even closer. He attempted to take her hand, but Caterina brushed him off. He had the audacity to look hurt. "I'll always care, Cat."

"Stop." She knew she should take a step back, but she couldn't. This was *Alaric*. She'd given him over two years of her life, and he'd completely taken advantage of her. "Where's Lizel?"

"We're not together anymore." Alaric took a breath. "She just broke up with me. Over text." He looked at her, his blue eyes piercing. "But if she hadn't done it, I was going to. Because I realized something."

"What?" Caterina's voice came out less cold than she wanted it to, more curious.

"I was a fool to let you go. I didn't know what I had until—until I wasted it all away. I've always loved you, Cat. I don't know why it's taken me so long to realize it." He did take her hand then; she was too surprised to stop him. His family insignia ring—big and bold and garish—dug into her skin. "We belong together, you and me. I don't believe one bit what I've seen in the papers about you and RC. That's not real. That's something like Lizel and I were—shallow, temporary. This"—he gestured to their interlocked hands—"*this* is what's real." When she didn't answer, he pressed, "Tell me what you and RC have is perfect. Tell me it's what you always thought it would be."

Caterina thought about RC, how he'd invited Roubeeni into the conversation she'd wanted to have with him. How she'd been ready to pour her heart out to him; how he'd stomped all over that without a second thought. "It's not," she said quietly, truthfully, looking into Alaric's eyes.

Here it was—the opportunity she'd thought about in her loneliest moments, something she hadn't even confessed to herself, let alone anyone else. Alaric coming up to her, apologizing, telling her he'd made a mistake. She'd imagined it a thousand times since the night of the yacht gala when he'd broken up with her. And now it was happening.

"You belong with me, Cat," he said, squeezing her hand gently. Sounds of the party—the laughter, the conversation—drifted into the hallway, but she barely heard them. "Not with him. And I belong with you."

Caterina knew she could erase the last few months. She could pretend they'd never happened. She could forget about RC, the hurt, the anger. She could forget Alaric had ever cheated on her. She could just . . . blissfully . . . forget. They could be the king and queen, together again, just like two years ago. They could start over. Alaric still got under her skin; he obviously still had a hold over her. Maybe that meant she loved him. Maybe that meant, like he said, they belonged together after all.

Caterina opened her mouth to say that—or something like that—and instead, heard herself say, slightly incredulously, "You haven't even apologized."

Alaric's mouth popped open, giving him the appearance of a fish gasping for breath. "What?"

She pulled her hand from his—his ring scraping her flesh—and took a step back, studying his face. "You haven't apologized for cheating on me. For the way you treated me. You haven't said 'I'm sorry' once."

He huffed a laugh and crossed his arms, his wiry muscles pressing against the sleeves of his sweater. "Okay, then. I'm sorry."

And just like that, all of Caterina's twisting, turning, churning thoughts quieted. She could see clearly again. Maybe RC wasn't for her, but neither was Alaric. She didn't belong with him. Maybe she didn't belong with anyone. She was done being tossed around; she was done falling for the wrong guy. She was done with guys like Alaric, period.

She found herself smiling a little. "Thank you. Thank you for teaching me a very valuable lesson."

He raised one haughty eyebrow. "Which is?"

"Your hold over me is gone, Alaric. You mean about as much to me as . . ." She pointed to a bronze sconce on the wall. "As that. I'm done feeling things because of you. So thanks for showing me that, once and for all."

He spluttered disbelievingly. "You're going to regret this. You think you're going to be happy with that RC guy?"

"Maybe not." Caterina's eyes pricked with tears again because she had really, really wanted to be. "But I think I'll find a way to be happy by myself, regardless."

And then the tears were threatening again. She pushed past Alaric and walked to the bathroom, Mia close on her heels.

•   •   •

Once they'd politely asked the bathroom attendant to leave, Caterina sat on the tufted bench in the basil-and-lemon-scented bathroom, using the Kleenex that Mia offered her to wipe under her eyes. "It's just so much. It feels like everything's happening at once."

Mia squatted next to her and rubbed her back. "But you handled it so well. With Alaric, out there." She thrust her chin toward the door. "He doesn't deserve you."

Caterina shrugged as a new rush of tears doused her cheeks. She was past Alaric; she'd finally broken the fetters he'd placed around her. The pain in her heart wasn't about him anymore.

"No, really. He doesn't deserve you. And neither does RC." Mia paused, as if weighing her next words. "Women in your position, Caterina, often do best alone. Love is a complication you can't afford."

Caterina pressed a tissue to her eyes, feeling the truth of Mia's words burn into her. "I—maybe you're right. It's all too messy and awful." She let out a shuddering breath, the ache in her heart unrelenting. "I can't believe that happened. With RC, I mean. I was trying to be open with him, to tell him how I feel. And he brings the *press*?" She shook her head. "It's so unlike who he really is. I just—I can't wrap my head around it."

Mia rose from her squat and perched on the vast marble counter, looking at her sadly. "When people show you who they really are, you should believe them. I'm pretty sure someone very wise said that."

"I know. But he was one of the sweetest people I knew, Mia. He was so kind and genuine and completely guileless. The Rahul I knew would never have brought a reporter in when he knew I wanted to speak with him privately. It just shows me how much

I've—I've—" She broke down then, unable to continue. Caterina wasn't one to sob, but her chest heaved from the fruitless effort of trying to hold back more tears. A fresh onslaught rolled down her face, fat and warm, drenching the top of her dress.

"We should leave." Mia got off the counter, her face a mask of concern. "You can't be around all these reporters like this."

Caterina followed her, because she didn't know what else to do. She couldn't shut herself away in this bathroom all evening, she knew that much. "But what about Ava and Heather? They rode here with us."

"We'll send Pietro for them," Mia said. "And don't worry about Harper. I'll go talk to her really quick. You just text Pietro and go get in the car. I'll be there in a moment."

Nodding, thankful she had someone to take charge right then, Caterina went to find her driver.

She waited in the back, with the privacy screen raised, because she couldn't stand to have Pietro looking worriedly at her in the rearview mirror. Even worse, she was afraid a single gentle question from him would reduce her to even more of a puddle than she already was.

A minute later, he had hopped out and was holding the door open for Mia, who got in and patted Caterina's hand. "There," she said, her amber eyes sparkling. "All taken care of. Now let's go."

"Where to?" Caterina asked, feeling exhausted to her core. "My dorm?"

"No. Let's go to my apartment." Leaning forward, Mia gave Pietro the address.

"Your place?" Caterina sat back against the seat. A text

message from Rahul pinged on her phone. Without even looking at it, she silenced her phone and slipped it into her bag. "I haven't been there yet."

Mia smiled back sweetly. "I can't wait to show you around."

RAHUL

He slammed the door of his Lyft and rushed back up the drive and into Harper's house. Doing a quick sweep of the guests in the foyer and then the great room, he could see Caterina wasn't there. He hopped off the step into the crowded living room, walked down the small hallway, and peeked into the empty bathroom, then crossed back quickly. He walked to the conservatory, but it was empty.

He was on his way back into the living room in search of Everett or Harper, slipping his cell phone out of his pocket to text Caterina, when he ran into Roubeeni. "Hey, Roubeeni. Do you know where Caterina is?"

She shot him a confused look. "Do I know you?"

"Oh, right." Rahul ran a hand through his limp, flat hair. After visiting Oliver's shop, he'd made a pit stop at Rosetta Academy to quickly wash up before he'd headed back to the party as himself. "Um, it's me, RC. Actually, call me Rahul." He adjusted his glasses, feeling self-conscious.

He could see her trying to take in this new information as her eyes ran over his un-made-up face, his glasses, his hair. "Wow. It really is you, isn't it?"

He managed a smile. "Yeah, I think so. But where's Caterina?"

"She left some time ago with her friend Mia."

Rahul sighed. "Right. Mia. Seems like she just cropped up out of nowhere, and now she's always around."

Roubeeni smiled and played with her big gold necklace. "Funny, that. I make it my job to know who's who in this crowd, so I did a little bit of sleuthing. Turns out she's renting a place in Rosetta, and she dates a young guy in town as well, though not someone in this crowd. He owns a store . . . Cassa something? His name's Oliver. Anyway, Mia hasn't been in town too long—"

"Wait." Rahul looked at her, his heart hammering in his chest. "Did you say she dates Oliver? Oliver Lemaire, who owns Cassa del Tesoro?"

Roubeeni smiled and snapped her fingers, her gold ring winking in the light. "Yes! That's it. Do you know him?"

Rahul began to dial Caterina, his body feeling cold. "Sorry, Roubeeni. I need to make a phone call."

The line rang, and rang, and rang.

CATERINA

"So this is your place." Caterina walked into the tiny one-bedroom apartment and looked around. It smelled faintly of beeswax and had only the bare essentials in place—a small couch, a coffee table that was leaning to one side, a corner lamp, and a small credenza near the kitchen. "Oh, shoot." She turned to look out the still-open front door. Pietro was idling at the curb. "I forgot to tell him to pick up Ava and Heather at the end of the night."

"I'll take care of that," Mia said, patting her arm. "You go inside and make yourself comfortable." She ran down to the curb, knocked on the window, and began speaking to Pietro.

Caterina watched her, smiling a little. Pietro looked at Caterina through the open window, and she waved to show him she was okay with what Mia had told him. Pietro nodded and pulled away from the curb.

Sighing, Caterina went to sit on the cheap sofa, laid her head back, and closed her eyes, wondering if she should check the text message from Rahul. But no. She'd silenced her cell for a reason; she had absolutely no strength to talk to him right now. Her cell phone would remain in her bag, at a safe distance.

A few moments later, a shadow fell across her face. She opened her eyes to see Mia gazing down at her, her hands on her hips, a peculiar smile on her face.

RAHUL

"Dammit." He ended the call as it went to voicemail for the fifth time. "Dammit."

Roubeeni was already gone, so he made his way to the great room again, hoping to find Leo and the others. Maybe they'd know how to get ahold of Caterina or even exactly where she and Mia had gone. He *had* to talk to her.

As he crossed the great room, looking for his friends, Rahul noticed that people were clustered in groups, talking in urgent tones. He slowed down a little, to try to catch what they were saying.

". . . such a horrible thing . . ."

". . . think he'll survive? . . ."

". . . Dr. Finer works at the ER at St. Francis, so he's in good hands . . ."

Rahul frowned. Who were they talking about? He stopped and tapped an older man on the arm. "Excuse me. I'm sorry to interrupt, but what's going on? Did someone get hurt? I stepped away for a little bit."

The man turned to him, his expression grave. "One of the party guests had a severe anaphylactic reaction to the cake. They had to call the paramedics. He was rushed to the hospital."

Alarm bells began to clang in Rahul's mind. "Who was it? Do you remember his name?"

The older lady the man had been talking to leaned in and said, "Leroy or Leon, I think? It was hard to tell in the hubbub. He was here with a group of friends—an Indian girl and a very large young man were also in the group, I believe. They all went with him to the hospital." She paused, frowning at whatever she saw in Rahul's face. "Are you all right, dear?"

Rahul was already backing away before she finished talking. "They went to St. Francis?"

The two older people nodded.

"Thanks." Rahul turned and ran through the room, toward the front door.

The Lyft driver was the slowest driver in the history of humankind.

Rahul leaned forward. "Would you mind driving a bit faster? My friend is in the hospital."

"I'm going the speed limit," the driver said in a monotone, without taking his eyes off the road. "I never go above the speed limit. Did you know seventeen percent of all vehicle crashes happen in winter conditions?"

Rahul massaged his temples. "Yes. I'm aware." Great. When he needed to get there ASAP, he got the one speed-conscious Lyft driver in human existence. Sitting back, Rahul texted Caterina again. It was the seventh text he'd sent in a row, but he didn't care. He was worried, and he didn't care if he seemed desperate.

Hi, me again, he typed. Please text me back even if you're mad. I just need to know you're okay. Mia is NOT who you think she is—stay away from her.

He checked the time again. It was past ten o'clock now; Oliver's shop would be closed. And it's not like Oliver would tell him anything anyway. He thought back to his visit there, how Oliver had asked him for information about Caterina.

He'd asked weirdly personal questions—were she and Rahul in love? Had Rahul had a chance to meet Caterina's father yet? Was Caterina heavily involved with her dad's political campaign, and did Rahul think he'd be invited to campaign parties and events? Rahul had no idea why he was asking—he still didn't, but he'd left there without the hair gel.

Whatever information Oliver was after, and for whatever purpose, it was clear he didn't have Caterina's best interests at heart. And Rahul knew he could never betray Caterina that way. Even if his loyalty to her meant he had to be . . . well, himself. That was why he'd washed up at school; after realizing the true price of Oliver's hair gel, he hadn't been able to wear it a second longer. He glanced at his reflection in the rearview mirror and ran a hand through his hair. No more RC. Ever. Could he live with that?

As the driver took the turn into the hospital entrance, the answer came to him: he had to. If he had the unfettered choice to be RC, he'd take it; of course he would. But not when that choice came with hurting the people he loved most in the world. And if rejecting Oliver and the gel meant he could protect Caterina in some fashion, at least temporarily, then he was glad. Although the knowledge that (a) Oliver and Mia were a couple and (b) the last time he'd seen Caterina, she'd been with Mia, made him very, very worried.

Opening the door, he rushed from the car into the hospital, his heart in two places at once. He didn't know where Caterina was, or how to help her in this moment. But maybe he could make amends with his friends while he figured it out.

CATERINA

Caterina smiled a little uncertainly at Mia. "Hi. Is Pietro heading back to wait for Ava and Heather?"

Mia shook her head, still smiling in that way. "You really have no idea, do you?"

The smile faded off Caterina's face. Her sixth sense was telling her something wasn't right—not right at all. "No idea about what?"

Instead of answering, Mia walked to the small credenza between the tiny living room in which Caterina sat and the adjacent kitchen. She pulled out what looked like a thick, plain black scrapbook, brought it over, and tossed it onto the coffee table with a loud *thunk*. "Open it."

Caterina didn't care for Mia's tone, but she sensed now wasn't the time to bring that up. With hesitant fingers, she picked up the book, pulled it into her lap, and opened it. There were pictures of her when she was young, maybe no more than ten years old. Caterina frowned. "Why do you have pictures of me?"

Mia paced in front of her and the coffee table, back and forth like a lioness in a cage. "That's not you. That's me."

Confused, Caterina flipped the page. There was another picture of the same dark-haired girl—apparently Mia—with a tall woman Caterina had never seen before. The woman had familiar, bright amber eyes and a thin smile, her dark hair cut into a stylish bob. She wore a businesslike pantsuit, and was posing with a young Mia in front of a stately stucco home. "What is this?"

"Me and my mother. Keep going. *Avanti!*"

Caterina did, only because her confusion and curiosity had overtaken her sense of caution and unease. There was a see-through plastic pocket on the next page, and in it, something golden and shiny. Reaching in with her fingers, she pulled it out and set it in her palm. It took her another moment to remember exactly what it was. She looked up at Mia, a knot of ice forming in her stomach. "This—this is my bracelet. The one I lost at the Riviera two years ago."

"Yes, it is."

Caterina turned back to the scrapbook, the bracelet clenched tight in one fist, and flipped another page. There were clippings and printouts on the next double-page spread, articles about Caterina, her father, or the two of them together from the last few years.

There they were at the Met, her in a red ball gown and him in his best suit. Another one of them at the hospital in rural Alabama her father had helped open. A third of just Caterina, being interviewed about her must-haves for her winter wardrobe last year. She looked back up at Mia, her mind spinning, panic beginning to coat every muscle, her brain screaming, *Run!* But of course she couldn't run. Mia was blocking the exit, and Pietro was gone.

"What is all this?" Caterina asked in a quiet voice that she hoped sounded calm and in control. "Why do you have these things—the articles, my bracelet?"

Mia was pacing once again, the tulle skirt of her dress trailing behind her. At Caterina's question, she stopped and turned, crossing her arms. "Because," she said slowly and deliberately, her eyes smoldering with a cold anger, "you're living the life I was meant to have."

Caterina looked at her, uncomprehending. "What are you talking about?"

"We're sisters, Caterina. We share blood."

The bracelet slipped out of Caterina's fist and fell to the carpeted floor, where it lay in a small, shining puddle. "What?"

Mia continued speaking. "We have the same father—Donati LaValle."

"That's . . . that's not possible." Her father would've told her if he had another child, for God's sake! It was ludicrous. "My father never mentioned you, not once."

Mia let out a bitter laugh. "Yes, I know. I was his big mistake." She walked forward, her eyes narrow slits. "Do you know what that was like, growing up and not knowing half the equation? Growing up with the shadow of that question mark, never fully feeling like I knew myself because I had no idea who my father was? All I knew of him was that he left when my mother got pregnant. He rejected me completely before he even knew me. And because of me, he rejected my mother, too."

Caterina thought about the woman with the bright amber eyes. "Your mother didn't tell you who your father was?"

Mia pushed a hand through her long blond hair. "Not until two years ago. Before that, all she told me was that she was ecstatic to be pregnant with me, but my father wasn't. So she told him to leave, that she'd raise the baby on her own, and he did. She was a diplomat—independent and strong, and more than capable of taking care of herself and her child. She didn't need him."

Caterina put a hand to her head. She could barely keep up with the information that Mia was slinging at her like tennis balls from a machine. "But I thought your *father* was a diplomat. And that your mother was a homemaker."

Mia laughed again. "Why? Because your *friend* Oliver told you so?"

Caterina sat up straighter, the scrapbook sliding off her lap and onto the couch. "How do you know Oliver?"

In response, Mia fished her phone out of her pocket, pressed a button, and showed the screen to Caterina. It was a picture of Mia with Oliver. He was kissing her cheek, and she was laughing. It appeared to be taken on the very couch on which Caterina was sitting. Satisfied with Caterina's expression, Mia put the phone back into her pocket. "I moved to Rosetta last fall, after high school graduation. It wasn't hard to find you, with your flashy cars and your glamorous parties and your frequent trips into town. Your postcard-perfect life.

"You seemed to like Oliver's store; I made it a point to go in there myself one day. Oliver and I began a friendship, and this winter, we began dating. It wasn't hard to get him to feed me bits of information about you. Men are particularly foolish around beautiful women. When he told me you'd be going to the Hindman Gala, I knew my time had come to step out of the shadows."

"You moved here with the sole purpose of tracking me down?" Caterina asked, her mind reeling.

"Of course I did."

"Why?"

"*Why?* Why do you *think*?" Mia asked, her voice rising. "My entire life I'd been told all I needed to know of my father was that he didn't want me. That he was a coward who had no interest in being a father. All my life I wondered what had been so vile about me that he hadn't even bothered to look back once he left. Do you know what torture that is for a child? To never be told the truth, to go to sleep every single night with a fistful of questions and hurts that would never be answered, never be soothed? And then I find out he already has a daughter! And nearly my age!"

Caterina shook her head, confused. "But you said you didn't know who your father was. So how could you know about me?" Her face cleared as pieces of the answer came to her. "You said your mother told you who he was two years ago. And all these clippings"—she gestured to the scrapbook at her side—"are from then. And the bracelet. Were you at the Riviera that summer?"

Mia began pacing again, her face mottled red with her rage. "My mother and I were at the same restaurant as you and your friends. She had an immediate reaction to you when she saw you at your table; it was like someone had walked over her grave. Her face was white, her hands clamped around her wineglass. I begged her to tell me what the matter was. She must've been discombobulated enough that the truth slipped out. She said you were Caterina LaValle, the daughter of Donati LaValle—someone she'd known years ago. And that he was my father. She'd seen the both of you in the papers over the years. That's how she recognized you." Mia paused, remembering. Her voice was much quieter when she continued. "I couldn't believe it. You were right there, in front of me. And after all these years, I *finally* had my answer. My father was Donati LaValle. You were evidence that he actually did want to be a father; he just didn't want to be *my* father." She glanced at Caterina. "When you went to the bathroom, your bracelet fell off your wrist. I walked by and swiped it, as a memento of sorts, since my mother refused to allow me to speak with you. But already I knew I would be researching you and your father as soon as I got home. I knew that wasn't the last time you and I would meet. So I bided my time and I waited for the pieces to align, for my life to bring me here, to you."

Caterina sat there in silence, barely able to process everything. The entire evening felt surreal, as if Dali had come along, painted a vignette of her life, and then pushed her into it. "But none of this is my fault," she said at last, her mouth feeling heavy and inflexible as stone.

"It may not be your fault, but I grew to despise you, from the moment I saw you in that restaurant. It was so obvious all the boys were in love with you and all the girls wanted to be your best friend. You just swanned about with no regard for anyone, with eyes for no one except yourself. You were shallow, I could tell—spoiled and pretty and self-centered, like a little bird in a golden cage." Mia was practically spitting the words now. "The research I did confirmed everything I thought. You were so *sure* of yourself, so absolutely confident about your place in the world. You were Caterina *LaValle*, daughter of a multimillionaire, attending a prestigious boarding school, dating the gorgeous Alaric Konig. Nothing ever went wrong for you. And you spent not one iota of your time worried about who you were or whether you were wanted. *Everyone* knew who you were and everyone wanted you. And there *I* was, completely invisible. Completely unacknowledged; completely rejected. Completely cut out of the LaValles' lives. It was unfair. And I knew it was up to me to set the balance right again."

"What do you want?" Caterina asked, noting the slight quiver in her voice. Her heart was beating so fast, she was afraid Mia would see it through her dress. "Money?"

Mia scoffed at that. "I don't want a cent of your father's money. Not everything is about money, and not everyone can be bought off with it. Perhaps it's time you learn that lesson."

"What, then?" Caterina asked, licking her dry lips. "Why tell me all this now? What's the point of any of this?"

Mia walked over to the matching shabby armchair where she'd left her purse and pulled out a business card. She tossed it onto the coffee table in front of Caterina. It said *Roubeeni Kaur, Glitz magazine*. "I have an interview tomorrow." Mia smiled. "A tell-all. How Caterina LaValle deceived the world with her fake, nobody boyfriend. How she concocted the pathetic, paper-thin scheme because she was desperately hoping to distract from the *real* story: how being dumped by her studly boyfriend, Alaric Konig, sent her into a tailspin." Leaning forward, Mia said in a stage whisper, "She even had to be hospitalized and force-fed, the poor, wretched thing." She straightened, examining her nails. "And from there . . . well, Roubeeni has contacts. I have a bigger story, don't I? A scandal that could destroy Donati LaValle's political career and expose him for the cheating, ignominious bastard he really is."

Caterina sat up straight, her eyes narrowing, her fists clenching around the photo album. "The lifestyle reporter at the *Times*—Bruce Amos. He mentioned that to me at the wedding reception. Were you the one who fed him that story?"

Mia waved her hand airily. "I might've told Lizel, who told Alaric, who told Bruce. I wasn't at that particular event, but word travels, doesn't it?" She looked at Caterina again, her eyes flashing. "Your entire world is just so flimsy. You're a paper doll, Caterina. All it takes is one storm to completely disintegrate you." She paused, letting that sink in. "I just want you to see what I've done to your life before the interview has even happened. I want you to *appreciate* the fact that you're truly alone now. I've gotten rid of your friends. I've gotten rid of the boy you loved. I've been invisible to you all my life . . . and now *I'm* all you can see. I'm all you have *left* to see."

Caterina shook her head, her body trembling, though whether it was from fear or anger, she couldn't say. She could walk past Mia, to the door—she wasn't being physically restrained—but every instinct in her body told her not to make any sudden moves. She was suddenly, vividly aware that she had absolutely no idea what Mia was capable of.

Mia smirked at her shocked silence. "Take your phone out of your bag." When Caterina didn't immediately do it, she gestured with her hand. "Go ahead."

With a shaking hand, Caterina pulled the zipper back on her clutch and pulled out her phone. There were several text messages she hadn't heard come in since she'd put her phone on silent.

Harper: Wow. So my party's boring, I'm needy, and my mom's an untalented hack? And you didn't even have the courtesy to tell me bye, you had to send Mia to do your dirty work? That's really messed up, Cat. But at least I know the truth now

Ava: you just left without saying anything??

Heather: we have to make our own way home now which would be fine if you had told us you didn't want to give us a ride back. This is not cool

Rahul: Caterina I'm sorry please come back so we can talk

Rahul: Caterina can you please talk to me

Rahul (one hour later): We need to talk about Oliver. There's something weird going on

Rahul: Caterina, Mia cannot be trusted. Where are you???

And several more in the same vein.

She set her phone on her lap and looked up at Mia, her blood beginning to boil and turn effervescent. "So you were responsible for Rahul breaking up with me. What exactly did you say to him?"

Mia didn't answer, just smiled coolly at her. "The details aren't important. You weren't right for each other anyway." She put her hands on her hips. "So, tell me. What does it feel like, being so alone in the world with only your darling sister for comfort? What does it feel like, knowing that by this time tomorrow, all your dirty little secrets—real and imagined—will be in the grasp of a gossip magazine reporter? You won't be so beloved by the entire world anymore, Caterina. You're going to feel the sting of cold, sharp rejection on a *global* scale. What will you do then? How will you handle it?"

Caterina felt her heart ice over with hatred at Mia's words. This was what happened when you extended your hand to others in friendship or love. This was what happened when you were honest and truthful. Vulnerability papered over the truth; it put a silken blindfold over your eyes so you'd mistake wrath for warmth and obsession for friendship.

All at once Caterina knew the moment she got out of here, she would use every resource at her father's disposal to take Mia and Oliver down. When she was done with them, there would be nothing left. Just a smoldering pile of ashes.

CHAPTER 22

RAHUL

The white-haired nurse at the desk wore scrubs with ducks and balloons on them. Her name badge read MARSHA. "Ah yes." She typed at the computer with one finger over and over: tap-tap-tap. "Yes, I see your friend here—Leo Nguyen." She twinkled up at Rahul. "And you're on his visitor list, Mr. Chopra. You can head down there. Room 305."

Rahul hit the counter with his open palm once in relief. "Yes. Thank you." He rushed down the hall, the smell of antiseptic burning his nose. He realized as he went that he hadn't even asked Marsha how Leo was doing. He'd just been so anxious to get to Leo's room and see his best friend with his own two eyes. But then he was at the door to room 305 and he pushed it open, charging in—and nearly collapsed with relief.

Leo was sitting up in his bed, an IV in the back of his hand and several other wires attached to his chest. There was a smile on his slightly swollen face, and he was in the middle of regaling Grey, Jaya, Sam, and DE—all of whom were clustered around his bed—with some story about a pigeon that had stolen his hat. They all turned at Rahul's noisy entrance, and, after a pause,

Leo's smile grew wider. "Aha. I knew he would come visit me."

Rahul walked forward and gave Leo a hug, as awkward as it was with all the machines connected to him. "I'm so glad you're okay." He stepped back, feeling an ache in his throat. "This is all my fault. I'm so sorry."

Leo frowned. "Did you stuff the cake in my mouth? Command my throat to swell up? My airways to constrict?"

DE raised her eyebrows. "I don't even remember you being there, to be honest."

Touché. "No." Rahul rubbed a hand along the back of his neck. "But it was lychee-guava cake. I heard them say that. Lychee is botanically a fruit, but for purposes of immunology, it's considered a tree nut. Not many people know that. I did, but I was . . . distracted, and I didn't clock it like I should've. I should've warned you. I knew you were allergic."

Leo patted Rahul's hand. "It's okay. The doctors say I am going to be just fine. It was the first time I had such a serious reaction, but they are giving me an EpiPen for any future attacks. The waitress just said it was guava cake, which is why I ate it in the first place." He shook his head morosely. "I always knew my love of sweets would come back to haunt me one day. I just didn't know it would be one day so soon."

"I'm glad you're going to be fine." Rahul perched at the foot of the hospital bed, the bedsprings squeaking under his added weight. "But it's not okay, what I did. How I've been acting." He looked around at all his friends, whose faces were grave but not unkind. "I . . . kind of got lost in my own head there. It was exhilarating being this other guy people were just instantly drawn to, who just fit into every situation he was put in, who was so deserving of Caterina. You guys kept telling me I was changing, that I wasn't the friend I needed to be. We even fought about it, but I just kept brushing you off. I thought you were being selfish. But the truth was, I wasn't there for you and *I* was selfish and self-centered and it led to this. . . ." He took a deep breath in and let it out slowly. "It's just now hitting me how much I've gotten away from the important things. I'm so sorry."

Grey grunted cryptically, but then Jaya nudged him and raised her eyebrows. After a moment, he cleared his throat. "What I mean to say is, it's all right. We all misstep sometimes."

Jaya smiled. "And it's nice when people forgive us for our missteps." She laid her head on Grey's chest.

DE stuck her tongue out at Rahul. "Fine. I'll forgive you too. But only because RC is so hot."

Leo laughed. "He was, that." Sam nodded her agreement. There were dark circles under her eyes; obviously, she'd been worried sick about Leo.

Rahul felt a wave of regret again, at his selfishness. *Lychee-guava cake.* Rahul would never have missed that, but RC's head was too full of thoughts about his own life to make space for anyone else's.

DE tore open a packet of lurid green hospital Jell-O, which somehow made her bright red hair stand out even more in the sterile hospital room. "So how did you even make such a complete transformation? Was it all makeup? Because you could totally have your own YouTube channel if that's the case."

"I don't know. It's all so weird," Rahul said, frowning. "There's a shop in Rosetta that Caterina visits a lot, and the owner gave me this gel that was supposed to have magical properties. But the guy, he's . . . I don't know, there's definitely something weird going on with him. I'm actually really worried about Caterina."

He filled them in on everything he knew, how Oliver had asked him all those invasive questions about Caterina, how he'd seen her disappearing with Mia and how he'd found out Mia was dating Oliver, and how Rahul couldn't track Caterina down. "I don't know what else—"

His phone rang, interrupting him. Caterina's name popped up on the display. "Oh shit, it's her." He swiped to answer the call and held the phone up to his ear. "Hello?"

Rahul frowned; he couldn't hear Caterina. But he *could* hear a familiar female voice in the background speaking intensely, almost on the verge of shouting but not quite. Looking around at his friends, he motioned for them to be quiet and hit the speaker-phone button.

CATERINA

She hoped Rahul understood what she was trying to do. She'd inched her pinkie toward her phone as Mia paced and talked, her words vicious and angry as a welt. Very carefully, Caterina had swiped to her contacts and pressed "call" on Rahul's name. That was all she had.

"You've got your head so far up your own ass," Mia was saying, "that you didn't even think *twice* when I sent Pietro away. You just expected me to do your bidding. Let loyal Mia tell him to go get Ava and Heather from the party. Let loyal Mia go tell Harper we're leaving. Let loyal Mia speak to my boyfriend. And yet I barely told you anything about myself. I barely shared a word about who I was or what was important to me. Did you notice?" She threw up her hands. "Of course not. Why would you? You're *Caterina LaValle*."

She said Caterina's name like it was the vilest, most disgusting thing she could think of. "It's always about the LaValles. No one else exists. Well, *I* exist. And you have no choice but to acknowledge me now. You have no choice but to accept that the LaValles are not as powerful or as perfect as they want the world to think they are. Soon your entire social circle will know that."

And she ranted on.

RAHUL

Rahul hit "mute" on his phone and stood. "I'm getting Caterina out of there."

DE raised an eyebrow while she ate the last of her—Leo's—Jell-O. "How are you going to do that, exactly? You said you didn't know where she was."

Rahul gestured to his phone, trying to tamp down on impatience while he answered her question. But every moment he spent here was a moment he wasn't at Caterina's side. She was obviously in trouble, and he needed to get to her. Right now. "That's Mia speaking. She said Pietro took them somewhere, so I just need to find Pietro and he'll tell me where to go."

"How will you know where Pietro is?" Leo asked, looking concerned.

"He lives in an apartment near school. I've heard Caterina talk about it before."

Grey stood. "I'll go with you."

"As will I," Jaya said, standing too.

"Me too." DE set down the empty Jell-O container and hopped off the other side of the bed.

"Well, I will have to stay here," Leo said mournfully, gesturing to his IV. "But take my keys and use my SUV."

"I'm staying with you," Sam said, gently patting his arm. She walked to his coat, which was draped on a chair in the corner, pulled out his keys, and handed them to Rahul.

"I am sorry to miss out on the action, but you go kick that Mia's *le cul* if you need to," Leo said.

Rahul nodded. "Thanks, Leo. I owe you." Then, followed by most of his friends, he headed out of the room and down the hall at a run.

Generally, Rahul had a healthy respect for the road and for the three-ton tubes of metal that sped along it, piloted by deeply flawed, easily distracted, illogical, overly emotional humans. But tonight he was fully embracing that deeply flawed, easily distracted, illogical, overly emotional side of him as he sped down the interstate toward Rosetta. Tonight Caterina needed him.

"Whoa there, buddy," DE said, leaning over from the passenger seat to check the speedometer of Leo's black Range Rover. "You wanna slow down a bit?"

"I'm only going eighty-five, and the speed limit's seventy-five," Rahul answered, keeping his eyes on the road. He still wanted to get there alive. "Don't worry. I have excellent focus."

He thought he heard Grey chuckle from the roomy back seat. Then he said, "Mia's still just raving. Caterina seems to be asking questions to keep her talking. Nothing new."

Rahul clenched his teeth. He'd given his cell phone to Grey to monitor, so that he wouldn't be even more distracted than he already was. Mia raving might be the status quo, but he'd still prefer Caterina not to be in the same room as that freak. At least, not without him there to protect her.

It was obvious that Pietro had been asleep, though he tried to assure the group of teenagers at his doorstep that that was not the case. "I was watching TV," he insisted, his voice husky and his hair sticking up in twenty-eight different directions. As if to underscore his point, a laugh track from a TV in the small living room behind him reached their ears. "What is happening?" He squinted around at them all. "Where is Caterina?"

Rahul took a breath. "That's what I want to know. I think she's in trouble, Pietro."

After Rahul had given him a quick rundown on what was going on, Pietro threw on a coat and some boots and insisted on coming along. "I will not let that *stronza* hurt little Miss Caterina," he kept saying firmly, closing the door behind him with a final click and brushing past them all and into the parking lot. "I am coming."

He got into Caterina's SUV and drove in front of Rahul, who was secretly seething at the residential speed limits in town. But he'd listened in on Caterina's conversation with Mia, and it appeared they were still talking. Mia hadn't hurt her, as far as he could tell.

Please let Caterina be unhurt.

Finally, finally, when Rahul thought he'd go mad, Pietro pulled the SUV over at the side of a small street lined with even smaller apartment buildings, and Rahul followed suit. The balconies, when the apartments had them, were empty, and the windows were mostly bereft of any decorations except institutional blinds. Rahul got the sense that this was a place where people came when they were passing through to something else—a place of transition, of ghosts.

Pietro got out of Caterina's SUV, and, putting the Range Rover into park, Rahul flung his door open and rushed over to him.

"It's this one." Pietro lumbered toward the ground floor apartment on the left, its outside painted a sickly green color. The blinds were drawn, but Rahul thought he could see movement beyond them.

"Thanks, Pietro. I got this." Without waiting for a response, Rahul raced past him, up the drive.

CHAPTER 23

CATERINA

"All I wanted, my entire life, was to know where I came from," Mia was saying, her eyes burning with anger and hatred. "I wanted to know who I was. That's not too much to ask. Every child should know that. And instead, I got lies and evasions and a father who refused to acknowledge my existence. Do you know what that felt like?"

Caterina thought about it. She thought about all the presents her father bought her to show her he was thinking about her when she was away at school. She thought about the vacations they'd taken together. The care he'd used when he'd first told her that her mother had died when Caterina was very young. The way he'd promised he'd never let her feel the loss of a mother because he would be both parents to her.

He'd fulfilled that promise. Never once had Caterina missed having a mother; never once had she questioned her identity or who she was. She was Donati LaValle's daughter, Caterina LaValle: That was the quintessential truth she'd known since she was old enough to form an identity. It was inscribed in indelible gold ink on her bones. It was part of her marrow.

What might it have been like if she'd been raised in shadow, in doubt? Without her father telling her to be proud of who she was, that she was meant to rule the world? What might she have twisted and broken into? Someone like Mia, perhaps?

She opened her mouth to say something—she wasn't sure what yet—when there was a tremendous bang and the front door flew open. Caterina jumped, her hand flying to her throat.

Mia spun around, her eyes narrowed, her cheeks still pink with emotion. There, on the other side, with his foot up in the air, was Rahul.

"*What* are you doing?" Mia spat.

"Move." Rahul brushed past her and ran to Caterina, who felt a swell of relief so sharp, it made her eyes water. He knelt before her, looking her over, his eyes wide in fear and concern. "Are you okay?" He put his hands to her cheeks and looked into her eyes. "Did she hurt you?"

Not trusting her voice, Caterina just shook her head. He had come. He had come for her. And then there was a trail of people rushing into Mia's tiny apartment: Grey and Jaya and DE and even Pietro. They all regarded her with anxious eyes.

Rahul put his arm around Caterina's shoulder as she stood, shaky and unsteady on her feet as the adrenaline receded. She was safe now. "We're leaving now," he said to Mia, his voice authoritative and firm, so reminiscent of RC. "And I'm calling the police."

Mia smirked at him. "I didn't do anything criminal."

"I'm pretty sure we can make a case for kidnapping," Rahul retorted, a muscle jumping in his jaw. He was angry like Caterina had never seen him, angry on her behalf. The thought made her heart squeeze in her chest. "And a case for extortion with your boyfriend, Oliver."

"I am calling the police right now." Pietro fished his cell phone from the pocket of what looked like his pajamas.

"Wait." Caterina held up a hand, and Pietro looked at her, confused. "Don't do that."

Rahul frowned. "Caterina, we need to make sure she's put away."

Caterina looked at Mia, at the anger in her eyes, in the set of her jaw, the way she held herself, like a feral, cornered cat, coiled to strike. "No," she said softly, gazing into her sister's eyes and seeing shades of herself and her father there. "No, we don't."

Mia looked a little unsettled, as if any smidgen of kindness was reason for suspicion. "Why? What do you want?"

Caterina walked forward, toward Mia, and felt Rahul's arm slipping off her shoulder. She wanted it back, desperately. But she had things to say. "When you first began talking about who you were and how you'd tracked me down, I felt nothing but a sense of violation . . . and anger. A lot of anger. I don't think either of those feelings is misplaced. What you've done is . . . reprehensible." Mia's face hardened at her words. "But the more I listened to you," Caterina continued, "the more I realized how much pain you were carrying around with you everywhere you went. What my father did to you—that's also reprehensible. That's also a violation, of the sacred pact between parent and child." She sighed, running a hand through her hair. "At first I didn't want to believe you. Maybe you were lying. Maybe this was all some big scam. But even in my heart, I knew what you were saying was true. The pictures of you as a kid—you look exactly like me, except for a slightly different nose and hair a slightly lighter shade of brown. And I could tell from the force of your anger that you weren't lying. You didn't want money, like you said. You say you want to expose me as pathetic and sad and deceitful to the magazines. You want to tell them about my father and what he did to you. But I think deep down? All you want is to be seen.

"I've spent my entire life being seen. I had to grow up under the pressure of an audience who appeared to love me, but who, I knew, would turn on me in an instant if I made a mistake. It made me grow a thick outer shell. I learned—from my father, from my own life experience, from the media—to never trust anyone. To never show anyone how I truly feel." She glanced at Rahul and then back to Mia. "But every moment of my life that has been hard or has broken my heart has come because of my inability and unwillingness to share myself with other people." She took a breath. "So I'm trying something new. My first reaction was to think, 'I can't wait to get out of here so I can utterly obliterate this woman.' But you're not just some woman. You're my sister."

There was a gasp from DE and a rustling among Rahul, Grey, Jaya, and Pietro, all of whom were finding this out for the first time. Caterina smiled at them all before turning back to Mia and extending her hands. "What you've done, following me, lying to me, getting close to me to chop everyone else out of my life, agreeing to tell a reporter lies about me—that's all still wrong. You were wrong to do it. But I'm not going to add to the pain, to the distress, of this situation by calling the police on you or anything else that won't bring more light and air and love into this. I want to make this right, Mia. And we're going to make this right, together, by doing what makes us most vulnerable. For me, that means taking your hand and inviting you into this family. You're a LaValle by blood, and it's about time someone acknowledged that."

Mia looked down at Caterina's extended hands, palms up in

the air, midway between them. Then she looked back up at Caterina. "This is some kind of trick. You're just afraid of my interview tomorrow." Her voice was flat, unemotional, but Caterina saw a flash of something very much like hope in her eyes.

"It's not and I'm not. You can still go to that interview, if you want," Caterina replied, her heart hurting for this girl who was just a product of her upbringing, like Caterina was, like all people were. "But whatever you do, Mia, my life has been changed forever because I know of you now. I have a *sister*." She paused. "I'm sorry it's been so hard for you. You deserve a lot more than what you've gotten from life so far."

Slowly, slowly, expecting Mia to pull away or slap her hands at any moment, Caterina reached forward and laid her hands in Mia's.

Mia looked shocked, as if she couldn't believe any of this was happening. "So . . . ," she asked. "What now?"

Caterina had expected the question. "If you're okay with it, I'd like to set up a meeting with our father. I won't tell him you're coming; you can do that or we can do it together in person, whatever you want. But I think it's about time he acknowledged you. Don't you?"

"Our—our father." Mia shook her head, her voice bitter. "He'll never agree to see me. If he didn't want me when I was a precious baby, why would he want me now?"

"People change," Caterina said simply. "I don't know how he feels about you now. I don't know if he lies awake thinking about the mistakes he made. But we won't know unless we try. And no matter what, however he handles meeting you, that's on him. It says nothing about you."

Mia stared into her eyes for a long moment. And then she

nodded, taking her hands away from Caterina, but not before Caterina noticed they were beginning to sweat. "Whatever. I'm not sure he even deserves it, but I'll think about it."

Caterina smiled. "Okay." Then, getting serious, she added, "You have a lot of pain inside you that you haven't been able to talk to anyone about. I would too, if I was in your place."

Mia shrugged but didn't say anything. That was okay; Caterina knew she would need time to be able to be vulnerable.

"We have a really good therapist at the school," Caterina continued. "Her name's Ari. She's excellent with family issues, especially. If you want, I could set you up with an appointment. You're not a student, but these are extenuating circumstances. And she might know another therapist in the area you could see long-term."

"Ari's really good," Rahul put in, and Caterina could tell he was making a monumental effort to be polite because it was important to Caterina. "I've seen her a lot."

"I'm not like you," Mia said to the both of them, her voice hard. "I don't do the touchy-feely, therapist-in-a-cardigan, talking-about-your-feelings stuff."

Caterina wanted to laugh at the idea of someone calling her touchy-feely. "Ari's not your typical school psychologist," she said instead. "She's really easy to talk to; you'd like her." Mia remained stonily silent. Caterina nodded. "Well, the offer stands if you think about it and change your mind."

Mia narrowed her eyes. "Why?" she asked. "Why are you being so nice to me?"

"Because I think your obsession with me and my life, your obsession with wanting to be seen, comes from a place of pain and fear," Caterina said, aware that Ms. Rivard, her psychology teacher, would be proud to hear her talking like this. "And that's different from someone who's just a bad person."

Mia chewed on her bottom lip. "I . . . I don't know what to say," she said finally, in a soft voice that sounded almost nothing like her.

Was it a manipulation? Caterina didn't know, and in that moment, it didn't really matter to her. She smiled and patted her sister's arm. "You don't have to say anything. Text me when you've had some time to think." She paused. "You'll be sticking around, right?"

"Yeah. I think I will. For a little while, anyway." She took a breath. "Don't bother trying to track Oliver down. He's gone."

Caterina frowned and felt Rahul shift beside her. "Gone?"

"Yeah, he left his shop behind and just took off. When I told him I was bringing you to my apartment to tell you the truth about who I was and what I'd done, he said things had gone far enough, that he didn't want to get in trouble with you or your father. I'm sure he'll land on his feet wherever he washes up, though. It's not the first time he's had to reinvent himself."

"Really," Caterina mused, though she supposed none of this was surprising. Oliver had always seemed to be made of shadows and mist, in a way. The man who could procure anything, for a price. She turned to go, the others turning with her.

When her hand was on the doorknob, Mia said, "Wait." Caterina turned to see her holding out the gold bracelet in the palm of her hand. "This is yours. You should take it."

Caterina took the bracelet and put it on her wrist. "Thank you," she said. "I'm glad something I treasure has come back to me." Then she slipped out of the apartment with her friends, leaving her sister standing alone, watching her go.

CHAPTER 24

CATERINA

Outside, the group huddled together at the curb by a big black Range Rover. They were all eyeing her with concern. Even Daphne Elizabeth.

Rahul stepped closer to her than he already was, searching her face, a furrow between his brows. "Are you okay?"

"I am." Caterina looked at him, at his endearingly floppy hair, at those gentle brown eyes behind his glasses. He was Rahul, not RC. How had that happened?

As if hearing her thoughts, Rahul said, "I want to talk to you."

"And I want to talk to you." Caterina took a breath and fiddled with her gold bracelet. "But I need some time to think." She had just told Alaric she'd never be with someone like him. Rahul appeared to be himself right now, but when would he become RC again? She'd been the cause of all of that. There was a lot to unpack together and look at, and she knew she needed a good night's sleep or two before she was ready and clearheaded enough to tackle it all.

Rahul's face fell, and she wished she could take him in her arms. "Right. Of course. Take all the time you need."

Caterina bowed her head and then turned to the others. "Thank you all for coming out here. It means so much to me." Her eyes flickered to Daphne Elizabeth, acknowledging the other girl's presence for the first time in months.

Daphne Elizabeth looked like she might collapse in a heap. "Um, yeah, no problem. Sure. I'm, ah, glad you're safe."

Pietro stepped up to her and gestured to her SUV, which she saw now was parked in front of the Range Rover. *"Ti porto a casa?"*

Caterina took a deep, shuddering breath, filling her lungs with the crisp, clear night air. "Yes. Please take me home."

RAHUL

He sat with his head in his hands, his elbows on his thighs, staring at the maroon-flecked gray carpet in his dorm room. Behind him, his poster wall was back to being its nerdy self. Gone were the tear-outs from *GQ* and *Polished*. It was all *Make* and *New In Chess* now. His dresser was bare, without RC's accoutrements of an expensive watch and the pot of Estonian hair gel. Everything was 100 percent Rahul Chopra. RC was gone.

Rahul's feet were tapping, tapping, tapping with the restless energy that coursed through his muscles. "She isn't going to call. This is it."

"She *will* call." Grey put a giant hand on his upper back. He was sitting beside Rahul as he had been most of the afternoon. They were both pretending to study, but of course, neither of them was really getting much done. It was Sunday afternoon; Leo wouldn't be discharged from the hospital until tomorrow morning.

Rahul looked up at him. "It's been fourteen hours. She isn't going to call." He'd told her the night before to take all the time she needed, but he'd secretly been hoping to wake up to a text or a phone call from her. It was past lunchtime now, and she hadn't called yet.

Grey looked helplessly at him, his broad shoulders taking up most of the room. "Maybe she just needs a little more time."

Rahul shook his head and put it back into his hands. "I fucked up, man. I fucked up the best thing that's ever happened to me."

The clock kept ticking.

CATERINA

"Thank you for coming to see me." Caterina looked from Ava's closed-off face to Heather's, her heart pinching at the distrust and suspicion there. "I appreciate it."

They were at Hospitalitea, the tea shop where, eons ago, she'd had tea with Mia. Now fading afternoon light filtered in from the windows, warming her worn wooden chair.

"You ditched us last night," Heather said, her voice hard and cold. Her hand sat in a fist on the smooth tabletop. A plaid scarf was woven around her neck, a protective covering she refused to take off.

Ava took a sip of her peppermint tea, her thick, brown curls shining in the sunlight. "Why'd you do that?" Her voice was softer, sadder, than Heather's.

Caterina put a hand over her cup of white pear tea, feeling the steam warm her palm. "It's a long story. But basically, I didn't know that the message you got was that I was leaving. It was supposed to have been that Pietro would pick you up later that night, whenever you wanted. I had to leave because Rahul and I—" She stopped, realizing how little her friends knew because she'd kept everything from them. Looking at them, she said, "What I'm trying to say is, I'm sorry."

Ava's mouth popped open; Heather narrowed her blue eyes. "For?" Heather said. She hadn't ordered tea, as if she didn't plan to stay too long.

Caterina lifted her palm and ran her fingers through the steam that curled above her cup. "For everything." She met Heather's eyes and then Ava's, making sure they knew her words came from her heart. "For how this friendship between the three of us has developed. I've always wanted to be on top, and being untouchable came at the expense of being real with you guys. It came at the expense of being a true friend. And now we have this . . . this twisted relationship where we don't trust each other and we're just waiting for one of the others to take advantage of us. I know I've had the biggest hand in creating that."

Ava swallowed a sip of her tea and set her cup down gently. "Wow. I never thought I'd hear you apologize."

"Me either." Heather laughed a little, disbelievingly. "But . . . it's kind of nice."

"It is," Ava agreed, nodding so vigorously that her curls bounced. "But, um, it's not all on you. We were more than happy to go along with it. Just to get to be a part of your circle."

Heather rubbed the back of her neck, her short dirty-blond hair catching the sunlight. "Yeah. Me too. It's not the best feeling to see how weak I've been, but I really just wanted to be your friend. And that meant I did a lot of things and took a lot of things I shouldn't have."

Caterina leaned forward and put her hands on theirs. "We can change. It doesn't have to be like that. We only have a few months left here, at Rosetta Academy, but we can have the kind of friendship now that we should've had all along."

Ava smiled at her. "I think that would be really cool."

Heather gave her a half smile. "Totally agree."

Caterina sat back, satisfied, and took a sip of her tea. "So let me tell you everything that's happened."

For the first time, she was completely, totally honest with her girlfriends, vulnerable in a way they'd never seen her. With every word she spoke, Caterina knew she was mending the fabric of their friendship, stitching the three of them together, closer than ever before.

The Next Evening . . .

CATERINA

"I don't know, Caterina." Mia looked in the vanity mirror of the Bugatti and arranged her bun first one way, then another. "Maybe we should've given him a heads-up about who I was. And that I was coming."

"We talked about this, remember?" Caterina studied her half sister, her gaze calm and steady. "You were the one who said it'd be better this way."

Over the past two days, Caterina and Mia had spent many, many, many hours talking. Mia had so much anger pent up in her, but she acknowledged that she'd gotten a little obsessed after the Riviera, and all of the things she'd done probably signaled that she needed to get help and process the things she'd kept bottled inside for so many years. She'd canceled the interview with Roubeeni and had instead visited the school psychologist at Rosetta Academy, who'd spoken with her briefly before referring her to a specialist in town. According to Mia, she felt lighter and freer than she ever had after having just scheduled the appointment.

It was strange, but Caterina could see a difference in her too, though it was obviously early days yet. It was as if just talking to Caterina honestly had eased some pressure off a highly volatile system. Mia already seemed less combative, more questioning. If not apologetic exactly, then . . . softer. Gentler. Caterina hoped that, in time, an apology would come. And she sincerely hoped Mia would stick around for a while, at least until graduation. It'd give them the chance to get to know each other before Caterina went off to college and Mia went wherever she would go next.

They got out of the car and began walking to Hospitalitea, where they were meeting Caterina's—and Mia's—father. He'd just returned from a business trip to France, and all Caterina had told him was that she was bringing a friend along. She glanced at Mia, wondering if her father would be able to see what she hadn't—that LaValle blood ran in Mia's veins.

"There he is," she said as they entered the tea shop, the bell over the door tinkling prettily. Her father, *their* father, sat in a corner, wearing a cashmere sweater and dark pants, reading something on his phone.

He looked up just as Caterina closed the distance between them, his face breaking into a smile. *"Topolina!"* He rose and hugged her to him, squeezing so hard that the breath escaped her lungs. "You're looking well."

"As are you, Papa," Caterina said, then turned to motion Mia forward. "This is Mia. She's joining us today."

"Ah." Her father leaned forward to air-kiss Mia and then stepped back, a wisp of uncertainty passing over his features as he studied her stoic face. "It's a pleasure to meet you, Mia."

They took their seats. Caterina was glad the tea shop wasn't too crowded. There were two couples at tables far away, which was just enough to keep her father from making a scene, but not so much that they couldn't have a serious conversation.

Papa smiled and gestured to the two flowered teapots already at the table, on their tea-light heaters. "I hope you don't mind that I ordered your favorite," he told Caterina. "White pear. And I also ordered the rose-and-honeysuckle blend. It's supposed to be good for jet lag, they tell me."

"Ah." Caterina poured herself a cup of white pear and then one for Mia. After she took a bolstering sip, she patted Mia's knee under the table and said, "So. Papa. There's something Mia and I need to tell you."

Her father looked from her to Mia and then back again, understanding dawning. "Are you a couple? Because you know I have no problem with that, Caterina."

Caterina shook her head and said solemnly, "No, we're not a couple." She paused. "But we *are* related." Mia stiffened beside her.

The look of understanding was gone from her father's face. At once, he was on guard. "What do you mean, you're related?"

"I'm your daughter." Mia's voice was just a fraction higher than its usual pitch, though it didn't quiver at all. She'd probably role-played this conversation many times over the last two days. "My mother is Ginevra Mazzanti."

Caterina was proud of her. She knew the sheer amount of courage it must take to look at someone, especially someone like Donati LaValle, and tell him you were the daughter he abandoned nearly two decades ago.

Papa's face turned a startling shade of purple. "That is—that's absolutely preposterous! How can I be sure this isn't some scam? Do you know how many phone calls and letters I get every year from so-called relatives, begging for money?"

"That's not why I'm here," Mia said sharply before Caterina could step in. "I don't want a penny from you." With slightly trembling fingers, she reached into her purse and pulled out what looked like an old letter. "I thought you might say something like this, which is why I brought proof." She handed the letter to Papa, who took it in a huff.

He opened it and read it, his face growing pale. Then he looked up at Mia. "How did you get this?"

"My mother kept it all these years. She didn't show me until two years ago, when we saw Caterina at the Riviera and the truth about my father's identity came spilling out of her, finally."

Her father ran a hand across his face, then looked back down at the letter. Finally, he set it down on the table, his face showing a thousand expressions at once. He looked at Mia. "What do you want?" he asked, his voice hoarse.

Caterina felt a pang of disappointment and pain. Disappointment that her father, her Papa, as strong and powerful as he was, couldn't do the right thing. He couldn't simply say sorry, couldn't admit he'd been wrong. And pain for Mia, who still wasn't getting what she wanted. "Papa." Caterina had spoken before she was aware she was going to speak. "I think you owe Mia an apology."

Mia held up a hand. "Don't! Don't make him apologize. I'm not some poor, rejected child who needs something from *this* man." She looked at Papa with disgust.

"What am I apologizing for?" Papa asked, leaning back in his chair.

Mia turned to him, her eyes flashing. "For deserting me and my mother? For telling her you weren't ready to have a child, only to have Caterina a year later?"

"I was *married*," Papa hissed. "To Caterina's mother. I couldn't just leave her and go shack up with your mother. Do you understand that? It was a mistake, what happened. And I was young and trapped."

Mia laughed, the sound bitter. "Oh, so she trapped you, did she?"

"That is not what I meant! I meant I was in a bad situation   "

"Stop." Mia leaned forward. "Don't say any more. You're a sorry excuse for a man, always have been. And *this* has been a mistake." She scraped her chair back and stood, looking down at Caterina. "Thanks for trying, Caterina. But I knew it wouldn't work. See you around." She grabbed the letter off the table and, without a backward glance, she was gone, hitting the door of the tea shop with her palm to open it and striding out onto the sidewalk, her chin held high.

Caterina turned back to her father. "Why?" she asked softly. "Why couldn't you apologize? Do you know what hell she's been through all these years?" She scraped her chair back too and stood. "I'm going after her."

"Caterina." Her father grabbed her hand and looked pleadingly at her. "I wanted to spend my energy, my focus, on you. And then your mother died and I was left alone to take care of a baby. Coming to America was the best way I knew how to help you."

"And no one was helping Mia," Caterina said.

"She had her mother."

"But she didn't have you. And for all these years, *I* did. It's deeply unfair, Papa. I hope you see that one day. And I hope you do the right thing and show her your true feelings. Being vulnerable isn't all bad, you know. In fact, it may just open doors in your life you didn't even know were there. Until then, goodbye." She pulled her hand out of his grasp and turned to leave.

"Caterina," he said when she was a few feet away.

She turned to look at him.

"I'm sorry," he said. "I don't want this to come between us."

She looked at her father, at the lines bracketing his mouth, feathering at the corners of his eyes. He'd always been her hero, a man who could do no wrong. But seeing him now, in this new light, Caterina realized something: He was deeply flawed, as human as anyone else. He was capable of making mistakes. But most important of all, she realized she didn't need to make the same mistakes as him. She was free to live her life by her own doctrines, by her own rules. "It won't, Papa," she said quietly. "But I'm not the one you need to make amends to. Now, if you'll excuse me, I should go comfort my sister."

Caterina turned and walked away, not in anger as Mia had, but in deep sadness. This fracture between Papa and Mia, she knew, was not hers to heal. And yet, perhaps, she could support her sister as Mia made her peace with whatever the future held for her.

As Caterina walked out into the chilly morning, she tipped her head back and let the sun drench her skin for a moment. Then she called, "Mia!" and began to walk down the sidewalk toward her sister, her hand extended.

CHAPTER 25

RAHUL

A single text had never caused him so much gut-churning, face-melting, teeth-grinding anxiety.

Meet me at Lake Rosetta tonight, 7 p.m.?

That was it. That was all she wrote. So he was just standing here at the lake, an hour early, waiting. Because what else was he going to do? Pace his room until he wore his carpet down to the bare floor? Talk Grey's and Leo's ears off even more than he already had? Take DE's advice to go skinny-dipping at the school pool after hours (apparently, it helped her whenever she was stressed, which . . . okay, great for her, but Rahul would be way too freaked about breaking the rules to do something like that)?

No, none of those were options. The only reasonable thing to do had been to walk out to the lake. He wished more than anything that he had some hair gel to use, to just wear RC as armor this one time. But standing there, looking out onto the nearly frozen surface of the lake in the near dark, Rahul shook his head. He was done with all that now. He'd made his peace with it.

He stuck his hands into the pockets of his coat and tipped his head back to look at the ancient pines surrounding him. A chilly wind blew his hair across his glasses, nipped at the tops of his ears and his nose. There were ripples on the lake's dark surface, like ruffles in silk.

There was nothing to do but wait. And if Caterina told him they were done, that he'd ruined things, he would have to accept it. He'd come so close to grasping the dream, but he had to face the facts: it might just escape his grasp, slipping through the gaps between his fingers like smoke.

CATERINA

She emerged from between two towering pines into the clearing that held Lake Rosetta in its cupped hand. It was only seven p.m., but the sky was already the color of an angry bruise, stars embedded in it like jewels. There was a close-to-full moon out, casting silver light on everything.

It took her a moment to notice him. Rahul stood with his back to her, his hands in his jacket pockets. What was most startling of all was the *way* he was standing—his shoulders back, his spine straight. He was standing tall, like . . . like RC. But then he turned sideways and the moonlight glinted off his glasses . . . and he looked like Rahul.

What would he say? How would he receive what *she* had to say? There was no way to predict whether RC or Rahul would be with her tonight.

Caterina stood there for a moment longer, watching him. Then, taking a deep breath, she said his name.

RAHUL

Rahul turned at the sound of his name, and his breath caught for a moment. Caterina was walking toward him, dressed in jeans and a deep green wool jacket she'd belted around her waist. Her hair was done in a ponytail—a stylish one, but still, a simple ponytail. And she was wearing a lot less makeup than she usually did. She looked younger, somehow, and so much more vulnerable. Rahul had to tamp down a powerful urge to put his arms around her, to shelter her from the world.

You don't have the privilege of that job, he told himself. *You might never have that privilege again.* The thought was like an arrow piercing his heart.

"Hi." He watched her face as she drew closer, slipping his hands out of his pockets.

"Hi." She didn't smile. Her boots crunched lightly on the frost-hard dirt. She came to a stop a few feet away from him. "Thanks for coming to see me."

This was a goodbye conversation. He could feel it in the air, its scent mingling with the musty lake water smell. It was a let-you-down-gently, this-is-never-going-to-work talk. Rahul steeled himself. He would take it well, as well as he possibly could. She'd already given him so much, and he was truly grateful. "Of course. How are you? How are things with Mia?"

Caterina dug the toe of her boot into the ground. "Mia's . . . good. All things considering. She's going to stick around, I think, and I'm glad."

Rahul frowned. That he couldn't understand. Picking up a

cold rock, he tossed it from hand to hand. "Really? After what she did?"

Caterina shrugged, sticking her hands into her coat pockets. "Well, it's complicated." She walked forward so she was beside him, facing the near-frozen lake, a glittering piece of black stone in the night.

"Still." Rahul shook his head, skipping his rock across the surface of Lake Rosetta. Thin ice dotted its surface like lace flowers, and his rock broke them apart as it went. "I can't believe the lengths she went to. It seems really messed up."

"I don't think Mia wanted to seriously hurt me. I think she just wanted me to feel all alone and rejected, like she has all these years." Caterina huddled into her coat as a brisk wind picked up, shaking the trees around them, whipping exposed skin. Rahul resisted the urge to put his arm around her. Instead, he picked up more rocks and skipped another one across the lake. "And it worked," Caterina continued. "For a few brief moments in that apartment, I felt my heart ice over again. I felt utterly, utterly alone."

Rahul let the rocks drop and walked closer to her. "But you're not," he said softly, gazing into her deep brown eyes that looked almost black under the night sky. No matter what happened, he would always be there for her if she wanted him to be. As a friend, as someone she could call on if she ever needed something.

Caterina smiled faintly. "When you came in, followed by the others, I realized something: Being vulnerable and open hadn't made me alone. It hadn't trapped me in a room with someone who hated me. Being vulnerable had brought me all of you. You were all there because I'd reached out and opened myself up a little bit in the last few months." She glanced away, the long line of her throat pale as marble in the starlight. "I didn't always know how to be a friend. With Ava and Heather . . . our friendship was the way it was—shallow and weak—because that's the kind of friendship I nurtured. I wouldn't ever let them get too close to me. I hoarded what I thought was power by keeping them at arm's length. But it turns out it's not power at all. It's loneliness. It's desolation. And I don't want to live like that anymore."

Rahul swallowed. He'd never heard her talk like this before. She sounded like a different person, almost. "At Harper's party," he began, wanting to explain, to tell her that he was just trying his best, "I thought it was what you'd want. I thought you had some news about your father or his business and that if I brought the media in, I'd show you I could be like that Trevor guy. Or like Alaric. That I could become a part of your world."

Caterina looked at him sharply, her small hoop earrings swinging with the movement. "Why would you want to be like Trevor or Alaric, Rahul?"

He shrugged and stuck his hands in his jacket pockets again. "They're so comfortable in their own skin. They have that easy confidence I've coveted my entire life. Everyone wants to be part of their orbit. I felt that for the first time with RC." He took a breath, wondering if he should say the next thing he was thinking or if it would scare her. He decided to say it anyway. "I felt, for the first time, like I was deserving of Caterina LaValle."

Caterina pulled her coat closer around her, her pale hands clamped around the edges. She looked down at her boots briefly before looking up at Rahul again. "Do you know what I was going to tell you at the party?" she asked quietly, taking a big step closer to him so they were barely apart at all.

Rahul shook his head. Her tone, and their sudden closeness,

gave him butterflies in his stomach, a chaotic, writhing, teeming tornado of them. He wasn't sure he could speak.

A crisp wind blew, taking strands of Caterina's hair and brushing them against his cheeks, smelling of soft, sweet honey. "I wanted to tell you that the day you broke up with me, at the art museum, I was going to break up with you."

"Oh." The butterflies evaporated. Rahul felt small and foolish again. What had he *thought* she was going to say? "That makes sense. Because it was all payback. You didn't want to—"

"Rahul," Caterina said, looking into his eyes. A simple chain glittered at her throat. "Shut up for a moment, please."

"Yeah, okay."

"I was going to break up with you because I knew I was hurting you. The reason you'd become RC in the first place was because of me. Because I didn't believe that you, Rahul, were enough to parade around to reporters and the other people at the gala. The reason you wanted so violently to leave behind Rahul, the sweet, guileless, innocent, kind Rahul I knew"—here she caressed his cheek gently and his heart leaped—"was my doing. I'd shown you what RC could be, and that made Rahul unbearable to you." Her voice bent a little, as if she were overcome with emotion. Rallying, she continued. "And I couldn't take that anymore. I couldn't watch you self-destruct. I thought maybe with some distance from me and my world . . . you'd return to yourself. And maybe you'd return to *me*."

He couldn't speak. He could hardly trust himself to breathe. What was she trying to say?

Oblivious to his internal turmoil, Caterina went on. "When I saw you at Harper's party, you were still RC. You still hadn't returned. And then I thought maybe the way to get to you, to

Rahul, was to be completely honest with you. After all, RC was me being dishonest, me trying to hide the truth. And the opposite of that was . . ." She paused, taking a deep breath of the lake-scented air. "To tell you how I feel. To lay my soul bare. To know that doing so might mean rejection and doing it anyway."

Rahul swallowed, his mouth suddenly feeling like a piece of desiccated wood. An owl hooted loudly in the trees above them, but he barely noticed. "And . . . and how *do* you feel?"

Caterina didn't hesitate. "Looking at you is like looking at the rising sun after the longest, darkest night. You bring me so much pure *joy*. I don't think I knew what happiness was until I was laughing with you about Carter's beard and its unerring resemblance to the Juniper-Hawthorn Rust fungus. Or learning about bacterial immunology while we were at that club in Denver.

"But it's not just about the things you say—it's the way you *are* in the world. The softness, the thoughtfulness, the sweetness you have about you, that balances out my own hard edges. If I'm the Ice Queen, Rahul, you're the warm waters I want to melt into. Saying I've never felt this way about anyone before is an understatement, but when I look at you . . . I see the future. And if that's not love, I don't know what is."

He gazed at her for a full minute, not saying anything. He couldn't; there were literally no words in his brain.

CATERINA

Caterina studied him in the near dark while he stared at her, speechless. There was a gentle splash in the lake as some creature dove into its murky depths.

"I've scared you," she said finally, looking away. It was what she'd been afraid of. It was all too much—her feelings, her honesty. But at least she'd been brave. At least she'd been vulnerable, even if it came with rejection. She'd said what was in her heart, and she knew she'd never regret that.

"Yes," Rahul said at last. "You've scared me." She began to nod and tell him she understood, but he continued speaking, his voice clear and strong. "You've scared me because I just realized, for the first time in my life, that I have so much to lose. You've scared me because you told me you love Rahul, that you see a future with him, and I was so close to destroying that Rahul forever." He shook his head, a look of wonder on his face. "What's crazy is, I never realized before Saturday night that RC's a part of me. Maybe a part that's been hidden all these years, but he's already in there. When I came to get you at Mia's apartment? Kicking open that door? That was such an RC move, but I didn't even think twice about it."

Caterina smiled. "Yeah. I'm guessing you were pretty RC to have influenced your friends and Pietro to come with you too. Seeing you standing here, tall and proud and sure? That's RC."

Rahul considered this, a slight frown on his face. "But the makeup and the clothes and the gel made me so much more handsome. And that handsomeness definitely opened some doors, especially with your crowd." He looked at her and shrugged.

"You let me be the judge of who's more handsome, Rahul. Believe me, I've dated some classically gorgeous guys who seemed troll-ugly to me by the end of our relationship. I think you're fucking beautiful. Besides," Caterina continued with fire in her voice, "I don't *want* someone who'll slot in with my crowd. I want someone who challenges me. Someone who makes me want to be the best version of me I can be. And that's not RC. That's Rahul."

A slow smile began to spread across his face, like sunshine seeping into the morning sky. "And I'm the one you love."

"Yes," Caterina said hotly. She wasn't done telling him how she felt about people who didn't accept Rahul. "And everyone who's ever said or implied you should be someone besides exactly who you are is wrong. That includes me. And Everett McCabe. And your parents. Your parents have *no right* to use your cousin's picture in place of yours. Or to hide you here. If they were here now—"

But she didn't finish her thought because Rahul put one hand at her waist while the other cupped the back of her head. He pulled her to him, a little roughly, his mouth on hers in the next minute. His teeth gently teased apart her lips and his tongue found hers. Caterina let herself sink and sink and sink into that kiss that felt like the universe speaking to her. Her arms cinched around his waist, her hands traveling up his back, feeling the firm muscles there. She gasped a little as he dipped his head down and nipped at her earlobe and kissed her neck, murmuring her name against her skin. Caterina's mouth turned up in an ecstatic smile. This was real. This was all happening.

Then she struggled to push him away, trying to clear her foggy, love-saturated head. "Wait. I really mean it. Your parents are wrong, Rahul. Do you understand that? They're wrong about you. You're perfect as you are. You're enough as you are. *More* than enough." She was almost desperate for him to understand this. "And I'm sorry I was one of those people who told you that you weren't enough, however implicitly. I was wrong. I was ridiculously, stupidly, horribly—"

He silenced her again with a kiss, this one deep and slow like a ballad. She put her hands on his solid chest and sighed, feeling her knees go weak as he kept on kissing her, his eyes closed, his mouth firm and sure.

Finally, he pulled back and smiled at her, his brown eyes shining. "I understand," he said softly, one thumb caressing her bottom lip, featherlight. "And Caterina?"

"Hmm?" With Rahul kissing her, she was having trouble keeping her thoughts in the here and now when they very much wanted to be in the there and then.

"I love you."

RAHUL

She gasped softly, the most beautiful sound he'd heard. Her eyes went wide, the stars reflected in those velvet irises. "Really?" she whispered, going still.

"Really." His hand lingered on the regal column of her neck as he ran his thumb just under her jawline, thrilling as he saw her eyes drift to his lips.

She reached forward and bridged the gap between them, her hands going around his waist, pulling her to him, closer than close. Her voice was a song as she whispered, "I love you too, Rahul Chopra. I love you, I love you, I love you."

One Week Later . . .

CATERINA

Caterina lay with her head on Rahul's lap. Spring was edging its way into Rosetta, and the occasional sunny 55-degree weather day had students sprawling on picnic blankets out on the green. He was playing lazily with her hair as he spoke to Grey about a chess game, winding locks of it around his fingers. Beside her, Ava was talking to Zahira, Jaya, Heather, and Samantha about her latest YouTube curly hair tutorial. Caterina closed her eyes and smiled to herself, the sun warm on her face. The scent of pine drifted in wafts on a cool breeze. Life, in this moment, was pretty perfect.

"Who is that DE is talking to?" Leo asked, his voice brimming with curiosity.

Caterina cracked open an eye and turned her head to look. DE was by the dining hall in the distance, speaking to a tall, golden-skinned boy she'd never seen before. "He's handsome," she found herself saying, and then laughed up at Rahul. "Not even close to you, naturally."

Rahul grinned and kissed the tip of her nose, his tie brushing her forehead. "Thank you."

Heather was spying on DE and the boy using the zoom on her phone's camera. She whistled. "Wow. He's really got a CW-TV-show-hero thing about him, doesn't he?"

"No kidding," Ava agreed, raising her perfectly groomed eyebrows. "I mean, I can appreciate that he's aesthetically pleasing, even if he does nothing for me."

Her girlfriend, Zahira, threaded her fingers through Ava's and made a noise of agreement in her throat.

"I wonder if it's that new guy," Jaya said, frowning a little as she sat up straighter on the blanket. "Remember?"

"Oh, you mean the mobster," Leo said, and Sam scoffed and hit him gently on the arm. "Or the spy."

"Stop spreading rumors, Leo," she chided him, laughing.

Grey put an arm around Jaya, pulling her snug against his chest. "Do you guys think he might be the one to help DE out of her romantic slump?"

Caterina propped herself up on one elbow and watched the two of them talking intently. "I don't know . . . but I hope so." She glanced at Rahul, smiled, and spoke quietly, just to him. "I want everyone to be as happy as us. Is that odd?"

His eyes softened behind his glasses, and he bent to place a gentle, sweet kiss on her lips. "No," he said, stroking the back of her cheek with his fingers. "When you're as happy as we are, it seems selfish not to want to share that with other people."

Caterina's smile grew. He'd read her mind. She lay back down and closed her eyes again, letting the sun warm her face and kiss the backs of her eyelids, reveling in the sheer beauty of the moment. As Rahul's voice washed over her like a warm ocean wave, Caterina LaValle felt in her bones that there was so much beauty yet to come. She couldn't wait.

ACKNOWLEDGMENTS

And just like that, the second book of the Rosetta Academy series is done . . . in a global pandemic, no less!

As always, I could never have done this without the help of a whole host of people. In no particular order, thank you to:

Thao Le, my literary agent extraordinaire—you're always in my corner when I need you and I so appreciate that.

Jen Ung, my editor—I'm so lucky to have worked with you from my very first book all the way to this, our fifth YA book together!

Cassie Malmo, publicist and delightful ray of sunshine—thank you for all you've done and continue to do for my books.

To my YA street team—you guys are my shining stars. Thank you for always being there, being enthusiastic, and supporting my stories! Special shout-out to Roubeeni, Ari, Latesha (aka Tesha), and Morgan, all of whom won a cameo in this book. Hope you like what I did with it!

To my family—love you, love you, love you. What show should we binge-watch together now that I'm off deadline?

To all my readers, new and old—thank you for coming along for yet another ride! I hope I did right by you with Caterina and Rahul's happily-ever-after. I can't wait to share what I have cooking next.